Knot Just Their Nanny

Reverse Harem Omegaverse

Eve Newton

Copyright © 2024 by Eve Newton

All rights reserved.

No part of this book may be reproduced in any form or by any electronic or mechanical means, including information storage and retrieval systems, without written permission from the author, except for the use of brief quotations in a book review.

For those who have stuck by me through 100 book releases. It's been a trip.

Blurb

CELEBRATE EVE'S 100TH BOOK RELEASE WITH KNOT JUST THEIR NANNY!

I can pinpoint the exact moment I went from his nanny to something else… when I purred directly in his face.

I mean, a burp would've been preferable for the first time ever. He is a rejected alpha mate, having been abandoned with his baby daughter, and I just purred at him. The weird thing is… he growled back. So, where does that leave us? Caught between a baby and an alpha in pain, that's where.

Oh, and did I forget to mention the other two alphas, his best friends, who seem to have moved in as well at some point during my reign as baby nanny and who seem more than interested in this development?

Three men and a baby? Nope. An overwhelmed alpha trying to do everything himself? Check. A complicated situation is about to turn upside down, and I have no idea where to go from here. I sure hope they do.

This is a non-shifting light and steamy reverse harem omegaverse standalone. Please note this is set in England in a completely fictional world, the characters are British and use British English.

Introduction

Omegaverse: A Brief Overview

Background:

Origin: The Omegaverse, also known as A/B/O (Alpha/Beta/Omega), originated from fan fiction within various fandoms.

Setting: It exists across various genres and settings, from contemporary to futuristic, and even fantasy worlds.

Key Concepts:

Hierarchical Structure: The society in Omegaverse is structured around biological roles:

Alphas: Typically the dominant, strongest group with leadership qualities. They are often portrayed as protective and possessive.

Betas: The most common designation, considered 'normal' and versatile, without the specialised traits of Alphas or Omegas.

Omegas: Often the rarest and characterised by submissiveness in this dynamic. They have the ability to become pregnant, regardless of their gender.

Dynamics: Relationships and social interactions are heavily influenced by these biological roles, affecting power dynamics, social status, and personal interactions.

Biological Aspects:

Heat Cycles: Omegas experience periods called "heats" that make them fertile and irresistibly attractive to Alphas.

Knotting: During mating, Alphas have a biological mechanism designed to lock them together with Omegas, enhancing the chance of pregnancy.

Scent Marking: Characters in this universe can often recognise each other's roles by scent, which plays a significant role in attraction and emotional responses.

Mating Bites: During the mating ritual which binds the characters together, they give each other mating bites, usually on the neck to show their commitment.

Preface

This is a light romance reverse harem omegaverse with one omega and three alphas.

There is no MM and no OWD (the ex-mate is well and truly out of the picture).

Hope you enjoy my 100th book as much as I've enjoyed writing it!

Lots of Love
 Eve

Chapter 1

Zara

The door closes softly behind me, but I don't move an inch, taking in the small flat and the alpha sitting, flicking through channels on the TV. He barely looks up as he hears me enter, but that's fine. I'm saying what I've come here to say, and nothing will stop me.

"Zara," Eddie starts, looking up briefly from his channel surfing, his tone already laced with that casual arrogance I've come to loathe. "What took you so fucking long? Where's the snacks?"

"Eddie, we need to talk."

He raises an eyebrow, turning his focus to me, leaning back against the cushions. "Sure, love. What do you have to say that's so important?"

I don't sit down. Standing by the door so I can

leave as soon as I'm done, I give him a level stare. "This isn't working for me anymore. Our relationship has been more draining than fulfilling, and I can't continue pretending otherwise."

Eddie's face shifts, the half-serious expression is melting into something else—something less pleasant, as I expected and why I planned this meticulously so I could get away.

I keep going, my voice a firm thread in the quiet of the room. "I'm moving on from whatever this has become," I continue. "I need to do what's best for me, and that means ending things between us."

"You're breaking up with me?" he asks incredulously. "You're fucking overreacting as usual because I haven't paid you enough attention."

My jaw clenches tightly. His eyes are doing that thing where they try to look sincere and hurt, but I see right through it now. "Am I?" I keep my tone even.

"Absolutely," he says, rising, taking a step closer, trying to close the space between us. "We have something special, and you're trying to throw it all away because of a few rough patches?"

I shake my head slightly; a chuckle almost escapes me. It's funny how clear things become once you make up your mind. "A 'few rough patches' is a bit of an understatement, don't you think?"

Eddie runs a hand through his hair – a nervous habit when he knows he's losing ground. "Look, I'll change, I promise. We can start fresh, pretend none of this ever happened."

The old me might have fallen for these lines, but she's not here anymore. "Pretending doesn't change reality, Eddie. It's time I face it."

He lets out a frustrated sigh, realising his usual tactics aren't working. "Zara, baby, come on. Don't do this."

The term of endearment is empty, like it belongs to another lifetime. "Bye, Eddie," I say as I open the door and step out.

"Where are you going?" He follows after me, his voice pitched with a hint of desperation.

I ignore him as I walk steadily out of the building, knowing even if he follows me, I'll still get away from him.

"Zara, get back here—" he yells. "You're being a complete bitch."

A few weeks ago, that would've hurt me, and I'd have done anything to make it up to him; sorry for speaking out, but I know now who he is and what he does. He is a gaslighting narcissist, and I need to get away from him.

I *am* getting away from him. I have it all planned and have left nothing to chance. I've closed the lease on my flat, sold all my furniture, and sold anything else that wouldn't fit into my tiny car.

I stride toward my white Fiat 500 parked along the curb, the cool morning air brushing against my skin. It's just a car, nothing special, but I smile as I unlock it and climb in. This little car is mine, all mine – a ticket to wherever I want to go, a companion on the road to freedom.

Settling into the driver's seat, the fabric of the upholstery feels familiar beneath me. My smile widens as I turn the ignition, the engine hums to life, steady and reliable. I've got a full tank, a playlist of my favourite tunes cued up, and the open road ahead.

"Zara!" Eddie snaps, marching towards me. "Where do you think you're going? No one else is going to want you if you walk away from me, you know!"

Ignoring him, I lock the door, and without a look back, I pull away from the curb and turn the corner to head towards the motorway and the new life that I'm about to carve out for myself.

"Here we go," I murmur.

The outskirts of the city buzz around me as I navigate through the streets one last time. The towering buildings, the endless sea of people—they're all part of a chapter I'm closing now. With each mile, the urban landscape of Greater London starts to fade, giving way to new beginnings.

The motorway stretches out in front of me, a ribbon of possibilities. There's something invigorating about driving with no one to answer to, no one waiting on the other end to tell me what to do or how to feel. Just me, the road, and the promise of a fresh start in the Lake District.

I forget all about Eddie, knowing he will try to ring me, but I've already blocked his number. There's room for *my* thoughts now, my dreams, my doubts. No one to tell me how I should feel or that what I'm feeling is wrong. Nope. All that is behind me, and now I have something new and exciting to look forward to.

There's a new job waiting for me, a chance to be someone important in a little one's life. A rejected alpha and his baby girl. It's a new one for me. Usually, it's the poor omega who ends up with a rejection and a single mum, but not this time. It's going to be a delicate time while I navigate this situation, but I'm definitely down for it. The fact that it is a six-hour drive away from my old life helps me to be excited about this prospect.

I think about that baby daughter, who is three

months old and all coos and giggles. And then there's her daddy, the alpha without a mate anymore. I wonder how tough it's been to stand alone against the world, to care for a child without anyone by his side, to feel the pull of the rejection on the bond he shared with his omega. Is he broken? Angry? Gentle? And then I think of the utter bitch who left them. How dare she? What kind of mother does that to their baby? The only silver lining is that the baby won't ever know any different. She won't miss what she never had, but it will still be difficult, nonetheless.

My eyes scan ahead, catching the signs that count down the miles. The Lake District isn't just a dot on the map anymore; it'll be my new home.

Around halfway there, I pull into the Motorway Services, the car's fuel gauge nudging towards empty. I hop out, stretching my stiff legs from hours behind the wheel. The petrol pump clicks rhythmically as I fill the tank, a simple sound that marks the pause in my journey.

Inside the shop, I grab a packet of crisps and a chocolate bar—snacks that promise a quick burst of energy for the road ahead.

With a full tank and a stash of goodies, I set off again, the highway unfolding before me.

The landscape shifts, giving way to rolling hills and open fields. It's like a postcard from a storybook, the kind of place where everything seems idyllic, tucked away from the harshness of reality.

The hours tick by, and the rhythmic hum of tyres against asphalt lulls me into a semi-contemplative state. The Lake District is drawing closer with every passing moment. The signs announce my progress: 50 miles, 30 miles, 10 miles...

It's mid-afternoon when I pull over and open up the GPS to tap in the address of the small town nestled in the heart of the North Lakes. I wait as it brings up the route, and then I set off again, expecting to arrive in twenty minutes.

That's when my nerves hit, and at the same time, I spot a deer, an honest-to-God deer, on the side of the road.

"Deer!" I shout, even though I'm alone, grinning like a maniac. "Aww, a fucking deer. So cute." It's already darted off as my car trundles by on these godforsaken country roads that are barely wide enough for my tiny car. I take it easy, and after a particularly hazardous bend, I turn onto a wider road that would pass for a main road, I assume, and then concentrate on the directions the GPS is throwing at me, leading me onto a lovely road with new-build houses all lined up identical and not really what I expected. I imagined a quaint cottage that has seen more years than I've changed my underwear, but I guess that was a bit naïve. Navigating the roads, I inhale deeply and exhale, letting my sudden burst of nerves dissipate.

"They're going to love you, Zara Roberts. Chin up, back straight. You got this shit."

Chapter 2

Zara

When the GPS tells me I've arrived at my destination, I hesitate and then pull onto the open driveway of the house, next to a ten-year-old Range Rover. A newer blue sedan is parked on the verge, and I breathe out a sigh of relief. Peter and Susan, Benjamin's parents, are here. They said they would be, but I was nervous they wouldn't show. I turn off the car and sit for just a second, looking at the front door where my new life waits.

"Okay, Zara, this is it," I whisper, grabbing my handbag from the passenger seat. My case and a few boxes filled with my stuff can wait in the car for now. No need to drag everything up to the door looking like an eager beaver, for fuck's sake.

Stepping out of the car, I close the door and take

in a deep breath of cool air. The place is quiet, peaceful even, nothing like the hustle of London where every moment was a noise of honks and shouts. Here, it's the soft rustling of leaves and distant birdsong that greet me.

I walk up to the door and ring the bell, the sound echoing slightly as I step back and wait.

The door swings open moments later by Susan and Peter with the kind of smiles that make you feel like you've come home. "Zara, dear, welcome!" Susan exclaims, stepping forward to envelop me in a warm hug. Her omega scent of lemon muffins wraps around me and already it feels like home, her embrace as comforting as a cup of tea on a rainy day.

"Thank you so much," I say, returning the hug before pulling back to look at them both. "I can't tell you how much I appreciate this opportunity."

Peter takes my hand and squeezes it, his eyes crinkling at the edges as his sandalwood scent lingers around him. "We're the ones who should be thanking you. Not everyone would take a chance on a job up here, especially with our unique situation."

We shuffle into the living room, where the furniture looks cosy and lived in.

"Was your drive up alright?" Susan asks, gesturing for me to take a seat on the squishy leather sofa that appears to have had a lot of bum action. In the sense of being sat on...

Fuck, Zara. Stop with the nerves.

"It was lovely, actually," I reply, sinking into the cushions. "The scenery changed so beautifully the further north I got. And no traffic jams, which is a miracle in itself."

"Ah, the joys of country roads," Peter chuckles, taking a seat in the armchair. "They can be a bit winding, but the views are worth it."

"Absolutely," I agree, nodding enthusiastically. "I saw a deer!" I still can't get over the joy of this.

Peter chuckles. "Yes, quite a few of those around here. And sheep. Lots and lots of sheep."

"And cows," Susan pipes up with a giggle.

"It's amazing. I'm used to the concrete jungle."

Susan sits down beside me, her hands folded neatly in her lap. "Yes. Change can be good, especially in a place like this. It has a way of growing on you."

"It already has," I say with a wistful sigh. I hope this job works out. I'll be disappointed if I have to leave again.

"We want you to feel comfortable here," Susan murmurs, suddenly a bit nervous. "Benjamin has been a bit resistant this morning, but he knows this is what's best for him and Mia."

I nod understandingly. "Yeah, I get it. It's a tough situation, but I'm here now and I intend to make his life easier and to care for Mia with my whole heart."

She smiles, but I can tell she is still nervous.

That doesn't bode well.

I've met Benjamin only a couple of times, and that was online. He was gruff. But I put it down to being tired taking care of an infant all on his own. My entire interview process has been with Susan and Peter. Dozens of Zoom calls, and they drove down to London to meet with me in person the other week.

"Let me show you to your room," Susan says, rising.

"Okay." I smile and follow her up the stairs, her steps light on the plush carpet. I follow, my own footsteps muffled, a sense of anticipation building in my chest as we ascend.

We reach the top, and she guides me down the hallway, pointing out where things are—the bathroom, the linen closet, a small nook filled with books and games. But it's the next door she opens that catches my full attention.

"Here we are," she announces, gesturing toward the interior. "This will be your space."

I step over the threshold into a cosy room bathed in the soft afternoon light. The walls are painted a calming shade of cream, and a comfortable-looking bed sits against one wall, complete with fluffy pillows and a knitted throw. A table and chair occupy another corner, a lamp casting a warm glow over them.

"Your room is right next to the nursery," Susan continues. "It's important that you're close by, for Mia's sake."

"Of course," I reply, already picturing late nights and early mornings spent tending to little Mia's needs. "It's perfect. I can't thank you enough for thinking of everything."

Susan smiles warmly at me, a look of genuine caring in her eyes. "We want to make sure you have everything you need."

A moment later, Peter appears in the doorway, a suitcase in his hand and a box in his other arm, a friendly grin on his face. "Where would you like these?" he asks, looking around the room.

"Over by the wardrobe would be great, thanks," I say, pointing.

He sets them down with care, taking a moment to ensure they're not in the way. "I'll grab the others."

"Thanks. I appreciate it," I tell him, feeling the warmth of their hospitality wrap around me like a blanket. "You've both been so welcoming."

Peter nods, satisfaction etched in the lines of his

face. "Well, we're glad to have you here, Zara. It's been a really tough time for Ben. Susan and I are helping as much as we can, but Sue still works part-time, and I have to get back to the practice; I'm a vet," he adds in as if I didn't already know that from our conversations. I nod interestedly.

"We would help more, but life—"

"Of course!" I cut him off. "You absolutely don't need to explain anything to me. It's literally my job to help out with the baby, and that's what you hired me to do. I'm here now, and you have nothing to worry about."

Susan takes a small step towards me, tears in her eyes that make my heart break a bit for her. "I just wanted to say thank you again for coming all this way. We weren't sure we'd ever find someone willing to take on the role." She pauses, her gaze flickering away before meeting mine again. "After so many turned us down, and we had to look further afield, well, it's been tough."

I nod, understanding the subtext without needing further explanation. Rejected alphas can be challenging, their presence alone enough to unsettle most. "I'm here now, Susan, and I'm not planning on going anywhere. Mia needs care and consistency, and that's what I'm here to provide."

The relief that washes over Susan's face is clear and bright, like sunlight breaking through clouds. "Thank you, Zara. It means the world to us, truly."

And then the alpha himself strides into the room, grim and almost mean. Benjamin Scott. His eyes lock onto mine like he's trying to figure out a puzzle that he's not particularly enjoying.

"Zara," he says, the word more of a statement than a greeting. "You came."

Well, fuck. Nice welcome, asshat.

"Benjamin," I return evenly, holding his gaze. I remind myself that I'm here for Mia. "Of course, I did."

He grunts almost in annoyance. His glare doesn't wane, but I don't look away. Something about his reluctance to have me here, even though he agreed to my contract, tells me he has huge trust issues with people sticking around when things get tough, and that doesn't surprise me one bit. It also makes me sympathetic, empathetic, even, and I don't take it personally. His pinecone scent hits my nostrils as he shifts his enormous frame, and I gulp as my stomach does a little flip. His alpha scent appeals to my omega in a way that has never happened before, and that is the absolute worst thing that could possibly happen right now.

I exhale softly and drop my gaze. His is too intense, and the undercurrent of whatever that is drifting through the air is overwhelming.

"Come and meet Mia," Susan interrupts and I nod quickly and follow her down the hall, my steps light, curious about the little girl I'm about to meet. She opens the door, and I see her swaddled in a pastel blanket. Her tiny fist curls around an unseen dream, and I can't help but feel a tug at my heart-strings.

"Fast asleep," Susan murmurs.

"Not surprising at this age," I smile. "She's gorgeous."

I lean in close, and whisper, "Hey there, Mia. I'm Zara, and I'm going to be hanging out with you for a while."

There's something magical about being needed, about being the one to protect and nurture. This tiny girl doesn't care about alphas, omegas or betas; designations and all their complications and needs mean nothing to her yet. She just needs love, and I've got an endless supply.

I straighten up and turn to see Benjamin scowling at me in the doorway. But he doesn't say anything. He just walks away, and I sigh. He'll come around and see that my being here isn't a bad thing.

It will give him back parts of his life that he needs, to continue to provide for Mia and be a great dad, instead of an overwhelmed, exhausted heap of alpha male.

Chapter 3

Zara

The front door clicks shut, and Benjamin's parents' muffled voices fade away as they leave.

With a smile, I head to the kitchen, ready for something to eat. I gather up the ingredients for a couple of sandwiches. Not really sure if Benjamin expects me to cook him a big meal when I just got here after a long drive. The kitchen has that lived-in feel, everything right where you'd expect it to be. It's Benjamin's house, his space, but for now, it's mine too.

Benjamin appears like a ghost, silent and surveying, eyeing the sandwich ingredients scattered across the counter, he arches his eyebrow.

"Making sandwiches. If you want something

proper, I'll make it a bit later, if that's okay," I say to him.

He glowers at me. "How did you know what I like? You've made quite the assumption with my sandwich there."

Glaring right back at him, I bite my tongue. "Well, it's your fridge and only your fridge," I point out, popping the cap off the mayo with a little more force than necessary. "So, I figure you like everything in it."

Can't fault that logic now, can you?

We lock gazes, and I can't help the small sense of triumph bubbling inside me as it looks like the top of his head is about to explode. It feels good to knock him down a peg or two from that high horse he lives on.

"Fair enough," he grumbles. "But combinations are key."

"If you like ham and you like cheese, you'll eat a ham and cheese sandwich, got it?" I give him a sugary smile that hardens his gaze, but not in a bad way. He is realising that he can't push me around with his stinky attitude. I get why he is so defensive, but don't bite the hand that feeds you, for fuck's sake.

The door opening and closing makes me frown.

"Boy-o. You ready for the footie?" A deep male

voice calls out, and two alphas saunter into the kitchen.

"Oh, hello," one of them says, coming up short when he sees me. He is cute, with dark hair and green eyes. The other one appears more reserved, with blonde hair and blue eyes. "Zara, right?" Cutie asks.

"That's me."

"The nanny?" the other one asks with a lingering look at me before shooting his gaze to Benjamin with a look that speaks volumes, if you can understand the meaning behind it. Which, to be fair, I don't.

"Liam," Cutie offers. "This is Henry."

"Nice to meet you."

"Go and wait in the lounge," Benjamin mutters to the two guys, who disappear hastily, leaving me with one pissed-off alpha. "Make one for Henry and Liam, too."

Turning my back, I roll my eyes so hard I'm worried they might stick that way. We'll have a talk about manners at some point, but right now, I feel, is not that time. "Okay," I say instead and busy myself with the order. When I hear him leave, I turn to the fridge to grab two bottles of water. Then grimace and make it three. "You get one of those on account of being in pain. Rude to me again, asshole, and I'll make a sandwich with your meat and two veg."

He hasn't heard me, but I feel better muttering it out loud anyway. Plastering a smile on my face, I load up a tray that I find propped up behind the kettle and carry it into the lounge.

Sliding it onto the coffee table as the guys are riveted to some guy barrelling on about football stuff, I turn to sneak out.

"Thanks, Zara," Henry says without much fanfare, grabbing a half without looking away from the action.

Liam, on the other hand, breaks his gaze from the TV and gives me a smile that's got more charm than should be legal. "You're a lifesaver. I was about to eat the sofa cushions," he jokes, his eyes twinkling with mischief.

"Let's hope it doesn't come to that," I reply. "Think of the blockage."

He blinks.

I blink.

And then my cheeks feel like I stuffed my head into an oven.

Liam bursts out laughing, and I cringe inwardly. "Oh, fuck. You're quick, princess," he snorts as even Henry breaks away from the action to snicker. Benjamin, on the other hand, sinks further into his armchair with a dark look, stuffing his sandwich into his mouth.

"Enjoy," I mutter, before heading back to the kitchen.

"Don't call her that again," I hear Benjamin snap at Liam.

I narrow my eyes and feel somewhat delighted that the gruff alpha defended my honour. Not that I minded, or I'd have said so myself. I'm not shy in coming forward—not anymore, not after Eddie.

I leave the lads to their game, the shouting from the TV already a dull roar in the background as I make my way upstairs and to my new bedroom. The scent of fresh paint and a faint tang of polish from the furniture gives the room that 'just-moved-in' vibe.

Unpacking, I start with the clothes, folding and organising them into the chest of drawers and wardrobe. It feels nice, this simple act of putting my things away, like I'm stitching myself into the fabric of this place. Each folded sweater, each neatly arranged sock drawer—it's like planting a flag, declaring a bit of this space mine.

With every piece of clothing I put away, the room starts to feel less like a guest room and more like mine. It's a comforting process, finding homes for my books, my sketchpad, and the handful of framed photos I've brought with me. I line them up on the dresser, a smiling picture of my parents waving from between two potted succulents days before they died in a car crash.

I hope they would be happy about this move. I know they would be glad for me to get away from Eddie. Although now that I think about it, that relationship was a crutch for losing them. He found me raw and vulnerable, and he manipulated me before trying to destroy me.

"Asshole," I mutter, but shake my head to forget about him again.

I glance over at the baby monitor perched on the bedside cabinet. The screen shows little Mia, peaceful in her crib, chest rising and falling in the steady rhythm of sleep. Just seeing her there, safe and sound, eases the tension in my shoulders from her father's brusque and less-than-welcoming attitude.

I finish with the unpacking, only having my toiletries to organise, and step back to survey my handiwork. It's the kind of routine I've always found solace in—everything in its right place, a spot for every little thing.

Stuffing the suitcase into the top of the wardrobe, I start dismantling the boxes, hoping I'm not going to need them anytime soon if Benjamin changes his mind about me being here.

The baby monitor emits a soft crackle before the sound of stirring comes through. I'm on my feet in an instant, crossing to the nursery next door. Mia's awake, her little arms flailing, legs kicking at the blanket she is trying to get rid of. I scoop her up, and she coos, eyes blinking up at me.

"Hey there, munchkin," I murmur as I lay her down to change her nappy. Mia gurgles and kicks her legs, seemingly happy with the attention. I glance around and notice how Benjamin has laid out everything Mia needs within easy reach: nappies, wipes, and a stack of clean onesies on the changing table. Running down the side of the room is all the bottle-making stuff, and I'm glad to see he has one of those prep machines that gives you a ready-to-drink bottle in seconds.

Massive time saver.

"Your daddy's pretty great, really, isn't he," I tell Mia, even though she's more interested in trying to stuff her hand in her mouth than what I'm saying. But it's true—Benjamin's done well here. He's trying his best to be everything his daughter needs, and that's all anyone can do. I soften slightly towards the cantankerous alpha. It would've been worse if he couldn't wait for me to get here so he could take off, leaving me to take care of his daughter for him. So, I have to respect that.

Once Mia's all fresh and happy, I place her back in the crib to make up a fresh bottle, then I scoop her back up and cradle her close, settling into the armchair by the crib. She nestles against me, ready for her feed, and I feel a sense of contentment wash over me. This isn't just a job; it's my calling. I'm ready to dive in, to give it my all. After all, this little girl in my arms and the man doing his best for her, are worth it.

As Mia starts to suckle, I take in the nursery. It's a dream, with pastel hues and soft toys scattered around like clouds on a summer day. There's a sense of calm that I haven't felt in a long time.

I glance down at Mia, her tiny hand gripping my finger like she's holding onto the world. Her eyes flutter closed, the rhythm of her feeding steady and soothing. For a brief moment, it's just us, and the rest of the world fades away.

Benjamin has done more than create an oasis; he has made a safe harbour for his daughter, a place where she can grow, laugh, and be loved.

"It looks like we're going to get along just fine," I murmur, and even though Mia can't understand me, I feel like she agrees, which might go a long way toward getting Benjamin to warm up to me, too.

Chapter 4

Benjamin

The front door clicks shut, leaving silence to settle over the house as Henry and Liam leave. I'm agitated and frustrated, and being away from Mia for so long, even though she is right here, has left me feeling empty inside. I push open the nursery door, my movements quiet, not wanting to disturb her.

I pause when I see Zara, tucked in the armchair with Mia nestled against her chest. Her voice is soft, a gentle melody that wraps around the room, soothing and sweet. I watch them, a lump forming in my throat. It's a simple scene, but it hits me like a ton of bricks. The kind of care and attention Mia's getting, the kind I never expected would come from anyone else after everything, breaks me just a bit more inside.

"Zara," I start, my voice rougher than I intend. "I can take over with Mia."

She looks up with a smile. "You should rest, Benjamin. I'm here now, and I've got her."

My jaw tightens. "I know it's your job, but she's my daughter. I don't need a rest from my own child."

Zara gives me a look, one that's all patience and no judgment, but it still makes something twist inside me. "It's not about needing a rest from her. It's about you getting the rest you need so you can be the best dad to Mia. We're doing great, so you can take some time to just chill."

I want to argue, to tell her she doesn't get it, that she can't possibly understand what it feels like to have someone you trust walk out on you—on your child. But the words stick in my throat, tangled up with the sight of my little girl resting peacefully in the arms of someone who isn't running away.

Yet.

Not wanting to argue in front of Mia, I turn on my heel without another word and head back to my room, the weight of the day pressing down on me, Zara's scent of lavender swirling all around me, making me ache with longing. Not for her, but for the time when I had my mate, and Mia had her mother.

I close the door behind me, leaning against it as if

it could prop me up. My hands fumble with the baby monitor, its little green lights blinking up at me. I set it on the bedside cabinet, the soft hum of its static, a thread connecting me to Mia, to the piece of my world nestled safely in Zara's arms.

I collapse onto the bed, my body sinking into the mattress. The exhaustion washes over me, tugging me under, but I resist the pull of sleep as I stare at the ceiling, thoughts racing and my heart aching. The dim glow of the baby monitor cast shadows across my room as I try to quiet my mind, but the memories come anyway—images of her walking away, leaving us, leaving Mia, our little girl who needs her mum and got stuck with just me instead.

I know Zara is good with her. I can see that with my own eyes, but trying to find comfort in the thought feels like a betrayal, like I'm passing my daughter off to a stranger. I know I'm being unfair to Zara, that she's only here to help, but the hurt is like a broken bone that never set right. It makes me lash out when I don't mean to and makes me say things sharper than I feel.

Exhaustion finally drags me down, and I drift off, the last thing I see is Mia's peaceful face on the screen, not knowing if I'm more relieved or resentful that she's sleeping soundly without me.

***

The darkness is thick around me when my eyes snap open. How long was I out? It feels like minutes, but the silence tells me it's been hours. My hand goes straight to the monitor, holding it up to my bleary eyes. Mia is in her crib, fast asleep, but what catches me off guard is Zara. She's curled up in the armchair, her body a soft curve under the throw blanket that my mum made and put on Zara's bed to make her feel at home here.

The sight makes my heart beat a bit quicker. I didn't expect Zara to stay by Mia's side all night. That's something a parent does, not a nanny.

It's unsettling and comforting at the same time.

My feet hit the thick carpet in a rush, my mind already made up. I move quickly towards the nursery door and push it open with determination. The only sound in the darkened room is Mia's gurgling, which demands my attention.

"Shh, sweetie," I whisper, scooping her up into my arms. She's warm and wriggly, her tiny fist brushing against my cheek as if she's reassuring me she's okay. I can't explain it, but I need her close tonight, closer than just through a screen.

"Benjamin?" Zara's voice slices through the hush of the room. Groggy with sleep, she's instantly alert as Mia's noise wakes her. She's rubbing her eyes, the blanket slipping off her shoulders as she sits up.

"I've got her," I say, more gruffly than intended. I don't want to be harsh, not really, but gentleness feels like a language I forgot how to speak.

"Are you sure? I'm up," she begins, but I'm already shaking my head.

"I'm sure. Go to your room and sleep."

She gives me a frustrated stare. "Okay," she murmurs, standing up and stretching briefly. "Call if you need anything." There's a hesitation in her step, like she wants to say more, do more, but she doesn't. She pads out of the nursery, leaving us alone.

"Let's get you settled, sweetie," I murmur to Mia, holding her close. Her tiny hand curls around my finger, a grip so strong and trusting. "It's just me and you, Mia. Always."

Back in my room, the crib is nestled close to my bed. I hadn't been sure about having it so near, but right now, it feels like the only place it should be. Gently, I lower Mia into it, her little noises filling the space between us. Her eyes blink sleepily up at me, and for a moment, everything else fades away. It's just her and me, and that's all that matters.

"Sleep tight, my little star," I murmur, tucking the blanket around her. She wriggles for a second before settling down again, her tiny chest rising and falling with each breath. This tiny person has become my world, and I'll do whatever it takes to make sure she's safe, happy, loved. Always.

My breath steadies as I lie back on the bed, exhaustion seeping into every bone in my body, the mating bite on my neck throbbing with the rejection of my omega mate.

My thoughts drift to Zara. She's here, in my house, taking care of Mia when I'm supposed to be the one doing all of that. Mum and Dad didn't take no for an answer and said I needed the help. They're not wrong. I've been running on fumes, and the work at the firm isn't going to wait much longer.

My eyes drift shut, but behind them, there's an endless reel of thoughts. It's more than just professional with Zara. She cares, really cares, and I don't know how to feel about that. Can I stand having her around? She's nothing like Nicole, Mia's mum, who left without so much as a backward glance. Will Zara leave as well? Will my bad attitude force her out of here?

"I'll never leave you, Mia." It's a promise, an oath sworn in the quiet of the night. Nicole might've walked out on us, but I won't. Not now, not ever. No matter how hard it gets.

Mia makes a small sound in her sleep, a reminder that she's here, she's real, and she's mine. My heart swells with love for this little being who depends on me for everything. She's my responsibility, my joy, my pain. I have to do everything in my power to give her the best life possible, even if it means accepting help from Zara.

I roll onto my side, facing the crib, watching Mia sleep. Maybe tomorrow I'll figure out how to handle all this—how to deal with Zara, work, and being a solo parent.

For now, though, I let the rhythm of Mia's breathing lull me into a restless sleep.

Chapter 5

Zara

Staring at the ceiling, it's impossible to fall back asleep. Trying to earn Benjamin's trust is like beating my head against a brick wall, but I've been here two minutes, so I have to be patient. I'm usually well-liked, though, and don't have conflict with anyone, Eddie notwithstanding, of course. It's starting to give me an ache and not in a good way. The omega designation in my DNA is desperate for him, an alpha, to accept me. I know I'm a people pleaser, but this is different. This is... his scent captivating me in ways that I need to push aside and forget about.

Groaning, I roll over on the small double bed.

Thud.

"Ah!"

My face is on the carpet from falling off the bed,

and the sheets are still tangled around my legs. I'm glad Benjamin didn't see me face plant. He wouldn't trust me with his baby if he had. It's weird, though. Holding a baby and dealing with children is when I'm at my most confident and capable, so he needn't worry.

"Shower," I mumble, untangling my legs and standing up. I sort out the covers on the bed and then gather up my towel and toiletries, slinging my dressing gown around my shoulders so I'm not sneaking back to my room in just a towel.

I slide out of my room, sneaking down the hallway to the bathroom.

The bathroom is cool and inviting, and as I strip down for the shower, I let the frustrations of the past day fade away with each layer of clothing. The hot spray of water soothes away the stiffness from sleeping in the armchair next to Mia. She had been niggly and fractious, and I didn't want her disturbing Benjamin, who I could hear snoring all the way down the hall. The poor man must've been exhausted. So I stayed, and it calmed her, and I'd do it again. This isn't a 9-5 job where I can clock in and clock out. I'm here for all the hours, and I hope Benjamin gets it through his thick alpha skull sooner rather than later.

The water rushes over me, drowning out everything but the beating pulse against my skin. It's a cleansing ritual that helps clear my head.

Once I'm done, I dry myself quickly and slip on my dressing gown to head back to my room. Making it there without incident, luckily, I dress in white leggings and oversized tee. Today, I have to make more progress with getting Benjamin on my side.

Today's the day I make us a team, for Mia's sake.

I head to the kitchen to start breakfast, hoping the smell of coffee and toast might lure out one grumpy alpha.

Halfway through popping bread into the toaster, there's a small squeal from the baby monitor clipped to my waistband.

I snatch it up to see Benjamin returning to the nursery with Mia. He is a totally different man than the brooding asshole he shows to me. Chuckling and tickling her, rocking her and dancing around as she flaps her arms. It's beautiful.

So his bad attitude is reserved just for me. But I understand. I have to. He feels guilty for needing help, and he thinks I'm going to leave like his mate did. I watch as he settles her in her cot, and then I go back to making toast as I hear him come down the stairs.

"Morning," I say brightly as he comes into the

kitchen with bedhead, tartan pyjama bottoms, and nothing else.

Don't look. Don't look... My gaze lingers on his abs before being drawn back up to his face by the intensity of his stare.

He glares at me as if he had forgotten I was even here. "Oh, you."

It takes a second of epic face control, but I don't grimace at him. I smile. An over-the-top cheesy grin that he seems to recoil from, like it's going to melt him or something. "Coffee?" I chirp.

"Tea."

Of course. If I'd offered the other way around, he'd be just as obtuse.

"I'll make it. I like it a certain way."

"Doesn't everyone?" I ask brightly, reaching for a mug anyway and handing it to him.

He looks at it for a moment and then leans past me to replace it and pick up another one. It's fair. Everyone has their favourite mug. But now it's my turn to recoil as his pinecone scent hits my nostrils and makes my heart beat a bit quicker. I stumble back and he looks at me like I've lost my mind, so I busy myself wiping down an already spotless counter.

"So, what are your plans for today?" I ask, glancing over my shoulder at him.

Benjamin doesn't respond immediately. His focus is on the task at hand as he meticulously stirs tea around in the mug. The way his fingers deftly work the spoon is almost mesmerising.

"Work," he grunts finally, not looking up. "Got to catch up on a lot of paperwork."

I nod understandingly, setting out plates and butter for the toast that's just popped up, golden brown and perfect. "Okay. Will that be here, or are you going out?"

He glances at me, a flicker of something indecipherable crossing his face before it settles back into that stern mask I'm getting to know all too well. "Here," he says curtly, taking a sip of the steaming tea he just made.

As I spread butter on the toast, I think about that flicker I saw. Was it vulnerability? My omega instincts are itching to soothe him, to show him he doesn't have to be strong all the time. But I tamp down those feelings. He's not ready for that kind of comfort for this hurt yet—at least not from me.

"Okay," I murmur, wishing he'd give me *something* to work with. I slide a plate of toast over to him.

He glares at it like it's poison, and I sigh. He is impossible!

But then he snatches it up and bites into it as he walks away, his mug in his other hand. Wonderful.

What a great way to get him on my side by making him hate me even more.

I stand there for a moment, letting out a small, frustrated huff. It's like navigating a minefield with this man. But as I glance at the empty space where he stood moments ago, I forgive him for being a dick. He's like a locked door with no key in sight. But something tells me there are treasures behind that door; it's not just stubborn pride and angst. There's caring in him—I've seen it with Mia—and if I'm patient enough, I'll see it directed somewhere else.

Shaking my head, I quickly eat my toast and tidy up, knowing Mia will probably be up soon and looking for her bottle.

A soft gurgling sound from the monitor alerts me, and I quickly wash my hands before heading back to the nursery. Mia is awake, wide-eyed and kicking her chubby legs.

"Good morning, sunshine," I coo as I pick her up. She rewards me with more cute baby noises that melts any remaining irritation from my encounter with Benjamin. I quickly make up a bottle with one hand while I keep hold of Mia. We settle into the comfy armchair, and she latches onto the bottle with gusto. It's these moments, the quiet ones with Mia, that fill me with warmth.

As Mia sucks eagerly on her bottle, my

thoughts stray to Benjamin again. Despite the rough edges to his attitude, there's a tender side I witness only in his interactions with his daughter. I wonder if anyone else sees that side of him or if it's locked away, accessible only by this tiny, innocent being.

Once Mia has her fill, I gently pat her back until a soft burp escapes her lips, and she nuzzles into my shoulder.

I lay Mia down in her cot again and stroke her forehead; she's contented for now. Feeling brave—or perhaps I'm just being stupid—I decide to join Benjamin downstairs. Maybe if we're in the same room without the pressure of conversation, his walls might lower just a bit.

Padding softly down the stairs in my slippers, I enter the living room, which has been turned into an impromptu office. Papers are scattered across the coffee table where Benjamin sits hunched over his laptop.

"Do you need anything?"

I curse myself for asking, but I can't help it. It's in my nature to nurture.

He glances up briefly, eyes narrowed behind his glasses, but he shakes his head curtly before returning his gaze to the screen. "No," he mutters.

"Will you be going to the office tomorrow?"

He looks up at me with a frown. "Why do you ask?"

"Uhm, your mum said that you'd run out of paternity leave and were now on holiday leave. I'm here now. You can go back and do your work without worrying about Mia."

Stop talking, Zara. You're making it worse.

His gaze hardens, and I'm sure he's about to lash out with a comment about not needing my permission to go back to work or something equally as prickly. But instead, he shocks me and sighs, the sound heavy like it's been dragged from the depths of his soul.

"I know that," he says, his voice softer than I expected. "I've been... adjusting. It's not as simple as just going back."

I nod, fighting the urge to step closer and offer more than just assistance. I want to offer comfort, but I know that's not my place. "I understand," I say, keeping my voice gentle. "If you need anything, I'm here, okay?" It seems that I need to constantly remind him I'm not going anywhere.

"Thanks," he grumbles, turning back to his screen.

I take it as my cue to leave and retreat back to the kitchen, where I can be useful. Busy hands keep nosy thoughts at bay—or at least that's what I tell myself as I start prepping for lunch.

Chapter 6

Zara

As I chop vegetables for a simple salad, my mind wanders back to Benjamin. His thank you, grunted though it was, felt like a small victory, a chink in his armour that was beginning to show. But it's not about winning with him; it's about understanding and being there for him and Mia.

I'm so engrossed in my thoughts that I don't hear him approach until Benjamin clears his throat from the kitchen doorway. I jump, nearly slicing my thumb.

"Shit!" I exclaim, putting down the knife and checking for signs of blood. I'm not great with that. Passing out occurs and all that, so I'm glad that I didn't cut myself.

"Careful," he says, an edge of actual concern in his voice that has me blinking at him in surprise.

"What are you? A ninja?"

He snorts. "Hardly."

"Did you need something?"

He hesitates, shifting on his feet, and then gestures vaguely at the fridge. "Water."

"Sit down. I'll get it."

Benjamin reluctantly perches on one of the stools at the island, watching as I get him a bottle of water. The silence is awkward but not unbearable.

"Thanks," he murmurs as I hand it to him.

I nod and return to my task, resisting the urge to fill the silence with pointless chatter that won't get me anywhere. The sound of crunching vegetables under my knife is soothing in its monotony.

We stay like that for a few minutes—me chopping and him sipping water—before he speaks up again.

"You're good with her," he says abruptly. "She seems to like you."

I look over my shoulder, surprised by the compliment. "Thanks. She's easy to love."

He nods, absently running a hand through his hair, and for the first time, I see something other than a soul-deep scowl on his face.

"I wasn't sure about having you here to help," he

admits quietly. "I should be able to handle it all on my own."

I set the knife down and lean back against the counter. "It's okay not to have all the answers or do everything solo, Benjamin. Everyone needs help sometimes."

He looks at me, and I see the tiredness in his eyes. "Yeah, well," he starts but doesn't finish.

Silence falls between us again, but it's a little less tense now. A shared understanding is beginning to weave its way through the air. He takes another sip of water.

Benjamin watches me as I resume chopping. I can feel his gaze on me. It's not as uncomfortable as I would have expected having someone watch my every move, not when it's him anyway. Pretty sure if some rando appeared in the bushes, stalking me, I'd take umbrage, but with Benjamin, it's... dare I say it? Nice.

"I'll get back to work," he mumbles and leaves me alone again to finish up the lunch prep. My phone buzzes on the counter next to me, and I frown at it as I keep chopping.

No Caller ID.

"Well, if you don't want to be identified, I don't want to answer you, fucker," I say, but my blood runs a bit cooler. Could it be Eddie? I blocked his number, but he still has mine. He could quite easily ring me from another number.

Cursing myself that while I thought I had everything planned, I clearly missed the memo that screams if you're running from a toxic ex to *change* your number, not just block his.

"Dumb, dumb, dumb," I mutter. "I wonder where the nearest shop is." I didn't see one on my drive in yesterday, but I'm going to have to find out.

Steeling myself as I replace the knife on the counter and march into the lounge to confront Benjamin, I ask, "Where is the shop?"

He turns his head, his eyes narrowing ever so slightly as if trying to figure out the urgency behind my question. "There's a corner shop in the village. It's about a twenty-minute walk," he replies, then pauses. "Why? Do you need something?"

I nod, trying to appear nonchalant. "I need to grab some essentials."

Benjamin studies me for a moment longer and then nods. "We'll get Mia in the pram, and we'll all go."

"Uhm," I murmur, surprised. "It's okay; I can go by myself. Just point me in the right direction."

"Mia needs to get out for some fresh air."

"Mia and I can go. You're busy—"

"We'll all go." His tone has gone back to the flat,

almost order, and it makes me swallow back my annoyance that he doesn't trust me with Mia. But I get it. He doesn't want me disappearing with his child without him. Maybe one day when I've earned that trust, but that's not today. Or tomorrow. Or probably even next month.

"Okay," I agree with a soft smile. "Do you want to get the pram out? I'll finish the salad to eat later and get Mia ready."

He grunts in acknowledgement and goes back to whatever he is doing, leaving me standing there, trying not to think about how this short trip feels like some kind of bizarre outing.

Pushing thoughts of Eddie out of my mind for now, I head back to the kitchen to finish up lunch. I plate up the salad and some cold meats I find in the fridge and then head upstairs to get my shoes on, and a jumper, and maybe a jacket. Spring in the Lake District is decidedly chilly.

After bundling Mia up in her warmest clothes, we head down, my handbag swinging against my side as I hold Mia close. Stepping outside onto the driveway, I see Benjamin wrestling with the pram. He's muttering to himself, and I let out a light chuckle. Who knew a pram could take down an alpha's poise?

When he sees me standing there, trying not to laugh, he gives me a scathing glare. "This bloody thing," he grumbles. "Designers of these need a good talking to."

I grab the other side of the pram, and together, we unfold it with a satisfying click. Benjamin looks at me with an eyebrow raised. "You can do that one-handed? What are you? A pram master?"

Giggling stupidly, I brush my hair behind my ear. "Nope, just practised. This isn't my first pram-deo."

"Huh?" He looks at me like I've lost my mind.

"Uhm. A play on rodeo..." I trail off, cheeks hotter than hellfire.

"Oh," he says and gives me a charming smile that floors me completely. My stomach drops, and the omega inside me lights up like a fucking Christmas Tree. We stare at each other for a few moments before Mia gurgles happily in my arms. He hesitates only for a second more before taking her from me and securing her in the pram. She coos, pleased as punch to have both of our attention.

"Well then," I say, clapping my hands together for lack of knowing what to do with them now Mia's not in them. "Shall we?"

We set off down the road, past the identical-looking houses and then turn the opposite way to which I came in and down the lane that leads into the village. Against my better judgment, I steal a glance at Benjamin, pushing the pram. Now that he's out of his usual environment, there's a change in him. He seems less tense, more part of the world around him.

"So, will you be going to work tomorrow?" I ask, just to break the silence.

He falters for a moment and frowns. "I haven't decided yet."

"You can, you know. Mia and I will be fine."

He stops on the narrow pavement and glares at me. "Look, Zara. I get that you mean well, but you've got to stop pushing me."

"What?" I blurt out, surprised by the aggression. "I'm not pushing you anywhere. I'm only saying that you can go without worrying."

"I'm still going to worry," he snaps. "I will always worry. And I don't need you making it worse by trying to shove me out of my own home and away from my daughter. Why are you doing that? Hmm?"

Staring wide-eyed, I fail to come up with an answer for him, which enrages him further. "That's not what I'm doing," I say softly. "But you need to be able to provide for your daughter, and that means keeping your job."

His eyes practically burst into flame, and I wish the pavement would open up, swallow me and deposit me somewhere far, far away from the angry alpha.

"Oh, really," he hisses. "How about you mind your own fucking business and leave me the hell alone?" He tries to turn on the pavement, but there is little space between the road and the hedge. He executes a dramatic four-point pram turn, getting angrier by the second before he marches back the way we came, leaving me on the pavement to stare after him in shock.

"Fuck," I breathe out. "That went horribly wrong."

Yeah, no shit, Zara.

I gaze after him, wondering if I should follow or stay the course and give him some time to cool down. That might give him the opportunity to lock me out of the house, though, and then I will have literally nothing but the clothes on my back and my car.

As if the universe is intervening, my phone buzzes again with the No Caller ID number, reminding me I need the new SIM card. Panic clawing my insides, I keep heading towards the shop, hoping I'll find it without getting wildly lost in the countryside and that by the time I return, things with Benjamin will have simmered down. I clutch the phone tightly against my palm, fighting the urge to throw it into the nearest bush. It's not the phone's fault that my life is a mess, and it's certainly not

Benjamin's fault either, even if he's currently at the top of my shit list.

While walking briskly, my panic only grows as the phone doesn't stop. A text message eventually comes through.

Pick up. We need to talk. You know you don't want this.

"Ugh! Fuck off," I say through gritted teeth. It hardens my weakening resolve to turn around and catch up to Benjamin before he packs up all my stuff and chucks it out on the driveway.

The shop comes into view, and relief washes over me like a wave. The bell above the door jingles as I enter.

I force a smile and approach the counter. "Hi, I need to buy a SIM card."

A friendly-looking middle-aged woman with spectacles sliding down her nose—nods and points to the array behind her.

After purchasing the SIM card and giving a polite nod to the woman, I take a moment to swap them out and take a deep breath before heading back to Benjamin's house. Maybe he'll be calmer now—maybe we can sit down and talk like adults without him snapping at me and without me making dumbfuck comments about him not being sacked from his job.

"What were you thinking?" I cry out as I stumble down the pavement back the way I came.

As I eventually turn back onto his street, all is quiet, and my belongings are nowhere to be seen. With my heart hammering and my palms sweating, I reach for the door handle on the front door.

It opens, and I gulp back the sob of relief.

The house is silent, so I creep upstairs to my room to take my shoes off and ditch my bag.

I hear Mia crying in the nursery suddenly, that same fretful wail she had last night, and my instincts kick in.

I dash towards the nursery, my pulse racing. As I fling open the door, Mia's cries crescendo into a full-blown howl. Benjamin looks frazzled and about to go into a meltdown. He's trying to soothe her with gentle bounces and soft shushes, but she isn't having any of it.

"Here, let me," I say, a lot more softly than before. I can't stand to see them both so distressed.

He looks up at me with weary eyes, and for a second, I think he's going to argue and tell me to piss off out of his face, but instead, he hands Mia over without a word.

Mia settles down almost instantly in my arms. I rock her gently, whispering soothing nothings into her little ear. Benjamin watches us with a complex expression that I can't even begin to unpack.

"How? I'm her father," he says, not bitterly but full of exhaustion.

"It's my scent. The lavender soothes them. It's why I stayed with her last night."

He breathes in noticeably, and his jaw tightens, his nose pinching as if he has smelt rotten vegetables.

Gee, thanks, asshole.

But I let it go because Mia needs me. "I think she might have started teething already," I murmur.

He frowns. "She's only three months."

"I know. It happens. We'll need to get some teething granules soon."

"I'll go now," he says immediately. "Where? The chemist?"

"Yeah, or any big supermarket."

"There's a Tesco not far from here. I'll go there."

"Okay, I'll put on my shoes and get Mia in the car." I turn to the door, but he shakes his head.

"No, she's settled now. Stay with her. I'll go."

I meet his gaze, and the argument and everything else just falls away as unimportant. He is trusting me alone with his infant, and I'm not going to hold anything against him. He is scared and tired and overwhelmed, and who wouldn't be in his situation?

"Okay." I sit down in the armchair and hold the baby close. He nods stiffly and, with a last look back, leaves Mia and me alone.

Chapter 7

Benjamin

I slam my car door a little harder than I mean to and wince. It's only when I'm pulling out of the driveway that it hits me how utterly fucking ridiculous today has been. From snapping at Zara, to walking out on her, only to end up handing over Mia like a deflated football, and now I'm off to Tesco like some errand boy because my daughter may be teething.

The drive is short but gives me enough time to stew over everything. Zara's scent is still loosely clinging to my clothes, and it's battling with the remnants of my anger. It makes sense that Mia would find it soothing; it's calm and gentle, unlike the storm that seems to perpetually rage in my soul these days.

Parking up, I haul myself out and into the bright lights of the busy supermarket. The place is packed out as expected on a fucking Sunday, and it's why I usually avoid them like the plague, but here I am, heading for the baby aisle and hoping to fuck I don't have to find anyone to ask them where the teething granules are. What are they even? It sounds fucking horrible, but I'm taking Zara's word for it because I've got fuck all else to go off.

I find the baby aisle and march up and down, dodging around people, trying to find the teething granules. When I find them, there are three different kinds, and I haven't got a bloody clue which one to get. With an impatient huff, I grab one of each—can't go wrong with that approach, right?

Standing impatiently at the self-checkout, I get to the front of the mile-long queue and zap the boxes, paying with my card, which was luckily still stuffed into my pants from the walk earlier.

Walk.

Fucking disaster, you mean.

"Who the fuck does she think she is?" I mutter out loud and get a weird look from the couple next to me, but I scowl at them, and they go back to their business.

Moments later, on the way back to the car, I calm down slightly now that the anxiety of being around so many people abates. It's one reason why I'm so reluctant to head back to work. I hate people. Henry and Liam are about my limit because I've known them since we learned how to walk, and Nicole bailing on us has exacerbated that feeling in me. Being alone with Mia at home has been soothing in more ways than one. Then Zara shows up, and my whole world has been turned upside fucking down. I don't want to go back to work where I have to be around people. I've been meaning to ask the boss of the small, yet extremely successful firm, if I could work from home for the majority of the time, but I haven't had the time or the inclination to attempt that conversation yet.

One thing I know, and it's why I was so unbelievably pissed off with Zara, is that she is right in what she said. I *do* need to provide for my daughter. She has only me. If I lose my job, we're toast. I'm mortgaged to the hilt, having relied on Nicole's income as well when we secured the five-bedroom property. We'd planned on more kids, and Nicole wanted an office where she could hopefully work from home when she started her VA career online. The house isn't huge; it's on a regular estate in lower middle-class Britain, and 'detached' leaves a lot to be desired. It's a marketing tool more than anything. You can just about fit a wheelie bin down the path between the houses, but it was *ours*. Our home. Our future.

And she shot it all to hell by being a selfish cunt

and walking out on her one-month-old infant and her mate.

Growling furiously, I slam my foot on the accelerator and squeal out of the car park like a boy racer.

Zara, holding Mia, flashes through my mind, and I slow down. How she instinctively knew what Mia needed was surprising and a bit awe-inspiring, if I'm being honest. It softens something inside me, though I'm not ready to examine that too closely yet. Let's face it, part of me doesn't want her here because she's another reminder of how shit I am at this whole single dad thing. She's like this fucking ray of sunshine on an otherwise cloudy day, and part of me wants to bask in it, but the other – the stubborn asshole inside – wants to shut the blinds.

I pull into the driveway with less of a squeal and more of a sobering glide.

Grabbing the boxes of teething granules from the passenger seat, I make my way inside. The house is quiet, almost too quiet for my liking. But then I hear it, a soft melody snaking its way down the stairs. Zara's singing again.

I climb the stairs on autopilot, drawn to that sound like a bloody satellite homing in on Earth. As I push open the nursery door, Zara cradles Mia against her chest, swaying gently back and forth in time with her lullaby. It's a picture of peace and contentment that makes my heart do this weird, fluttery thing that I will absolutely deny if anyone asks.

Zara looks up and smiles softly as she sees me in the doorway. "Hey," she whispers, as if loud words might shatter the magic of this moment.

"Got these," I grunt, holding up the boxes like trophies from some great hunt in Tesco's wild aisles.

She nods approvingly, and her smile widens just a tad more. "Three?"

"I didn't know which one was best."

She giggles softly and grabs the green and white box. "I'll try these first."

"How do you...? You know?" I glare at her as if she knows what the hell I'm talking about.

"Apply them?" she asks gently. "The easiest way is with your little finger. Hold her while I go and wash my hands."

I nod and take Mia from her arms, feeling the familiar weight and warmth of my daughter settle against me. Something akin to calm seeps through the walls I've built so high since Nicole left. Mia gurgles, and I can't help the twitch of my lips that might be the beginning of a smile. I can't let Zara see that, though; she'll think she's winning.

Zara returns, hands scrubbed and ready for baby dental duty. "All clean," she announces, her voice still soft but laced with an unmistakable note of mirth. It's as though she can see right through my gruff exterior as I lay Mia down on the changing table.

I watch, fascinated despite myself, as Zara opens the granules and pours them onto her fingertip. Mia's little mouth opens like she knows relief is coming, and Zara gently rubs the granules on her sore gums. To my amazement, Mia's fussing eases almost immediately.

"Look at that," Zara coos, "happy baby."

Still trying to keep up this façade that I'm not impressed as hell with Zara's omega magic, I grunt a response.

Zara gives me a knowing look, but doesn't call me on my bullshit. Instead, she picks Mia up and settles into the armchair with her. "If you need to finish up your work, I've got her now."

I want to argue. I want to say that I'm fine and don't need anyone's bloody help, especially not from an omega who has somehow wheedled her way under my skin without even trying. But the truth is, I'm knackered——completely bruised from the inside out, and Zara's offering a lifeline against the stubbornness that is trying to get the better of me.

I sigh, the sound more defeated than I intend it to be. "Yeah, alright." It's barely above a whisper because pride is a stubborn bastard, and admitting I need the help feels like admitting defeat.

Zara doesn't gloat or offer platitudes. She just nods, her attention already back on Mia as she continues to hum softly.

Heading back downstairs, I try to focus on the work that needs doing. Emails, project updates, plans that need reviewing, but the idea that I *do* need to go back into work tomorrow gnaws at my insides.

Before I chicken out, I shoot a quick text to Alan, the boss, so there can be no backing out. He will sack me if I backtrack now.

I'm interrupted by Zara's appearance, gentle and unobtrusive.

"Mia's asleep," she says quietly.

"Thanks," I reply with a gruffness that isn't quite as pronounced now.

"We make a good team," she ventures cautiously.

I couldn't agree more, but the words get stuck in my throat. If I admit them and she leaves Mia, leaves *me*, it will gut me completely. So, it's better to hold her at arm's length and try to place some trust in her to do the job she was hired to do.

Chapter 8

Zara

Groggily, I open my eyes, having slept in the armchair again to make sure Mia was comforted and felt safe and secure. I stretch and check the phone, still resting on the arm from where I placed it last night when I came back up after dinner. It's early morning, but not the crack of dawn. Leaping up, I glance around and hear the sounds of someone moving around the kitchen.

Heading down, pulling a hair tie from my pjs pocket, I scrape my hair back into a messy bun and enter the kitchen to see Benjamin making coffee.

I knew it! The bastard.

"Coffee?" he asks with a smirk, knowing he's busted.

"I'll have tea," I reply, just to be obtuse.

He snorts. "Okay, well, you know the drill with tea."

Narrowing my eyes, I set about making a cuppa as he moves on to the toaster.

"I'll be going in today," he says casually. "Maybe half a day. See how it goes."

I nod encouragingly. "Good stuff. We'll be here happy and safe when you get back."

He gives me a look that screams we'd better be, or there's going to be a storm raining down shit on my head from a dizzy height. I give him a bright smile that he scowls at. He is not a morning person.

Scratch that. He isn't an any time of day person.

"I would appreciate it if you let me know before you take her out. The garden is fine, obviously, but you know, for a walk."

"Of course."

"All the numbers are on the fridge." He points it out. "My mobile, the office, my parents and their work, Henry, Liam, the doctors, the nearest hospital, which is an hour away, so you know, anticipate, and 999."

"Anticipate?" How in the fuck am I supposed to do that? Buy a crystal ball?

He grunts.

"I changed my number. I've texted it to you and your parents."

"Yes, I saw. Why is that?"

The question is innocent enough, but I don't want to answer it, so I shrug. "Fresh start and all that."

"I'm going to shower," he murmurs and disappears upstairs with his coffee mug and toast in hand.

Seeing as he didn't make me any, I set about making my own toast and jump when the front door opens. I grab the nearest knife from the counter and stand poised to attack any intruder, but it's just Liam, sauntering in like he owns the place.

"Do you have a key to this place?" I snap.

"Yeah, and what are you going to do with that? Slather me with butter?" His green eyes light up, and that flirty smile adorns his face.

I glare at the used butter knife in my hand and haughtily place it down. "You wish."

"Maybe I do," he murmurs. "Where's Ben?"

"Showering."

Silence.

I turn to see if Liam has disappeared, but I see him still standing there, a curiously amused expression on his cute face.

"Oh? And you know that because...?"

"He told me he was going to shower. You just missed him," I snap.

"Okay, keep your pants on. Or not, you know, whatever makes you comfortable."

"How about you shutting the fuck up?"

"Ohh, feisty. I like that." He approaches and reaches over to snatch a piece of my toast and bites into it with a big grin.

"You are an ass," I mutter, but the fluttering feeling in my stomach at his closeness is hard to ignore. His scent is like hot earth after a summer rain, and it makes me want to leap on him and bury my face in the crook of his neck.

Flushing deeply, I turn from him and berate myself. This isn't like me. I need to keep it professional.

But Liam isn't a fool. He knows exactly what he's doing to me. "Fancy going out sometime?"

"What?" I stammer, turning back to face him to see if he's joking.

He's not. His face is serious. Contemplative and a bit wary.

I blink, unsure how to navigate this unexpected development. I'm here for Mia, not to get tangled up in whatever charming web Liam is spinning. But he's impossible to ignore, with that smile that could coax the sun from behind the rain clouds.

"Out? Like a date?" I question, and there's an edge of disbelief in my voice.

He nods slowly. "Yeah, like a date."

I chew on my lip, weighing the pros and cons. It's clear there's an attraction, but things are complicated enough without adding romance. Then again, I can't deny the spark of excitement at the idea. I don't know anyone up here apart from Benjamin and his parents. The prospect of a friend, someone to chat with about something other than Mia, is enticing.

"Think about it?" he murmurs.

"I don't think Benjamin would approve," I mutter back.

"Who says he has to know?" Liam asks and, with a saucy wink, leaves me to contemplate that very dicey situation.

Tea in hand, I circle the kitchen, my mind a whirlpool of Liam, Benjamin, and the offer that hangs in the air, tempting but with an undercurrent of danger.

Moments later, Benjamin strides into the kitchen, now dressed for work in a smart shirt that shows off his well-muscled frame. He's an alpha through and through - all imposing presence and barely restrained power. His navy blue pants are well cut and expensive.

Benjamin pauses and for a moment, he looks like he might say something. But then he just nods and grunts a goodbye before heading out, apparently meeting Liam in the lounge on his way out.

I'm left standing in the silence of his absence, my internal debate about Liam's invitation growing louder. Deciding to push it aside for now, I head back upstairs to Mia.

Liam and his date proposition can wait.

Chapter 9

Liam

Leaving the house with Ben as we car share to the office; I'm glad he's making the move to go back. I highly doubt on any level that he will stay all day, but it's a start. The poor dude has been through the wringer, facing something no one should ever have to. If it had been me, I'd have folded like a cheap tent, but he's holding up behind these mile-high castle walls he's built around himself. Never really an open guy, he is so much more closed off now, and it makes my heart hurt for him. Zara is little Miss Ray of Sunshine, though, and I knew she would bring a spark back to his life, even if it was to piss him off. It's a start. Sue and Peter consulted me and Henry before they even told Ben about Zara. We all agreed she was perfect. In person, she is even better than I could've imagined. Her scent, her tight little body and peachy ass, that face that could launch a thousand ships – not that I'm the kind to objectify omegas, mind you, but credit where it's due. She's bloody gorgeous, and it's doing my head in a bit.

I can't help but tease her; it's like she's this unwrapped lollipop, and I've always been one to poke at the world to see what happens. I sprung the date on her because I genuinely want to know what she'll say. It's not just about getting in her pants, although I'm an alpha drawn to her, so yeah, it's there, but she's got this air about her – like she knows exactly who she is, and that's fucking attractive.

Benjamin hasn't seen it yet, or if he has, he's pretending not to. The bloke's got more walls than a fortress, and for good reason. His heart was torn out and Zara is touching on edges that haven't felt warmth in ages. Then there's me, the alpha with a sense of humour as subtle as a house brick, wondering if there could be something more between me and Zara.

In the car with Ben now, driving towards the daily grind at the office, he's got his game face on as he keeps his eyes on the road—all business and determination. But he barely says a word.

"Thinking about Mia?" I venture.

He nods stiffly. "Always."

"And Zara?"

That gets his attention. He turns his head slowly toward me, eyes narrowing slightly. "What about her?"

I shrug nonchalantly. "She's good with her."

"How would you know?"

"If she weren't, you'd have her out on her ass quicker than lightning, so I'm making assumptions. Sue me."

Ben's jaw clenches, and he stares back at the road. "She's fine," he says in a clipped tone.

It's always 'fine', 'okay', or 'alright' with him. No fluffy words, just plain, to the point, bordering on rude.

I let the silence sit, only the sound of the car engine and the occasional squelch of tyres through puddles still sitting there from the downpour of Friday, filling the space between us.

But as we pull into the office car park and go about our day, my thoughts never stray far from the tiny omega nanny. She's a conundrum wrapped in an enigma and draped in a cashmere cardigan that hugs all her curves in all the right places. I catch myself wondering what her answer will be to my proposition. I'm not letting it drop. Not yet. I *will* ask her again if I don't hear from her. Not in a creepy, stalker-y way, but I need her to know I'm interested and that I'm not going to let Ben stop something that could be really awesome.

My hand reaches for my phone to text her, but maybe that's being too eager. I slide the phone back into my pocket and focus on the pile of paperwork piled up around me. It's not just about playing it cool; it's about timing and respect. I need to show her that I'm serious, not just chasing a whim or a fantasy of my best friend's nanny.

It's like my mind's split in two – one half on client portfolios, the other on Zara's soft laugh, the way she challenged me without a single hint of fear this morning. It's refreshing, and while I can see she has that softer omega side, she isn't afraid to stand up for herself.

The day drags on, and finally, it's time to call it quits. Ben looks like he's about to drop from exhaustion, stress, or both. I'm shocked he made it to this point and didn't cave and go home at lunchtime. Sure, he'd have had to come back and pick me up, but maybe that's why he stayed. He doesn't say much as we head back to the car.

As we drive home, we pass by rolling hills dotted with sheep, the landscape bathed in the golden hues of late afternoon sun. It's strikingly beautiful here in the Lake District – tranquil, serene – yet it feels like we're stuck in a bubble of tension that even this view can't dissipate.

I clear my throat. "You did good today."

He snorts. "Gee, thanks, Dad."

I chuckle. "No, seriously. I mean it. You went the distance."

"Only because I had to drive your sorry ass back home."

"Ha! I knew it."

We share a laugh, and his tension eases a bit.

"Zara texted me updates. It made it easier, you know."

"Yeah, I can imagine."

The rest of the ride is quiet, but there's a kind of peace between us, a momentary truce in the silent battle Ben's got going on inside. He's a fortress, alright, but every stronghold has its weak spots, and I reckon Zara is one for him. He just doesn't know it yet or won't admit it.

When we get back to the house, I come in for a quick beer before heading home. It's lonely in my flat; even though it's only a short walk from here, I'm still alone when I get there. We find Zara and Mia in the garden. Mia is bundled up in her pram as Zara feeds the ducks that have waddled their way over from the small lake at the back of the estate. The sight does funny things to my chest, like maybe I want something more domestic than my bachelor pad and string of meaningless dates.

Zara looks up and smiles at us. God, that smile floors me. "You're back."

Ben grunts a reply, scooping Mia up from the pram with an expertise only a parent possesses. But his usual stoic face softens just for a second as he kisses his daughter's head.

Zara's gaze lingers on me, a secretive smile on her face that tells me that she is thinking about the possibility of a date. I run my hand through my hair.

"Yeah," I say, voice casual, my gaze never leaving hers. "Looks like you've had a productive afternoon."

"You have ducks! No one told me about the ducks."

"You're a fan of ducks?" I ask, making a mental note for some reason, just cataloguing things away.

"Who isn't?" she responds. "Ducks, deer, cows, sheep. You don't get those in the middle of London. Pigeons, yes. Lots and lots of pigeons, but no ducks."

I laugh, and I'm glad to see the corners of Ben's mouth twitch upwards, too. It's a rarity these days. "We'll have to make sure you're fully briefed on all the wildlife around here then," I say, still watching Zara.

She laughs, the sound light and airy, like it could lift the lingering shadows in the corners of the garden. "I'd appreciate that. Countryside newbie here, remember?"

I raise an eyebrow and tap a finger to my lips, pretending to consider something deeply important. "Might require several guided tours. Deep immersion in the local culture, and all."

Her eyes dance with amusement. "Sounds very comprehensive."

Ben clears his throat, looking between us with an unreadable expression for a moment before fixing his gaze on Mia, who's starting to fuss for attention. He bounces her easily and diverts the conversation back to safer ground. "We should get inside before it gets too chilly for her."

Zara nods, her attention shifting back to her charge. She grabs the pushchair as Ben heads into the house and follows, pushing it along and getting it through the back door with ease.

I linger by the door, watching as Ben heads toward the stairs with Mia cuddled close against his chest. Zara hangs back a bit as she folds down the pram.

Once Ben is out of earshot, I lean in a little closer to Zara. "About earlier," I murmur, keeping my voice low.

Her cheeks colour just a tad, and she looks away briefly before meeting my gaze again. Her scent, that gorgeous lavender with honey undertones, wafts in my direction and I'm a lost alpha.

"Hmm?" she murmurs.

"Did you give it some thought?"

She bites her lip, a hint of a smile teasing at the edges. "Maybe I did. A girl can ponder her options, can't she?"

"Absolutely," I agree with a nod. "Options are important."

"We are talking about the same thing, right?" There's a playful glint in her eye that says she knows exactly what we're discussing.

"Of course we are," I flash a grin. "I wouldn't be so forward as to assume you've thought about anything else."

Her laugh echoes in the small space between us. "You're confident. I'll give you that."

"I try," I reply, my voice as smooth as I can make it. "So, should I take that as you're considering saying yes?"

She tilts her head, casting a thoughtful glance towards the upstairs where Ben has disappeared. "I am considering it," she confesses. "But there's a lot to think about, you know?"

"I know," I admit, "but sometimes overthinking can steal away the fun parts."

"Mmm." Her gaze meets mine again, full of

promise and caution mixed into one beautiful package.

I take a step back, giving her room to breathe. "When you're ready to stop considering and start experiencing, let me know. My number's on the fridge."

She giggles but sobers up quickly. "I will."

With that, she turns away from me, heading up the stairs with an unhurried grace that leaves me standing in the doorway, feeling like maybe the odds are stacked in my favour.

Chapter 10

Zara

Feeling Liam's eyes on me as I walk up the stairs is unnerving. It's different to the way Benjamin looked at me. His was scrutiny, sizing me up as a caregiver to his daughter. This is... heated. I won't deny it sends a thrill rushing through me. His scent notwithstanding, I find *him* attractive. He is fun and cute and the total opposite of Eddie. He wants to build, not break. But two things are holding me back, and one of them is currently standing at the changing table, cooing to his baby daughter. The other, well, let's just say I'm gun-shy after being gaslighted for all those months. Even though in my head I know Liam isn't Eddie, my heart just can't take another knock. It's already taking it all it can from Benjamin's brusqueness.

"I'll make her up a bottle," I murmur as I step into the room.

Benjamin only nods and carries on with his undivided attention to Mia. I set about prepping the bottle and watching as the hot water gushes into it, followed by the longer cooler water. This really is a marvel machine. Prepping by hand hours in advance is a real ball ache, truth be told.

Twisting the top on, I hand it to him as he settles into the armchair with her.

Benjamin's eyes flick up to mine for just a moment as he takes the bottle, and there's something there, something unreadable that makes me pause.

"About Liam..." he starts and stops as I give him a curious stare.

"What about him?" *Oh God, does he know Liam asked me out?*

"Take what he says with a grain of salt."

"What does that mean?"

"When he was talking about showing you around. Don't expect it. He's—"

"What?"

Benjamin glares at me for making him say it, but I need more information than he is currently providing.

"A serial dater." His gaze hardens when he

finally meets my eyes. "I don't want you thinking there's anything to his flirting."

I press my lips together, desperately holding onto the laugh that needs to come out. "Thanks," I choke out. "I can take care of myself."

"It's more for Mia's sake. I don't want him driving you away."

And there it is. He's not jealous, but he knows he has a good thing going here with me.

"I'm not going anywhere, and, for the record, it'll take a lot more than a few flirty comments from a cute guy to send me packing."

Something flicks across his face, but it's gone before I can see what it is. He nods and drops his gaze back to Mia. That's my cue to beat it.

"I'll get dinner on. Spaghetti Bolognese, okay?"

"Yes."

I roll my eyes and turn to the door.

"Thanks."

Snickering at the afterthought, I stick my thumb up, but don't turn back around. "No worries," I chirp and hastily make my way back downstairs, contemplating his remarks about Liam. They're not off-putting in the sense that I refuse to date alphas who like the omegas. There are things to consider, like the rut. It's not likely a single alpha is going to sit around and suffer through his rut, needing a knot when he can find a willing omega to stick his cock into. I wonder briefly about Benjamin's rut and how he plans to deal with that now that he has been rejected. But then I find this train of thought a bit weird and shake my head, gathering up the ingredients for the Bolognese.

The sizzle of the onions as they hit the pan is oddly satisfying. I focus on the task at hand, dicing tomatoes and adding them to the pan. Cooking is therapeutic, and soon, the smell of the sauce is making my mouth water. Stirring it gently, I put a pan of water on to boil before adding the spaghetti and glancing at the clock. Benjamin should be down soon.

When more time passes, and the spaghetti is ready, I chew my lip. He's still not come down. Draining it off, I throw it in the sauce to keep it from ruining and head up to the nursery.

The sight that greets me makes my stomach do a flip-flop. Benjamin is fast asleep in the armchair, his shirt unbuttoned, and Mia's chubby little cheek pressed against his chest while she sleeps. The skin-to-skin contact is adorable, and the fact that he knows what his daughter needs is heart-warming.

Not wanting to disturb them, I back out and pull the door softly closed. Going back to the kitchen, I dish up my dinner and eat it at the kitchen island, messing about on my phone. By the time I'm finished and have tidied up, Benjamin still hasn't come down. I leave the Spag Bol in the pan, where he can warm it later if he comes down and head to the lounge to read my book for a bit. It's the first time I've really had some time on my own where I wasn't sleeping. My mind wanders back to Liam, and I feel more and more as if this is something I *want* to explore. Slowly. A walk to the lake in the afternoon or coffee somewhere close by. But Benjamin won't like it, and that is something that I have to consider regardless of whether it's really his business who I date or not. If he's paying me to take care of his daughter, then I absolutely have to take his feelings into account.

Liam's idea of not telling Benjamin isn't a good one. Secrets come out, and it will probably be worse if Benjamin finds out later. But is that the only way I'll get to meet up with Liam? Maybe secrets at the beginning while we figure shit out aren't the worst idea.

"Fuck," I mutter, flinging my head back against the couch. I've been here for two days and already things are getting complicated.

The more I think about it, the more my head spins with the 'what-ifs' and potential complications of getting involved with not just an alpha, but Liam. He's got charm by the bucketload, but as Benjamin pointed out—there's a trail of broken hearts in his wake.

I shove the thoughts aside and try to focus on my book, but the words blur on the page. I can't seem to shake off the image of Benjamin asleep with Mia, nor can I ignore the slight twinge in my chest at how cute it is. For an alpha who's been through hell recently, he's holding up like a trooper.

The clock ticks away, and eventually, my eyelids grow heavy. Stretching out on the couch, I decide I'll shut my eyes for just a moment...

"Zara?" The soft voice snaps my eyes open, and I blink to find Benjamin standing over me. "Sorry to wake you. I just wanted to say thanks for dinner."

"No problem," I yawn, sitting up and rubbing my eyes. "Mia sleeping okay?"

"Yeah. I've put her in her cot."

"I'll go up. I'm beat."

"Uhm..." He says, giving me a weird stare.

"What is it?" I ask, wondering if I have Bolognese sauce up my face.

"I put the crib in your room. I hope that's okay. I just thought with you sleeping in the armchair... it's not good for getting any rest, and I know Mia is up half the night, so—"

"Thanks," I cut off his rambling with a smile. "I appreciate that."

"Just say," he says with an intense stare that gives me goosebumps. "Don't suffer because I'm not thinking far enough ahead."

"Okay," I say with a nod. "I will. Thanks."

He nods and moves past me toward the kitchen. "Night Zara."

"Good night, Benjamin."

I watch him disappear into the kitchen. Maybe there's more softness under that rough-around-the-edges exterior than I gave him credit for.

Dragging myself off the couch, I plod upstairs to my room. A little smile tugs at my lips when I see the crib nestled in the corner; it makes the space feel more like home. The baby monitor is on the bedside cabinet. Mia is sound asleep, her tiny chest rising and falling in a steady rhythm that calms me more than any meditation app ever could.

I change into my pyjamas and slide into bed, listening to the quiet of the house settle around me like a familiar blanket. My mind keeps rewinding to Benjamin's face when he was thanking me. It makes me wonder if we could become friends despite the awkward start.

As I settle down and try to sleep, my mind drifts back to Liam. Tall, confident Liam with that cheeky grin plastered across his stupidly handsome face.

What am I doing even considering getting

involved with someone who could potentially bring drama into this already complicated household? Still, part of me buzzes with excitement at the thought of seeing him again.

I'll sleep on it and see how I feel about it in the morning.

Chapter 11

Henry

It's getting late, but I've finally gone over Ben's financials with a fine-toothed comb.

It's not looking good. Without *her* income and interest rates going up, he's going to run into some trouble, especially with the drop in his own income from all the time he's taken off since that bitch walked out. I never liked her, but Ben wouldn't listen. She was self-centred from the start. But I'm not going to tell him I told you so. There is no point, and it would only make both of us feel worse.

Still, it's happened, and now things have to change. I don't believe getting rid of Zara is the answer, either. He needs her there so he can go and work. It's a bit of a tricky situation.

Picking up the phone, I dial Ben.

He answers straight away. "Hey."

"Hey. So, I've gone over the statements. It's not looking good, mate." Why beat around the bush? Pleasantries aren't going to make the money issues go away.

"Fuck," he sighs. "How bad?"

"Pretty bad. There's got to be cutbacks, but I don't think Zara is one of those."

A silence that is almost deafening.

"It's a lot of money," he mutters.

"I know, but without her, you can't go to work. So, we have to be practical here. She gives you the time to get back on track. Yes, it might end up a lean month or two while your salary catches up again, but she is a necessity you can't afford to lose."

"So where then?" The desperation in his tone rips at me.

"I need to dig deeper. In the meantime, don't be reckless. Stick to the basics. Yeah?"

"Yeah," he says. "Thanks, Henry. I know you've got better things to do with your time than help me figure this shit out."

"No, actually, I don't," I chide him gently. "I've got the expertise to do this, and you need someone who can see the wood for the trees."

"Thanks," he whispers and hangs up.

I sigh. I wish I could've given him better news. He needs a second income, but from where? Christ only knows.

I blink, focusing on the picture of me, Liam, and Benjamin down by the lake before Mia was born. Thick as thieves, even after *she* tried to undermine our friendship. I refuse to call her by her name. She doesn't deserve that respect. What she did was despicable, and if I ever see her again, I won't be responsible for my actions.

Tamping down the anger I feel over this situation, I inhale deeply, and then I have a Eureka moment.

"Fuck!" I snatch up my phone again and dial Liam on video call.

"Yeah?"

The TV is on in the background, too loud, and he's staring at it, not me.

"Give me your full attention, dickhead, this is serious."

He picks up the remote, turns it down, and faces me. "Who died?"

I grimace at him.

"Oh, fuck. Who died?" he asks, panicking.

"No one, you idiot. But Ben is in deep shit."

"Why? Did that cunt come back?"

"No," I growl, "and she'd better fucking not."

"Then what?"

"I have a proposition for you. Hear me out before you say no, okay?"

"I don't like the sound of this."

"Hear me out?"

"Okay," he capitulates.

"You are currently in a one-bedroom rented flat, a two minute walk from Ben's house. I'm your accountant, so I *know* your lease is up next month, asshole, so don't try me, okay? You are going to give up your lease and move in with Ben, giving him that second income he desperately needs to keep his house."

"What? Fuck off."

"No, listen to me. Shit is bad. Really bad. I've told him, and he wants me to see where he can cut back, but it's like trying to get blood out of stone, man. There is nothing else to cut back on, unless they all give up eating. Zara is non-negotiable, before you say it. He needs her so he can work."

"Oh, she definitely needs to stick around," Liam says with a salacious grin. "She is hot."

"Stop thinking with your fucking knot and be serious. You need to move in with him. Tell him your landlord isn't renewing your lease. He won't be able to refute that and will give you a roof over your head.

Temporarily, which will become less temporary when he realises he needs you there."

"So you want me to move in with Ben and his hot nanny that smells of lavender with honey undertones and whose pussy I want to ride during my rut, hoping she can ease my poor suffering?"

"Jesus," I growl as he laughs. "Liam!"

"Oh, lighten up, dickhead." He goes completely sober, which is rare for him. "It's really that bad?"

"Yeah."

"Then, of course, I'll do it. I'll tell Vic I'm moving out and confide in Ben tomorrow about how I'm being thrown out."

"Don't overdo it," I warn him. "Just say Vic wants to sell up in this economic climate."

"Got it, boss," he says. "Suppose I'll start packing up my shit. Can't wait to get under the same roof as Zara."

"Hands off the nanny, asshole. She isn't there for you to harass."

"Who said anything about harassing her? I asked her out."

I groan into my hand. "You didn't?"

"I did. And I think she'll say yes. Don't tell Ben. Not yet. He will probably freak."

"Probably? Make that definitely. Liam, you're playing with fire here."

"I know, but have you seen her? Fuck, I can't stop thinking about her."

"What a shock. You thinking about an omega," I say dryly.

"No," he says, drawing out as if I'm thick. "This is different. She has bowled me over."

"God help us," I mutter, re-thinking my grand plan.

Liam chuckles. "So, not that I really mind this order from you, Your Highness, but what about you?"

"What about me?"

"Why don't you pack up and move in with him?"

"I own my house. It'll take longer to sell it or find someone to rent it out. Although three incomes will make it easier for him, for all of us, really..." I trail off, contemplating the idea of giving up my house to move in with Ben and Liam. It's not that off-putting. My house is a two-bedroom terrace on the main road. It suits my needs. I don't need anything bigger, but I'm at that point in my life where I want to start actively looking for an omega to settle down with. I can hardly do that under Ben's roof.

"What?" Liam asks. "What's making you pause?"

"I want to settle down," I say with a sigh. "My business is doing well, I'm thirty-one, it's time."

"Yeah, well, when you find the one, please make

sure she isn't a cunt. I only have enough hatred in my heart for one."

Snorting as I know exactly how he feels, I reassure him. "I'll do my best. Thanks, Liam. I know I'm asking a lot."

"Fuck off. This benefits me way more than it'll benefit Ben, anyway."

"Doubtful, but good of you to say."

"No, really. I'm getting bored of my life."

I raise an eyebrow. "Really?"

"Yeah." He slumps back, holding the phone up. "It'll be nice to have the company."

I glance around my empty space and sigh. "Yeah, I know what you mean."

"I'll let you know what Ben says then," Liam states, clearing his throat. "Hopefully, he doesn't expect me to live in a box on the side of the street. Maybe I'd better wait to tell Vic and speak to Ben first."

"I doubt he will make you live in a box, but do what you need to do. I'll speak to you tomorrow."

"See ya."

We hang up, and I sit back, feeling relieved. My approach with Liam was harsh, but he responds better to being told what to do rather than leaving it up to him. He's a bit wishy-washy at decision making and we'd still be here next year if I'd left it to him.

Sitting back, I rub my hand over my face, tiredness pulling on me. I need sleep before I look through Ben's finances again. I don't want to make a mistake that could end up costing him. He's dealt with enough setbacks to last him a lifetime. I won't be the cause of anymore.

Chapter 12

Liam

I shove my phone into my pocket and flop down onto my bed, staring at the ceiling as I contemplate this new twist in my so-called 'boring' life. Yeah, I've dated plenty, had fun, enjoyed the perks of being an alpha without the constraints. But this moving in with Ben under the pretence of losing my place is a whole new level of plot twist in the drama that's been dull up until now.

Of course, I want to help out my friend, but the thought of Zara under the same roof is a pull I can't let go of. Her voice is like a melody that's stuck in my head.

I push myself up and start packing a few things into a duffel bag—just essentials for now. I can't arrive at Ben's looking like I'm moving in permanently straight off the bat, even though that's the ultimate goal.

Losing myself in the rhythm of pulling stuff out of the drawers and wardrobes, I end up packing up most of the room when the clock strikes midnight. I'm not a hoarder. I like things minimal and clean. It will make the move easier as I can probably fit everything in this flat into one room anyway. Minus the furniture, obviously, but I won't need that.

I glance around the mostly bare room. It's funny how a place can simultaneously be full of memories and yet feel so empty once you've decided to leave it behind. Crawling into bed, I close my eyes and try to get some sleep. I'm going to have to approach this carefully with Ben, not spring it on him. It's out of the blue, and I don't want him getting all flappy about it. But I'm glad Henry came to me about it. We need to help him all we can now, and while I'm as useless as a chocolate teapot with Mia, I can help out with other stuff apart from the bills.

* * *

When day breaks, what seems like only moments later, I'm up and stretching the sleep from my limbs. It's going to be a weird day. I've got that antsy feeling like I'm on the verge of something significant — new starts are always like that, aren't they?

I shower quickly, thoughts of Zara filtering in again with the steam. There's something about her that's different, refreshing. She's not like anyone else I've dated or messed around with. She's here for Ben and Mia, but there's an edge to her, a fire that makes my inner alpha sit up and take notice.

After dressing for work in a dark grey suit and white shirt, I grab a protein bar for breakfast and head out for the short walk to Ben's. The air is crisp, with that Lake District bite that wakes you up faster than a double shot of espresso.

Arriving at Ben's house, I let myself in and head to the kitchen, where things are already a hive of activity. Zara is making toast again, and this time doesn't try to attack me with the butter knife. Her hair is up in some artless bun thing that looks like it shouldn't work but utterly does on her, and she's wearing one of those floaty tops that suggest rather than scream her curves.

"Liam," she says, not turning around.

"Morning," I say, aiming for nonchalant but probably hitting awkward instead. "Ben here?"

She giggles. "Well, he does live here, so yeah. He's upstairs with Mia."

"Thanks."

I turn to leave as she gives me a curious stare. "Everything okay?" she asks, her brow furrowed with concern.

"Yeah, just some shit going on. Need to talk to Ben." It's casual, not setting off alarms, I don't think.

"Oh, okay," she says and goes back to the toast.

Heading up the stairs, I make my way down the hall to the nursery. I knock lightly, and he looks up from the chair where he's feeding Mia. He frowns. "You're early."

I stride in, all purposeful. "Yeah, got something to discuss with you, mate."

Ben's eyes narrow a bit suspiciously. "Alright," he says slowly. Mia gurgles in his arms, oblivious to the tension that's suddenly whirled into the room along with me. He passes her off to this contraption that rocks her gently, and she seems right chuffed with the swap as he straps her in.

"So, what's up?" Ben asks, turning to face me and crossing his arms, almost defensively, like he expects me to launch at him.

"My contract is up on my flat next month, and Vic isn't renewing it."

He frowns. "Oh, shit. Do you know why?"

"He wants to sell it and needs me out so he can get it up to code, or whatever."

"Is he allowed to do that on short notice?"

Well, fuck. I don't fucking know. Damn you, Henry!

"Uhm, well, the notice is four weeks…"

"That doesn't seem like a lot," he says, his frown increasing.

Okay, this is spiralling. "Regardless, I need a place to stay while I find something else. He's got people coming over and all sorts of crap I don't need."

I mentally roll my eyes at myself. This wasn't a well-thought-out plan.

"Well, I don't suppose I blame you. So you're looking for a place now?"

"Yeah, I wondered if I could move in here temporarily, you know, just while I find something."

"Here?"

"Yeah, you've got the space, I need somewhere to live that's not going to have contractors crawling all over it for the next month and I'd obviously help with the bills and shit." I shrug.

Benjamin rubs the back of his neck, looking pensive. "Well, I guess we could arrange something," he finally says with a shrug, though there's a hint of hesitation in his voice. "Might be good to have another pair of hands around here anyway."

"Thanks, mate," I say sincerely. "I appreciate it. It's just until I sort shit out."

"No worries." He claps me on the shoulder, the gesture firm and reassuring. "It's not like we don't have the room. But..." He frowns again. "Zara. Don't complicate things with her, please."

"What do you mean?"

"You were flirting with her yesterday. Don't. I don't want her mooning over you when she's supposed to be watching my daughter."

Every alpha cell in my body wants to tell him to get fucked, and that he doesn't dictate to me who I can and can't see, *but* the problem is, I know where he's coming from, so I nod. "Of course."

"I mean it," he growls. "Stay away from her."

I chuckle and hold my hands up. "Promise." It's a lie. I know it is. I intend to insert myself into Zara's life one way or another because I'm infatuated with her on a level that makes my cock stiff but also makes my heart jump. I've never had the heart thing before, so I think it has to mean something.

"I'll leave it to you to tell Zara we've got a housemate," he says and grins, the first real smile I've seen on his face in months.

"Nice, I'll remember that."

He waves me off and picks Mia up again as I make my way back downstairs.

Ben's warning is like a neon sign flashing in my head, but it might as well be background noise. I can already feel the pull toward Zara, some magnetic force that doesn't give a shit about anything but drawing me into her orbit.

She's still fussing over breakfast like she's head chef at some fancy restaurant. She looks over her shoulder and gives me a half-smile that does funny things to my stomach. "Hey."

"Hey. So, it looks like it'll be breakfast for four tomorrow."

"Huh?" She wrinkles up her nose as she stares at me.

"I'm moving in. Gotta get out of my place, and Ben said I could stay here until I sort something out."

"You're moving in?" Her voice goes up an octave, which tells me she is nervous about that prospect.

"Yep."

"I see." She takes a sip of coffee, eyes searching mine. "Well, that's up to Benjamin, obviously, but don't get in my way. This is my job, and I won't have anyone messing with it."

"Understood," I murmur, giving her a sexy smile that I can see affects her.

This is going to be fun.

Chapter 13

Zara

I'm trying to keep my cool, but this is a bloody disaster. I haven't even got used to living in someone else's house and now there's going to be another person moving in? And not just any person, but Liam with his cheeky grins and flirty comments that I should not be responding to. But I am. Responding, that is. And it's not good.

"Right," I say, clapping my hands together as if that will physically bring order to the chaos now threatening to topple me. "What's the timeframe for this move?"

Liam's smile widens, and he leans back against the counter. "After work."

"What? That's no time to prepare!"

He walks over, a little too close for my racing heart, and lowers his voice. "I'm sure you'll make it more than accommodating." He winks before heading off toward the lounge as if he doesn't have a care in the world.

Once he's gone, I finish eating my toast, all while planning what needs to be done before his arrival. I haven't even ventured into the spare rooms to see what state they're in. Do they need bedding? And OH. MY. GOD!

The broken lock on the bathroom door needs fixing! I hadn't paid it much mind before now, knowing Benjamin has an en-suite and wouldn't be using it anyway. It was completely devoid of any toiletries, and even the bog roll had a layer of dust on it when I first got here. But *now*! Oh, no. This needs sorting as soon as possible. I'm not that handy with a screwdriver, but surely it can't be that hard, right?

Right.

I won't be caught on the loo or in the shower by Liam bursting in to do his business.

Part of me wishes Benjamin had at least given me a heads-up, but I guess this was the heads-up. It sounds like Benjamin didn't know either until Liam arrived this morning.

I finish my breakfast at record speed, the urgency to 'make things accommodating' suddenly taking over my entire to-do list between taking care of Mia. I hurry upstairs, making a mental checklist of everything I'll need to do before Liam drags his alpha ass and all his baggage into this already crowded domestic scene.

"Hey," Ben says, and I glare at him.

He snorts. "Liam tell you he's moving in?"

"Yeah, you've just made a shit ton of work for me."

He frowns. "Fuck that. It's not a hotel. He can sort himself out later."

"Oh no," I say, shaking my head. "Not on my watch."

"He's not a guest. He's going to be chipping in and stuff."

"Did you know the lock on the bathroom door was broken?"

He shrugs. "I'll fix it."

Shaking my head, I say, "Go to work. I'll do it."

"Do you know how?" he inquires.

"I'll figure it out. Tools?"

"Under the stairs."

"Awesome."

He shakes his head and leaves me to it as I barge into the bedroom furthest from mine.

Taking it all in, I decide I can work with this.

I fling open windows for ventilation and search through the wardrobe for a duvet and pillows, which I find still wrapped in plastic. I unwrap them and shake them out, before searching through the linen cupboard at the end of the landing. Grabbing some spare covers, I quickly make up the bed and grabbing the duster and polish from the kitchen, I give the room a bit of a tidy.

Checking in on Mia, who is still sleeping, bless her little socks, I move onto the bathroom door lock situation. It's one of those simple internal locks, but it's completely jammed. Right, YouTube tutorial it is. I fetch Benjamin's toolbox from under the stairs. The man's got every tool under the sun but doesn't seem to have used any of them—and settle down with my phone for a quick crash course in basic DIY.

Armed with a modicum of newly acquired confidence and a screwdriver, I set to work on the lock mechanism. Half an hour later, after some muttered curses with my wrists aching, there's a click that sounds like victory. The lock turns smoothly in its casing when I test it.

"Ha!" I punch the air in triumph, my voice echoing, and then I clap my hand over my mouth, hoping I didn't wake Mia.

I check on her immediately, creeping into her room with the softness of a cat burglar. She's still fast asleep. I feel my chest swell with love for the little girl.

Once I'm sure she's okay, it's back to my list. I

tiptoe out, closing the door gently behind me and head downstairs to tackle the next job on my list. God, there's so much to do, but now that the bathroom lock is fixed, I feel like bloody Superwoman! Not all heroes wear capes and there's no cheering crowd. What a fucking let down.

I start pottering around in the kitchen, cleaning up after breakfast, wondering how I'm going to approach this whole 'Liam moving in' situation. A part of me is ready to take control of this whole fiasco, but another side—the side that blushes when he looks at me—is slightly panicked at the thought of sharing a living space with him.

I didn't get a chance to ask if I'm supposed to cook for him or leave him to his own devices. That doesn't feel right to me. It's in my contract that I make food for Benjamin. I'm happy with that, especially as it means one meal at a time, which I can then clean up after. If Liam saunters in with a different schedule, it's going to throw me right off kilter.

I decide to text Benjamin because, let's face it, I can't just stand around like a lemon, not knowing what the heck is going on. My thumbs fly across the screen with a rapid-fire message before I can second-guess myself.

Benjamin. Am I cooking for Liam, or what? I need details. Zara.

Sent.

The kettle whistles its shrill tune, and I jump, snapping my focus back to the here and now. Tea, that's what I need—a nice cuppa to steady the nerves.

As the tea steeps, Benjamin's reply pings through.

Whatever. Don't go out of your way.

Well, that's frustratingly vague. I take a sip of my tea, letting the warmth settle me.

My phone pings again. It's from Liam.

Feed me all the things.

Growling at the winky face, I inhale deeply. "Asshole," I murmur, but the smile tugging at my lips is hard to squash.

I've gone into panic mode because I'm nervous about being so close to an alpha who makes my omega purr inwardly. But now that I think about it, it will make getting to know him easier without having to sneak around. Maybe this is fate knocking.

I guess we'll find out.

Chapter 14

Benjamin

Taking off my suit jacket, I sling it on the small, rickety wooden chair in the gents as I stare at myself in the mirror. My eyes are bloodshot, and I'm pale and sweating. Loosening my tie, I roll up the sleeves of my crisp white shirt, not even wanting to think that Nicole ironed it months ago before she left, and it's been sitting in the wardrobe ever since. Running the cold tap, I shove my wrists under the torrent and try to regulate my breathing. My mating bite is throbbing, red and angry. Cupping a cold hand over the bite, I hiss but then breathe out a sigh of relief. The rut is getting close. Mere weeks away, and I hadn't even given it a single thought since Nicole left. What was the point? But the mating bite is protesting not only the rejection, but what in the hell I'm going to do to ease my need for a knot when the time comes.

A sex doll?

I mean, I've heard alphas do this, and there are toys that omegas use to ease their heat—massive dildos with bulging knots at the base—so why not a slicked-up sex doll for a rejected alpha to get his knot wet?

"Fuck's sake," I mutter and return my hand to the water, still gushing out of the tap.

The door opens, and Liam strides in, giving me the side-eye. "You all right, mate?"

"Yeah, I'm fine."

He huffs out an unusually frustrated breath and stands there with his hands on his hips. "Stop with the 'fine' and 'okay', okay? It's perfectly normal to be neither of those things. Especially with what you're dealing with right now. Your rut's coming up, you've got a little one at home and Zara's moved in to help. It's a lot to take in."

I can't help but scoff a little. "You make it sound like Zara moving in is the biggest issue."

Liam inclines his head, sizing me up with that familiar, knowing expression. "Isn't it? She's thrown your life off kilter. Have you even considered what *you're* going to do when her heat hits?"

My chest tightens at the mention of her name

and heat. Just thinking about Zara gets the alpha in me riled up; she's an unknown entity in my territory, and my instincts are all over the place. The way she doesn't take my shit is something else. I am still reeling from her boldness.

"There's a plan for her. I didn't even consider me. I was hoping it would just pass on by and I wouldn't know the difference."

"Biology sucks in the way that it's never gonna happen, Ben. You can't keep hiding your head in the sand."

Turning off the tap and drying my hands on some scratchy paper towels, I ignore him.

"She cares, Ben. And you need that right now. Someone to talk to, maybe? Just to ease a bit of this hurt."

I glance away, focusing on a crack in the tile flooring. I'm not good at accepting help; never have been. But there's no denying that Zara has already made an impact.

"A sex doll!"

"What?" Liam splutters, his eyebrows nearly reaching his hairline.

"A fucking sex doll designed specifically for alphas."

"You want to knot a sex doll?" His brow furrows deeply.

"You got a better idea?" I round on him.

Liam's response is a chuckle, low and teasing. "You've got a real live omega in the house, and you're thinking about plastic?"

I feel the frustration roil in my gut. "Don't be a fucking idiot. Zara is Mia's *nanny*."

"I'm aware."

"You are no help. Fuck off out of my face now."

"No can do. We need to sort this out. When?"

"Four weeks."

"Okay, so we've got time. How about you hire someone from *Omegas4U*?"

I give him a scathing glare. "No, thank you. Bringing a stranger into my home with my daughter down the hall is all kinds of not happening."

"Okay, point taken. You could go to a hotel?"

"No!" I clench my fists in his face in annoyance. "I've made up my mind. I'll get a sex doll… It will be fine."

"Well, it'll be something, but I'm not sure *fine* is the word you're looking for."

"Go away."

His shoulders slump, and I feel bad for pushing him away, but I just can't talk about this anymore. I didn't want to talk about it in the first place. Turning back to the mirror, I straighten my tie and adjust my sleeves, buttoning the cuffs again so I look the part.

Snatching up my jacket, I glare at Liam, who, for once, seems lost for words, and I stalk out, seeing as he isn't moving. Grabbing my phone out of the inside pocket of my jacket, I ring Zara.

She answers on the second ring. "Daddy," she says excitedly. "Switch to video!"

Daddy?

I switch the call to video in time to see Mia attempt to roll over from her tummy but not quite making it.

"It's early!" Zara chirps in that infectious way she has. "I was taking a video when you rang, but you get to see it live."

"Not in person, though," I grumble, and there's a pause.

Zara's face comes on the screen. "I know, but you're doing what's best for Mia by being there, and we're here having fun. She will show you what a big girl she is when you get back."

"Thanks," I say, my throat getting thick with emotion that I'm sick of feeling now. Hurt, guilt, misery. When will it end?

Zara's shoulders slump and she looks like she's about to cry, which makes me feel even worse. "I was trying to help, not make you feel worse. I'm sorry."

"No, it's not you," I'm quick to reassure her, as I don't want her to leave. I need her and not just for

Mia, I'm starting to realise, but for me. She stops me from falling into a pit of despair with her energy and cheer. "I truly appreciate it. Thank you."

She smiles, a bit wobbly, but it's genuine. "We'll see you soon."

"See you soon."

We hang up, and I feel oddly better about life in general for a few moments before reality bitch slaps me again, and I sink down from the momentary high. Heading back to my desk, I sit down, purposefully ignoring Liam as I get stuck into the latest project, but my thoughts don't stray far from the weird timing of Liam suddenly needing a place to stay. The more I think about it, the more I think Henry put him up to it. Not that I'll call either of them on it. It's a much-needed gesture, and if they want to play along like I'm helping Liam out of a shitshow, then I'll gladly do that. Truth be told, it's a fucking relief to know that, at least for a while, the bills won't be quite so tight. It makes me feel bad for growling at Liam. I turn in my chair and catch his eye, giving him a smile. He grins and laughs, shaking his head, knowing this is the best he's gonna get for an apology from me.

But then I realise it isn't good enough. Not if he's doing this to lighten the financial load.

Before I can second guess myself, I'm up from

my chair and making my way over to where Liam is sitting, buried in a mound of sketches.

"Hey," I say, the word feeling foreign as it dangles awkwardly in the air between us.

"Hey yourself," he responds, leaning back in his chair, one eyebrow arched in a silent question.

I rub the back of my neck, feeling awkward. "Look, I was a twat earlier. About everything."

Liam's face softens, and he leans forward, elbows resting on the cluttered desk. "We're all twats sometimes, Ben. It's part of our undeniable alpha charm."

I snort, unable to hold back a smirk. "Yeah, well, thanks for sticking around—even when I'm being particularly charming."

"My pleasure," he says with mock seriousness before a chuckle escapes him. "Get back to work, asshole. I don't want to stay late when I've got Zara's cooking to look forward to."

"If you're lucky. I have a feeling, since we threw this at her with no warning, it'll be cold soup and stale bread."

We share a snicker, and it's... nice. It feels normal, and that has been something I haven't felt in a really long time.

Chapter 15

Zara

I hadn't intended to make Benjamin so upset with the video call, but sometimes, you have to yank on the reins when an alpha is getting stubborn and broody.

I know he's got a lot resting on his shoulders, but Mia needs him to be sensible right now. I'm just trying to push him in the right direction. He might not like it, but someone's got to do it. The man could use a break from worrying every second of every day. I need to be more proactive. I'm here for Mia, yes, but I need to be here for Benjamin as well. Make his life a little bit easier.

I glance around, considering what to make for dinner tonight.

With everything that's gone on, I reckon comfort food is the order of the day. Something that'll give him a break from all the stress when he gets home.

I pull out my phone and start scrolling through recipes. Stew? No, too heavy. Pasta? Maybe it's a bit unimaginative.

"Ooh, nice." Cottage pie. I spotted another pack of mince in the freezer yesterday, so I quickly grab it and place it in a sink of cold water to defrost quicker. In the meantime, I set about peeling potatoes and prepping vegetables while feeding Mia and playing with her. She is babbling from her play mat, trying to tell me something very important in baby speak and honestly, who am I to ignore such an enthusiastic conversation partner?

"Really?" I say as I tickle her tummy. "And you think adding a bit of cheese on top of the mash would be even better?"

Mia giggles and flails her arms about as if to say 'obviously'. Wise beyond her months, this one.

Eventually, all the play wears her out, and she succumbs to the pull of sleep. I place her carefully in her crib in my room and make sure the baby monitor is on as I slip out and head back to the kitchen. Time is ticking on, and the mince is soft now, so I rip it out of the packet and chuck it into the waiting pan of onions to brown off before I add it to the carrots and stock. I stir it, watching the way the meat sizzles and mixes with the caramelised onions, releasing a homey scent that fills the kitchen.

The potatoes are soft now, so I drain them and start mashing, adding butter and a little milk until they're creamy and smooth. I grin as I sprinkle cheese on top—just like Mia 'suggested.'

As the pie bakes in the oven, I tidy up. The clatter of plates and cutlery is rhythmic and comforting.

I glance at the clock. Shit, time's running faster than I thought. I quickly set the table for three, Liam included. I'm nervous to see him now. This is going to be like our first date, with Benjamin tagging along for the ride.

When the door opens and the alphas stride in, my heart kicks it up a notch.

"Wow!" Liam exclaims, coming straight to the kitchen. "Fuck, that smells good. Knew you wouldn't let us down. Ben here thought we'd be on cold soup and stale bread."

Giggling, confused, I ask, "What?"

"Springing this move in on you," Liam explains. "Ben thought you'd be big mad."

I glance at Benjamin with a raised eyebrow. He glares back at me. "It's not my place to be mad. This is Benjamin's house."

"Call him Ben, for fuck's sake," Liam says. "Benjamin's his Sunday name."

Shaking my head with a smile, I will call him Ben when he tells me to and not a second before. "Mia's sleeping," I say, turning my attention to the alpha of the house. "She's not due a bottle for a while, so dinner's ready now if you guys want to grab showers beforehand?"

"Are you going to join me?" Liam asks, waggling his eyebrows.

"Fuck off with that," Benjamin growls. "Leave her alone."

"It's okay," I say, pressing my lips together, appreciating the defence but not needing it. He doesn't know that Liam and I are... whatever we are or will be. "But thanks. Nice to know there are still gentlemen out there."

"I don't want him fucking this up," Benjamin grouses. "That dinner smells too good."

"Agreed," Liam states. "I promise not to fuck anything up. Deal?" His green eyes pin mine, and the sexy, seductive gaze is almost more than I can handle. I gulp and feel slick dampen my pussy. He is affecting me way more than I'd like. My heat isn't due for another four weeks, and while Susan and I made a plan for that, where I will hole up for three days while she and Peter take over during the weekdays, Liam's presence seems to be dragging it closer to the surface.

I don't know if that's a good thing or a very, very bad thing.

"Go now," I croak, waving them off towards the stairs. Benjamin doesn't look particularly thrilled, but there's a subtle shift in his posture. The rigidity in his shoulders relaxes just a notch as the smell of dinner seems to erode away some of his earlier frustration.

Liam gives me a cheeky grin and bounds up the stairs two at a time.

Benjamin grumbles something under his breath that I don't quite catch as he follows Liam at a more sedate pace. I shake my head, trying to focus on setting the last of the table rather than the riot of butterflies Liam's flirtatiousness has set off in my stomach.

Once they're out of sight, I turn to Mia's baby monitor and check on her one more time before turning back to attend to the pie just as the oven timer pings. Pulling on oven gloves, I retrieve the cottage pie—all golden brown and bubbling around the edges—and set it down with a satisfied sigh.

Liam returns first, hair wet and dressed in grey joggers and a tight white tee. His hair is sticking up adorably, and through forces that are unknown to me at this particular time, make me smile and go over to him. I reach up, his six-foot frame towering over my five-one as I stand on tiptoes and smooth his sticky up hair down, lingering a bit too long.

His gaze pins mine again, heating my insides, my heart speeding up as our lips are too close together.

He grins. "Thanks."

"Anytime," I croak, drawing in his scent as he does the same to me. It's natural. It's the dance of the alpha and omega.

"Fuck, you smell good," he murmurs, closing his eyes.

"You sure that's not just the pie?"

He chuckles and opens his eyes. "Not the pie. You."

I tilt my face towards his, wanting him to kiss me. His summer rain scent is overpowering, telling me of his arousal that matches mine. His lips brush mine, but then Benjamin's footsteps can be heard coming down the stairs, and I stumble back, my cheeks on fire as I turn away and busy myself with the veggies.

Fuck. What am I doing?

Bad Zara. Bad, bad omega.

Chapter 16

Liam

The smirk that adorns my features as I watch Zara's cheeks burn with a blush that radiates all the way to her neck, is smugger than usual. She's adorable when she's flustered and fuck me if that doesn't make me want her more.

That scent.

I glance over my shoulder to see Ben trudging down the stairs, looking like a bear with a sore head.

"Smells fucking incredible," Ben mutters as he reaches the bottom step, his mood visibly lifting at the sight of the feast Zara has prepared. He slants a suspicious glance at me and Zara as if he feels he can't leave us alone for even a second. Mind you, he probably can't. If he hadn't arrived with epically bad timing, I'd have my tongue down Zara's throat right now, and maybe, if I'd got lucky, she'd have had her hand wrapped around my cock.

With a raging hard-on, that is uncomfortable as fuck, we sit down for dinner, and it's bloody delicious—Zara's got skills in the kitchen, that's for sure. I keep stealing glances at her throughout the meal, appreciating how she puts everyone at ease with her quick wit and easy smile—except when she locks eyes with me. Then there's that spark, that tension I'd love to explore.

I notice Ben is watching her too, not with lust or longing, but with something akin to admiration. It's like he didn't know someone could come in and just fit with him and Mia so seamlessly. He's been stressed since that bitch left him, but Zara being here seems to lessen the load somehow.

And now I'm here as well to ease the financial burden. Captain Liam to the rescue.

I need a cape. I'm a fucking superhero who needs a fucking cape.

My mind wanders as Zara regales Ben with tales of Mia and their day together. I won't say I'm bored, but it sort of leaves me out of the conversation a bit. Not that I mind. It gives me more time to steal glances at Zara while she shares her stories. It's as clear as the nose on my face that she adores that little girl, and I know that will go a long way with Ben.

"I'm sorry," Zara says, suddenly, her foot nudging mine under the table, jolting me out of my thoughts. "We're leaving you out."

"No, go ahead. I'm enjoying the food."

"No, it's rude not to include. How were both your days at work?"

Ben and I exchange a glare as if he is almost daring me to spill the tea on our rut and sex doll chat. Yeah, not likely.

"It was fine. Work, you know," I say, turning away from Ben and giving Zara a smile.

I catch the tail end of Ben's grunt of affirmation, his own response just as tight-lipped and cryptic.

"Sounds riveting," she giggles.

We move on from work talk quickly because, let's be honest, who wants to talk shop when you've got a delectable cottage pie in front of you and an even more tempting omega sharing the table? I notice how Zara's laughter rings clearer than the clinking of cutlery against plates, her giggle infectious, and for a moment, there's a sense of ease around the dinner table that feels like it could almost be domestic.

Almost.

Ben's perpetual scowl leaves a lot to be desired.

"So, Zara," Ben says, breaking a lull in conversation. "We'll need to get that bathroom lock fixed up for you."

"I fixed it already," she says with a proud beam. "Who knew YouTube was such a good tutor?"

"Oh, okay," he says. "Good."

I mentally shake my head at him. She is begging for some praise—not in a needy way, but in a way that tells her she did a good job.

"Nice," I say, holding my hand up for her to give me a high five. "Handy omega to the rescue."

She laughs and slaps her palm against mine, and it's like I've been hit with a million volts of electricity.

Okay, not quite because I'd be dead, but close. The skin-on-skin contact, however brief, has made this interested alpha tumble over a cliff I didn't know I was hanging from as I plummet headfirst into... something with her.

Her lips part, and she lets out a long breath. She felt it, too. I know she did. It was too electric for her not to have.

"Uhm," she stammers and stands up. "I'll clear up and check on Mia."

"I'll go," Ben says.

"Of course. Of course," she says, bobbing her head and avoiding everyone's gaze as she gathers up the empty plates and disappears like her ass is on fire.

My mind is racing a thousand miles an hour as I watch Zara's retreat. This is it, isn't it? The moment when you know you've found *the one*?

Sitting back in my chair, I'm floored. I can barely breathe. Ben leaves the dining room, and it's just me and my thundering heart and stiff cock, which might as well be a second presence right now, it's so huge.

Needing to move, I stand up, suddenly restless, right as Zara walks back in to tidy up the table some more.

She freezes when she sees me. I'm acutely aware of her gaze trailing up the length of my body, lingering on my cock area before it shoots up to my eyes, and she licks her lips enticingly before backing out, the condiments forgotten as I hear her race up the stairs and out of sight.

Chapter 17

Benjamin

As I ascend the stairs, my mind spins with thoughts of work, Zara, and bloody Liam, with his charming grin and flirty comments to my nanny. Something is brewing between them, and as much as I can tell Liam to fuck off, he's an adult. She's an adult. I'm nobody to tell them who they can and can't be interested in, but at the same time, she is Mia's nanny, and my responsibility is to my daughter and her wellbeing.

Reaching Zara's room, I push open her door gently and find Mia sleeping peacefully in the little crib. Her little chest rises and falls rhythmically, and for a moment, all is right with the world. She's why I have to pull my socks up, get my ass back into gear at work.

After watching her for a few heartbeats more,

feeling that paternal pride settle warmly in my chest, I venture further into the room. It's Zara's personal space, and I feel like I'm invading it.

Mia stirs as I move closer, and she wakes up, letting out a squawk that signifies it is bottle time. Smiling, I pick her up and disappear quickly into the nursery where I place Mia in the cot and prep a bottle before I scoop her back up to change her.

As I'm standing at the changing table, Zara bursts into the room and comes to a halt. "Sorry, I forgot she was in my room."

"Hope you don't mind I went in there to get her," I murmur, concentrating on the job at hand.

"No, of course not." Zara comes closer and stands next to me, gazing down at Mia with love in her eyes that warms my dead soul.

She's good with her, I'll give her that. She's got this maternal instinct that draws her to Mia, and Mia to her, like two magnets. Zara smiles at me. It's tentative and full of uncertainty, but something softer that makes me want to maybe confide in her like Liam suggested. But I don't even know where to start.

I shake the thought away as quickly as it comes. Instead, I focus on Mia as I sit down with her and place the bottle in her little mouth. She blissfully guzzles down the milk.

"You're doing great," she murmurs, but then her

gaze shoots to mine in panic. "I don't mean that in a condescending way, obviously. I mean, with going back to work and—"

"Thanks," I cut her off with a tight smile.

I don't want her pity or, worse, her reassurances. But somewhere, deep down, I know she's not offering either. She's just trying to be supportive. It's a foreign concept for me, but my body relaxes just a fraction under her gaze.

Zara's eyes soften, and I reckon she can sense my internal war. She turns to me as if she's got something important to say, then hesitates. The air between us is thick with unspoken words.

"Benjamin," she starts. "I know things have been, well, a bit topsy-turvy recently with me moving in and everything, but I just want you to know that I'm here. For Mia, *and* for you, for whatever you need."

Her sincerity hits me like a ton of bricks. She means every word, and what's more, I believe her.

"Thanks," I say again because what else can I say? Zara doesn't understand the complexity of what she's offering — an omega, willing to stand by a rejected, single dad alpha who's got more baggage than Heathrow airport.

She nods and steps back, giving me space to finish feeding Mia. It's a simple gesture but one that tells me volumes about her respect for boundaries —

something deeply appreciated, especially as her scent is overwhelming me in the peace of this room. The silence lingers comfortably as Mia finishes her bottle and lets out a satisfied burp. Zara takes her from my arms, and Mia snuggles instantly against her chest.

I watch them—the nanny and my daughter—and there's a warmth that refuses to be ignored. It wraps around my chest like a blanket fresh out of the dryer. Comforting. Welcoming.

Zara catches me staring and blushes slightly. "I'll just put her down for the night," she murmurs, heading towards the cot.

I nod, watching as Zara bends down to tuck Mia in. The tenderness in her movements, the soft croon she hums, is maternal and protective and catches me right in the heart. This omega is incredible with my daughter.

Mia's eyes flutter closed, her little hand gripping Zara's finger for a moment before sleep claims her. Watching them is like witnessing a private moment, and suddenly, I feel more than just gratitude or responsibility towards Zara. I feel this pull, this undeniable draw that I've been trying my hardest to ignore.

She stands back up straight, meeting my gaze with those deep-set eyes of hers that seem to look right into my soul. "I'm going to head to my room. It's been a busy day. Goodnight, Benjamin," she says softly before slipping out of the room.

"Night, Zara," I reply. "Oh, and yeah, call me Ben."

She giggles and nods once before she disappears.

I stand there for a while longer in the comfort of the nursery, lost in thought. There's something about Zara that disrupts the balance I've so carefully maintained since becoming a single dad. I'm not sure what that means or if it even means anything.

Once I'm sure Mia is settled, I reluctantly leave the nursery and head back downstairs, where I find Liam flicking through the TV channels.

"You and Henry concocted this grand plan, didn't you?" I ask him as I slump into my favourite armchair, an old, squishy, maroon leather thing that Nicole hated with a passion.

He pauses momentarily, which tells me everything I need to know. "What do you mean?" he asks.

Sighing, I rub my hand over my face. "Thanks."

He looks over at me and smiles. "Still don't know what you mean, but anytime, bro."

I nod, grateful to have these people in my life that, in my grief and despondency, I tended to forget about. It's time I remembered and stopped feeling so sorry for myself and acting like a dick to everyone around me. That gives Nicole power over me, and if there's one thing that I know, it is that she is dead to me. She will never be part of mine or Mia's life ever again. That determination lifts the cloak of doom a tiny bit and I sit back with a smile as Liam settles on an old football match from the 1980s.

Chapter 18

Henry

Bright and early, I arrive at Ben's house and instead of letting myself in like I usually would, I ring the bell. There is Zara to consider now, and she might not appreciate random alphas popping up in her face without warning.

The door swings open, and Ben, hair still tousled from sleep, gives me that look that says, 'too bloody early for socialising'. But he steps aside to let me in, shaking his head with a mock frown. "You could have just walked in, you know."

"Yeah, but then I'd miss the opportunity to see your charming 'I've just woken up face'," I jest, stepping past him into the familiar warmth of the house.

He rolls his eyes, but I catch the twitch of his lips fighting a smile. "Coffee?" he grumbles, already heading towards the kitchen.

Following him through, I sit at the island while he goes about making two mugs of steaming coffee. The silence between us is comfortable; we've known each other long enough that words aren't always necessary.

As he hands me a mug, I decide it's time to broach the subject that's really brought me here at this ungodly hour. "So," I begin, taking a slow sip to gather my thoughts. "How are things with Liam?"

Ben glares at me. "I know you two got together and concocted this plan. I bet it was your idea, and he went along with it."

"No clue what you're talking about," I murmur with a soft smile.

Ben's expression goes less hard. "Sure you don't." He takes a long gulp of his coffee, his gaze lingering on the mug as if it holds the secret to the universe or, more likely, just enough caffeine to kickstart his day. "You know," he starts slowly, "having Zara around is not what I expected."

"What did you expect?" I ask, genuinely curious.

He shrugs, a half-smile tugging at the corner of his lips. "I don't know—awkwardness, tiptoeing around each other? But she's a natural fit. Mia adores her."

I nod, sipping my coffee. "Glad she's working out."

Ben sighs, lost in thought. "Yeah," he says after a pause. "It's nice having someone else in the house who gives a damn."

There's a vulnerability in Ben's voice that hits me right in the gut. He's my best mate and seeing him struggle has been tough. "Yeah. I'm still going through the statements, but with Liam here, things should ease up a bit?" I pose it as a question because I will deny all knowledge that we set Ben up. I'm sure Liam will as well.

Before he can answer, there's the soft padding of feet on the stairs, and we both turn to see Zara entering the kitchen. Her hair is tousled from sleep, and her eyes are bright with that morning freshness that makes her look almost ethereal in the soft light filtering through. She is a looker, and her scent is as enticing as this steaming mug of coffee that's still too hot for me to drink.

Ben's face lights up in a way that's both subtle and completely obvious at the same time. "Morning, Zara," he says, his voice smoother than I've heard it in a long time.

"Good morning," Zara replies, her voice soft, almost musical. She glances over at me and offers a polite smile. "Henry, right?"

"That's me," I say with a chuckle. "The early

bird who apparently loves to torture Ben with unsociable hours."

She laughs. It's a genuine, melodic sound, and for a moment, I fall under her spell. There's something about her that just makes you want to stick around and listen for a little longer.

She moves to the kettle, filling it before switching it on, and then turns back to us. "Anyone for tea?" Her offer is as warm as the jumper she's got on, oversized and beige.

"Got coffee, but thanks." I'm curious about her. Liam is completely infatuated with her, and Ben has his head up his ass, so maybe it's up to me to be the clear-headed one and assess this situation with my analytical mind.

Ben nods in agreement with me, yet his eyes linger on Zara as she moves around the kitchen. There's an ease to her actions, a confidence in the way she handles herself that's both refreshing and a tad intimidating. "I'm good with coffee too," he says, but I can tell he's appreciating more than just her offer of tea.

Zara catches his gaze and grins, a playful light in her eyes. "Suit yourselves," she replies before fetching a mug from the cupboard.

I watch the interaction between them, intrigued

by the dynamic that's emerging. Zara seems to fit seamlessly into the rhythm of this household, bringing with her a spark that was sorely missing since *she* left Ben high and dry.

As Zara busies herself with her tea, I decide it's as good a time as any to engage her in some conversation. "So, Zara," I start casually, "how are you finding everything? Settling in alright?"

She turns to me, her smile unwavering as she nods. "Yeah, it's lovely here. Ben's been great, and Mia's an absolute angel."

"Good," I murmur. "You like the Lake District?"

She nods. "It's gorgeous here. The air is so clean and fresh, and the views are absolutely stunning. I can't wait to go walking."

Ben clears his throat. "Well, the weekend is all yours, so, you know."

She smiles and nods. "I'm looking forward to it."

I take another sip of my coffee, appreciating the warmth that spreads through me as I observe this new dynamic with a fascination that is bordering on obsessive. Seeing Ben's world brighten up with Zara in it, is something that makes me happy that my friend appears to be pulling himself out of the darkness he plunged into.

There's movement behind us, and I turn to see

Liam padding into the kitchen, yawning and stretching his arms above his head. His hair is dishevelled, and he's got that 'just rolled out of bed' look that somehow suits him.

"Morning," Liam grumbles, scrubbing a hand over his face before noticing Zara and instantly brightening.

"Morning," Zara echoes back to him, her smile growing wider as she greets Liam.

Liam crosses the room for his own mug, and the air subtly shifts with his presence. He's like an additional burst of energy, even though he's clearly in need of a caffeine injection. "How's everyone doing this fine morning?" he asks as he leans against the counter, eyes still heavy with sleep but glinting with interest. "Bit early, innit, Henry?"

"Just thought I'd stop by. See how everyone is getting on," I murmur, hiding my smile behind my mug. Oh, this is fun. The three of them have zero clue what it looks like to an outsider. Liam is practically drooling all over Zara while she pointedly ignores him, and Ben is trying his best not to be a grouchy fucker in front of the nanny.

It's fucking glorious to sit here and watch them at it, none of them knowing what to do next.

"So, I'll go and get showered, and Liam, you can

go after me," Zara blurts out after a weird pause where only I seemed to be enjoying myself.

"Or we could double up, save water." Liam gives me a bright smile.

"Fuck off," Ben grits out, but even that doesn't have the usual oomph behind it. More like it's an automatic reaction.

Zara laughs, shaking her head, her eyes sparkling with amusement. "Nice try, but I think I'll manage on my own," she quips, her tone light-hearted.

Liam winks at her, unfazed. "Can't blame a bloke for trying. But alright, I'll queue for the shower like a civilised human being."

I marvel at their back-and-forth. It's like a sitcom in here. Sarcasm and banter flying around the kitchen—it's a stark contrast to the dull mornings we used to have before Zara blew in like a breath of fresh air.

As Zara exits towards the shower, Ben turns his attention back to his coffee, taking a deep swig, as if it's some sort of elixir that can calm his rattled nerves. Liam's gaze lingers on her retreating form before he snaps back to reality with a sheepish grin.

"Well, this has been fun," I say, standing up and placing my empty mug in the sink. "I'll leave you all to it."

With a round of goodbyes that's as warm as the steaming mug I've just abandoned, I head out of the kitchen, leaving the others to their own devices. I've got a feeling they'll need a bit of space to navigate this new dynamic, and I can't wait to see how it plays out.

Chapter 19

Zara

The steam from the shower is enough to make me cough a bit—it's that hot. I'm trying to scald myself into stopping this thing with Liam. As much as I'm attracted to him, I just don't think Ben will be happy, and I don't want to do anything to cause him discomfort or pain.

"Friends. Friends. Friends," I mutter to myself as I scrub and scrub until my skin is red. "Just friends. It's fine."

When I climb out of the shower and dry off, my skin is tender, and I wince as I wrap the towel around myself, looking around for my dressing gown. I groan when I realise I left it on my bed, flustered to have a third alpha whose bergamot scent hit my nose in the early morning and mingled nicely with Ben's pinecone one, which threw my head for a loop. Then Liam strolled in, and I was toast.

This is bad. So, so bad.

Clearing my throat, I gather up my things. I know Liam will be lurking, waiting for his shower, and now I have to stroll past him in just my towel. Could you get more of a cliché if you tried?

Opening the door a crack, I leave it to my super sensitive omega nose to sniff him out. He is not hovering outside, so I open the door and run across to my room as fast as I can, slipping in and closing the door behind me. Leaning against it, I breathe out.

This is ridiculous.

I glare at the dressing gown, innocently strewn on the bed, as if it's its fault for abandoning me. I snatch it up and wrap it around myself as I find some clothes to put on.

With a deep breath, I try to push the embarrassment and the rush of hormones away. I need to get a grip. It's all well and good saying I'll keep things friendly, but with the way my heart is racing and my skin still tingling from his near proximity, keeping to that might be harder than I thought. There's only so much an omega can take before she goes into spontaneous heat.

I open my door again, this time fully dressed in my day clothes. I pick up the baby monitor to see Mia is still sound asleep and make my way back down to the kitchen. As I pass the bathroom, I hear the shower running, signifying Liam scrubbing up. For one second, just one tiny second, I pause and breathe in his scent, drifting with the steam under the door. Then, regretfully, I move on.

Ben is making cereal for breakfast, and the kitchen is quiet, except for the sound of his spoon clinking against the bowl. I shuffle in, my feet somehow heavier than usual, and I sneak a glance at his strong hands as he pours the milk.

"Morning. Again," I say, trying to sound more cheerful than I feel.

Ben looks up from his breakfast, a small smile tugging at the corner of his mouth. "Want some cereal?"

"Okay, thanks."

As Ben prepares another bowl for me, I make another cup of tea.

We eat in a companionable silence for a while before Ben speaks up again. "You seem distracted this morning," he says with a hint of concern.

I force a smile, not wanting to delve into the reasons why too much. "Just thinking about plans for today with Mia. I wondered if you'd mind if I took her for a proper walk out."

"Uhm. Where to?"

"I thought we could take a walk down that path that runs down the side of the estate, see where it leads."

"To the lake."

I blink and wait for more. When it doesn't come, I draw in a breath. "So, is that a yes or a no?"

He searches my eyes for a few seconds before he says. "Yes, I suppose so. Make sure you wrap Mia up warm and let me know when you leave, when you get there and when you set off home and arrive back here."

"Yes, Daddy," I tease with a smile.

He glares at me, but there's no animosity.

We finish off our cereal in relative silence as Liam strolls in, looking more hot than an alpha has a right to. His scent is strong from the heat of the shower and brings out the deep lust in me I have for this man. I avoid his eyes as I turn around and busy myself with packing the dishwasher. Liam makes toast and takes it to go as Ben is calling for him to hurry up.

"See you later, princess."

"Bye," I murmur and breathe out a sigh of relief when he leaves.

The slamming of the front door behind him is enough for me to cringe. He's going to have to get used to being a bit more stealthy. Frowning when I don't hear Mia stirring, I grab the baby monitor and glare at it, making sure the volume is turned up. It's way up, but still nothing. She's asleep, but I find that to be a little off character. I've only been here a few days, but already I know her routine. Shooting up the stairs, I enter the nursery and go to her cot. She looks flushed and not in the good way. Placing the back of my hand on her forehead, I rear back from the heat.

"Shit," I murmur and look around hastily for that box where I know all the baby first aid stuff is. Grabbing it, I unclip the lid and snatch out the thermometer.

"Come on, come on," I mutter as I wait for it to turn on and set itself. It's a forehead one, so I place it close to Mia's skin and click the button. It flashes red, and the screen says 39C. "Oh, fuck, fuck, fuck." Moving swiftly, I grab the baby paracetamol and double-check that three-month-old babies can take it before I place the syringe in the top and tip it upside down, measuring exactly 2.5ml. I leave the syringe sticking out of the top of the bottle as I gather Mia and place her on the changing table. She is responsive but listless. Popping the onesie open to cool her fevered skin, I grasp her chin gently and grab the syringe, slipping it into her mouth and squirting the liquid into the inside of her cheek so she can swallow it without choking.

She gulps and then lets out a wail to end all wails. I swear they can hear her in Outer Mongolia.

"Okay, baby," I coo, trying to soothe her as I pat her back gently. "Just let that medicine work, you'll feel better soon." She's crying in that way that makes every omega instinct in me go haywire—the need to protect and comfort.

With Mia still in my arms, I fetch a cool cloth from the bathroom to dab her forehead and cheeks, murmuring reassurances all the while. It's going to be okay, I tell myself as much as I'm telling her.

I do the quick check. No rash. No vomiting. No trouble breathing that I can see. No outward signs of illness. Possibly teething. It's been known to give babies fevers. Ben and I are fine, so probably not flu but possibly a cold that her little system hasn't come into contact with yet.

Ring Ben.

No, don't ring Ben. Not yet.

As I second guess myself, I check the time. I need to give the medicine twenty minutes and then check her temperature again to see if it's coming down. After that, I'll ring Ben if it's not lowering.

I walk with her, trying not to jiggle her too much. Her cries die down, and she falls asleep again, limp and hot but breathing steadily. Placing her back in her cot, I check the time again and pace some more.

At ten minutes, I feel her forehead and grab my phone. Dialling Ben's number, I steady my breathing. If I panic, he will flap so hard he will take off.

"What is it?" he asks after the first ring.

"Just to keep you in the loop, and don't worry, but Mia has a temperature. It's 39 degrees. I've given her 2.5 mils of Calpol. No rash, no vomiting, she's breathing fine. She's asleep. I'm just waiting twenty minutes to see if it goes down. If not, we may have to consider taking her to Urgent Care."

Silence.

Then. "I'm coming home."

"No, not yet. Give the medicine time to work. It's possibly teething, and the Calpol will work. I will ring you back."

"Zara—"

"Ben, it's fine, this was a courtesy call to keep you in the loop and to let you know I've given your daughter medicine, okay? Babies get fevers. It happens."

"Ring me the second you take her temperature again," he says stiffly.

"I will."

He hangs up, and I check the time again.

At eighteen minutes, I'm armed and ready with the thermometer, forcing myself to wait and not check her again already. By the time twenty minutes hit, I'm checking, and when it flashes red again and is 40C, I breathe in and grab my phone, dialling Ben.

The front door bangs open, and footsteps thud up the stairs, followed by his phone ringing, Ben blazes into the nursery, panicked and frantic.

Chapter 20

Zara

I hang up the phone and shove it in my pocket. "We need to take her to Urgent Care. Go and get the car seat."

"What's wrong with her?" he asks desperately. "Is she going to be okay? Fuck! Fuck! I knew I shouldn't have left her. I had this feeling this morning, but she felt fine and took her bottle—"

"Ben. Go and get the car seat," I say calmly as he runs his hand through his hair but doesn't make a move. "Go, now, please."

"Yes, yes." He shoots off downstairs, and I hear the clatter of the door opening again. Meanwhile, I do up the poppers on Mia's onesie and wrap her in a light blanket, not too thick, just enough to keep her safe from the chill outside. Every omega bone in my body is vibrating with the need to protect this little one.

Mia is fussing again, a low whine that tells me she's uncomfortable but not in immediate danger. I pick her up, trying not to jar her little body too much. "Shush now, darling," I whisper. "We're going to see a doctor, and they'll make you feel better."

Ben's back in what feels like seconds, car seat in tow. He's pulled off his suit jacket and rolled up his sleeves like he's about to do battle. His alpha instincts are probably through the roof right now.

"Is she okay? Is she worse?" he asks, his voice cracking with the fear every parent knows when their little one is sick.

"She's the same, Ben," I reply soothingly. "But we're not taking any chances, okay?" I hold out Mia for him to take so he can place her carefully in the car seat.

He cradles her close, breathing deeply like he's trying to reassure himself that she's still here and real. It breaks my heart a little because I can sense his fear as tangibly as if it were mine. His pinecone scent has filled the air with his panic, and it's making my head spin a little.

Ben carries her down carefully and steadily and clicks the car seat into place as I quickly make up four bottles and follow with the baby bag.

When I exit the house and close the front door, I see Ben standing there frozen for a moment before reality seems to settle back over him. "Right," he says firmly, nodding to himself as if trying to shake off the panic. "Let's go."

The drive is tense. Mia's soft fussing from the backseat is like a thread pulling taut with each mile we cover. Ben's knuckles are white on the steering wheel, his eyes focused so intently on the road that I'm not even sure he's blinking.

I reach over and lay a hand on his arm. "She'll be okay," I whisper, but he hears me.

He glances at me, then back to the road. "I know," he says, but his voice is heavy with worry.

Time passes too slowly. Ben wasn't kidding when he said the hospital was an hour's drive away. Thank God this isn't a life-or-death emergency.

We hope.

When we finally arrive, Ben parks the car, and I get out with the bag while he gets Mia, still in her car seat, to take to the Reception.

"Mia Scott," Ben states. "She's got a fever."

I take over and tell the Receptionist all that I know and have done.

When she tells us to take a seat in the child-friendly waiting room, I can't just sit there. I unbuckle Mia and try to give her a bottle, which she refuses. That's not good. She starts crying again so I walk with her, up and down, up and down wearing a path in the floor until finally her name is called.

"Mia Scott?"

"Here," I say as Ben races over to the nurse, and I join them at a more sedate pace.

"Could you follow me, please?" the nurse says with a smile that is meant to be calming but does little to calm Ben down.

We trail behind her down a corridor that smells like antiseptic. It clings to the brightly painted walls despite the cheerful drawings of zoo animals trying to convince us otherwise.

She ushers us into a small examination room where another nurse waits, this one holding a digital thermometer.

Ben's alpha control frays even more at the edges. "Please, just help her," he pleads.

I place Mia down on the examination table and the nurse checks her temperature. She gives no indication one way or the other. "Dr Evans will be with you shortly," she reassures us as she makes notes in her chart.

Ben and I sit on either side of the examination table. We're both staring at Mia, who's now settled on the table, looking small and vulnerable amidst the white sheet.

I take Ben's hand in mine, giving it a squeeze. He returns it, his grip firm, grounding me as much as I am him.

A few minutes later, Dr Evans walks in—a kind woman with kind eyes. She washes her hands before turning to us with a warm smile.

"How are we doing today?" she asks brightly as if we're here for a routine check-up rather than a feverish baby emergency. But her tone is just what we need, the normalcy of it all easing some of the tension in my shoulders.

"We're a bit worried," I manage to say. "Her fever was forty when we took it last."

Dr Evans nods as she slips on gloves. "Understandable. Fevers can be scary, but you've done exactly the right thing bringing Mia in." She approaches the table and starts examining Mia gently, asking questions as she goes.

"Has she had any other symptoms? Coughing, vomiting, diarrhoea?"

I shake my head. "Just the fever, and she's been fussier than usual," I reply. "And I think she's teething."

Dr Evans nods and checks for a rash anyway and looks in Mia's ears, then listens to her chest with a stethoscope. She's thorough but quick, making soft cooing sounds that have Mia staring at her with wide-eyed trust.

"I can't see any outward signs so it could be the teething or possibly a standard viral infection. You're doing the right thing by giving her Calpol at four-hour intervals, and you need to get fluids into her. Her nappy is wet, so that's a good sign, but you need to keep an eye on that."

"But she's refusing her bottle," Ben says, the worry flooding his voice.

"Try a syringe for cool boiled water, just little bits at a time," Dr Evans suggests easily.

"Yes," I agree quickly. "We can do that."

Dr Evans smiles and turns back to Mia, doing up her onesie again. "You've given your mummy and daddy quite a scare, haven't you, little one?"

"Erm," I start, but Ben shakes his head. I close my mouth, understanding he doesn't want to get into our situation, which is fine. As long as he doesn't mind the good doctor thinking I'm Mia's mum.

"If she is still refusing fluids and has stopped wetting her nappy by tonight, bring her back, and we'll admit her with an IV."

"Okay," I say with a brisk nod as Ben appears to go further into a meltdown.

Dr Evans writes up a few notes and hands us a small card with the emergency contact number for the paediatric ward. "Any concerns at all, don't hesitate to call," she says with such sincerity that it's hard not to feel comforted.

We thank her profusely and stand to leave. Mia is now cradled in Ben's arms and goes back to sleep instantly.

As we walk back through the corridors towards the waiting area, I can feel Ben's tension increase with each step. "She's going to be fine," I reassure him.

Ben offers me a weak smile. "Yeah."

We grab the car seat and bag we left in the waiting room in our hurry to get Mia seen and step into the sunlight streaming through the front doors of the hospital.

The drive home is less tense than the ride in, but still enough to send my omega instincts into overdrive. Mia dozes in her car seat all the way back home, and as soon as we arrive, Ben scoops her up. "I'll try her with a bottle."

"Okay," I say, smiling as I gather up the baby bag and follow him inside.

Back in the nursery, Mia refuses her bottle, protesting loudly and sending Ben into a further downward spiral.

Working efficiently, I get the cool boiled water into a sterilised bottle, syringe some of it out and hand it to him. He glares at it as if I handed him a snake.

"Here," I say, taking Mia from him and sitting in the armchair with her nestled close to me. I hold my hand out for the syringe and attempt to get water into Mia's mouth, but she's gritting her gums, making it impossible to get anything past them. "It's okay, we'll try again in a bit," I reassure Ben.

He nods, looking anxious. I pass her back over as I rise, and he takes her gently. He sits in the chair, just staring at her.

"I'll be back to give her another dose of Calpol in a bit," I murmur, leaving them alone as I make my way back downstairs.

Putting the kettle on for a pot of tea, Ben needs one and so do I after this hectic morning, I jump when the front door bursts open and Liam rushes in with Henry hot on his heels.

"Everything okay?" Liam asks, looking around, "Ben bolted like a bat of hell was after him. Henry and I have been panicking. Neither of you were answering your phones."

"Mia has a high fever, so we took her to Urgent Care. We're back now," I say.

He nods, running a hand through his hair. "Is she okay?"

"We think so. Just teething or a mild viral infection."

"Oh, good," he says, breathing out. "Kettle on?"

Smiling, I say, "Yeah." Giving Henry a quick smile and a nod, I pour tea into the pot and then one straight into a mug for Ben. Taking it upstairs, I enter the nursery quietly, and Ben looks up. "Need to keep your fluids up as well," I say softly.

"Thanks," he says. "Does she need more Calpol?"

"Yes. I'll do it. Put her on the changing table."

He nods, grateful that I'm not abandoning him to the task. I measure out the medicine and administer it gently as Ben stands close by, observing the process.

"I'll change her while I'm here," I murmur, and he nods.

We both bend down at the same time to grab a nappy from underneath, our faces close together.

His blue eyes gaze into mine, and my entire body goes on the fritz. I feel my insides vibrating, and I can't stop it. I purr directly in his face, loudly, contentedly, seeing the shock register in his features as my cheeks go flaming hot.

We both straighten up quickly, his eyes hooded, but before I can say anything, not that I even know *what* to say, he lets out a soft, possessive growl that sends a thrill over every inch of my body. His horror at his action mortifies me, and I stammer, thrusting the nappy at him and lunging for the door, which I swung closed when I came in. Grabbing the handle, I stupidly push it instead of pulling it. But it's too late to stop my body from moving towards what I expected to be the gap in the doorway. My head connects with the door as I yank it back, and I muffle my curse as a throbbing pain shoots through my head.

I can feel Ben's eyes on me, but I have to get out of there. This was unexpected, and the embarrassment that floods me is heinous.

I scamper down the stairs, tears pricking my eyes as I clap my hand to my head, feeling a big bump forming already.

Chapter 21

Henry

Liam and I are milling about the kitchen when Zara storms in with a massive bump on her head.

"Fuck," Liam murmurs, going to her and staring at it. "You've got a huge egg on your head."

"Thanks, asshole," she grumbles. "Is that what that splitting headache is all about?"

"How did you do that?" I ask, going over to her and taking her by the elbow to draw her over to a stool to sit.

"I ran into a door," she says.

Liam and I exchange a glance, which she sees and rolls her eyes at. "No, really. I ran into a door. It's fine. I'm okay."

"No, you look like you might be concussed," I say

and go to the freezer. Searching, I can't find any frozen peas, but I do find something I can press to the bump.

"I'm not concussed," she says. "I know first aid. For adults, children and infants."

"So do I," I say, surprising her.

She purses her lips and narrows her eyes at me. "I'm still not concussed."

"Here, hold this on it," I instruct, holding up the pack of frozen vegetables to her head.

"Ow," she groans. "What the fuck is this? Broccoli?" She pulls it away and glares at it.

"Well, you didn't have peas and unless you want to hold some frozen chicken fillets to your head, this will have to do."

"It's all knobbly," she complains, but doesn't move it.

"Should've gone with the chicken," Liam pipes up, leaning on the island and gazing at her with a laugh. "You've already got an egg, so it would be fitting."

"How about you shut the fuck up?" she snarls.

"Ohh, feisty omegas are my favourite," he practically pants.

Shaking my head at him and giving her an apologetic smile, I lean in a bit closer and adjust the frozen broccoli. "Also, you do have that Mother Hen vibe going for you."

She glares at me, but then giggles. It's the sweetest sound. "I'm never going to live this down, am I?"

"Nope," I say. "Not while Liam's around anyway."

Her shoulders slump. "It hurts."

"I know. I'll get you some painkillers."

"In that cupboard up there," she says, pointing to one near the fridge.

I busy myself with popping two tablets out and getting her a glass of water.

"Thanks," she says when I hand them to her. "You smell nice." She blinks and frowns, but shakes her head and takes her pills. "Like fresh linen infused with bergamot."

I tilt my head. "Oh? That's a new one." *Curious.*

She stares at me for a second. "You didn't know you smelled like bergamot?"

"No, the fresh linen part. No one has ever said that before."

"Well, I guess they weren't smelling hard enough."

I chuckle. "Guess not." I move away from her, finding this conversation unsettling—not because of what she said, but because she is literally the only one who has said it. What does that mean? Does it even mean anything? I grab a tea towel and wet it with cold water. Wringing it out, I then take it over to her and remove the offending broccoli to replace it with the cloth.

Water drips down her face as she smiles and says, "Thanks. The broccoli was defrosting, so it wasn't so bad."

Liam looks between the two of us, his expression unreadable. "I need to go check in with work after I bolted. I'll be back in a few."

Taking over with the towel pressed to Zara's head, I lean in closer. Call me crazy, but I want her to breathe in my scent, and fuck, I need to breathe in hers. That lavender and honey combo is mouth-watering.

"You're very cool and reserved, Henry," she says. "Good in a crisis."

"Okay?"

"The three of you make a good team. Ben is growly and brooding, Liam is fun and flirty, and then there's you, cool and reserved."

"You make it sound really boring." I joke, not sure how I feel about her observations.

"It's not boring," she says, shaking her head and then wincing. "You're stable and pragmatic."

"Oh, this keeps on getting better," I murmur. If she calls me cute with a great personality, I'm going to go and hide under the duvet for a while.

"Omegas like that. They want someone they can rely on, you know?"

"Hmm."

"You don't agree?"

"I think I'd rather be called growly and brooding or fun and flirty."

"If wishes were horses..."

"Indeed. How's your head feeling now?"

"A bit better."

"It's going to hurt for a while. Maybe we should take you up to Urgent Care just to be on the safe side?"

"No, it's a two-hour round trip. I'm fine."

We settle into an easy silence, the kind that isn't awkward but comfortable—like a warm blanket on a chilly evening. She relaxes on the stool, the towel still pressed lightly against her forehead.

If she says she's fine, she's probably fine. Still, I can't help the protective surge that ripples through me. It's unfamiliar and surprising.

From the corner of my eye, I notice Liam slink back into the kitchen after his call. "Why don't you go up and make sure Ben is doing okay with Mia?" I ask him.

"Sure," he says, glancing between Zara and me.

Liam's expression is a mix of teasing and suspicion, as if he's caught onto something more than just my nursing duties. But he doesn't question it, just nods and disappears up the stairs.

Left alone with Zara, I'm acutely aware of the quiet that's settled between us. It's not uncomfortable—far from it. It's like we're both soaking up the tranquillity after the chaos of a minor injury.

Zara chuckles softly. "This house is starting to feel like a hazard zone."

"Maybe we need to wrap everyone in bubble wrap," I suggest, and her laughter brightens the room even more.

"Probably not the worst idea I've heard," she says and stands up.

She wobbles slightly, and I reach for her. "Let's get you to the couch. You can rest up a bit."

"Yeah, maybe that's not such a bad idea," she murmurs. She lets me help her into the lounge, and I settle her comfortably on the couch. "Tea? You were making some earlier."

"Please," she says. "Thank you, Henry. I appreciate the care."

"Anytime," I mutter, meaning it with every ounce of my being. This tiny omega with the huge bump on her head has wrapped her way around my lonely soul, and now I understand why Liam is so infatuated with her.

She is perfect.

Chapter 22

Liam

I knock softly on the doorframe of the nursery to see Ben looking dishevelled and frazzled. He's staring at Mia in his arms, a bottle poised but being ignored.

"Hey."

"Hey," he whispers.

"What a day."

"Yeah." He looks up at me, panic, fear and something else all over his face. "She won't feed."

"Want Uncle Liam to try?" I offer. I mean, how hard can it be?

He shakes his head with a frown.

"Maybe the shock of seeing my mug will make her drink something," I prod. He is clearly really worried.

"Okay," he says. "Maybe."

He rises and indicates that I sit in the armchair. I do, and then he hands me Mia. "Hold her steady but not too tight," he murmurs.

"Got her." I stare into her little face, and she blinks sleepily. Ben hands me the bottle and slumps on the floor, leaning against the cot, looking like he has the weight of the world on his shoulders. "You okay there, pal?"

He shakes his head but doesn't say anything.

I turn my focus back to Mia and press the bottle to her lips. She opens up and latches on, suckling for all she's worth.

"Ha!" I whisper triumphantly. "Uncle Liam for the win. I need a fucking cape for sure now."

"She's feeding?" Ben asks, sitting up.

"Yep."

"Oh, well done," he says and bumps his fist against my shin before slumping back down.

"Wanna tell me what's on your mind? You know, while this cape is flapping about?"

He sighs. "Zara purred at me."

My heart skips a beat. "Oh?" My voice sounds hoarse to my own ears, but Ben doesn't notice.

"That's not the worst part. I growled back at her."

"Ohhh?" This just got interesting.

"It's not like that," he snaps, even though I've barely uttered a word. "I'm still mourning the loss of my mate. Ah, fuck this!" He rips at the collar of his shirt to reveal a red, angry-looking mating bite mark. "Shouldn't this be over by now?" His desperation hits me hard in the chest.

"I don't know, mate." I pause. "Do you want her back? You know, if she came crawling back, would you take her?"

"No," he spits out. "She is dead to me. If she even tries, I'll fucking kill her."

I try not to take that literally, but he's made his point.

"Have you got rid of all her stuff?"

His head snaps to the side. "What do you mean?"

"All her shit. Is there still stuff in your room of hers? That won't be helping you move past it, if her scent is still all around you."

His face goes pale, and he clenches his jaw so tight, I think I hear his teeth crack. But it tells me all I need to know.

"Pack her shit up, and I'll take it to the charity shop today."

He unclenches and looks defeated. "Do you think that's what's holding me back? Why this bite won't just fade?

I shrug and look at Mia because he is breaking my heart here. "I don't have the answers. But you gotta try, yeah?"

"Yeah."

He doesn't move; he just sits there like a lost man. I want to ask more about the purr and growl situation, but I can't. Not now. No wonder Zara was in such a mess she smashed a door into her head. That must've confused the shit out of both of them.

"Go on. You can do it."

"Yeah." This time, he stands and stumbles towards the door. He pauses and looks back. "Burp her when you're done. Hold her up to your shoulder and pat her back."

"I know, I've seen you do it."

"Thanks," he mutters and walks out slowly, as if he's walking towards the gallows. Maybe it does feel like that. This is the final step.

I focus on Mia, her tiny hands batting at the air as she finishes her bottle. She lets out a contented little sigh, eyelids drooping. "Right then, time for the grand finale," I whisper and lift her to my shoulder, patting her back just like Ben said. A delicate burp escapes her, and I laugh quietly. "Good girl."

I rise and place her carefully in her cot, hoping I'm doing it right. I'll send Zara up in a bit to make sure. Assuming she's all right with that massive bump on her head. This day has been pretty shit for everyone, it seems, and it's not even five o'clock yet.

Ben's departure hangs over me like a storm cloud.

I know he's hurting; that bite is more than a scar—it's a reminder of everything he's lost, but I'm willing to bet that once he clears out that bitch's stuff, he'll feel loads better.

Here's hoping, anyway.

Chapter 23

Benjamin

I stand there for a second, gripping the doorframe like it's the only thing keeping me upright. I'm not ready for this. I don't think I'll ever fucking be ready for this. But Liam's right; there's shit to be done.

Taking a deep breath that feels more like inhaling shards of glass, I trudge into the bedroom that used to be ours. Her scent lingers. There was a time when that fresh apple scent was my favourite smell in the world. Now, knowing I have to move forward once and for all, it's like acid burning through my nostrils. I told myself I was keeping her stuff around for Mia's sake, and while that was true, I also needed that. But it's holding me back and making me suffer even more.

I hesitate at the wardrobe, then yank it open with

more force than necessary. Some of her clothes still hang there, as if she might waltz in any minute, slip into one of her dresses, and smile at me in that way she used to before everything turned to crap.

Not anymore.

I rip hangers from the rail, clothes tumbling into a messy pile on the floor. Each piece feels like a betrayal. How could she do this? How could she leave us like this?

Questions I've asked myself a million times in the two months since she walked out without a word.

By the time I'm halfway through, sweat is dripping down my forehead, and my hands are shaking. The bite is pulsing on my neck with the sheer force of the mating that is unravelling. Each item I throw to the floor is a second closer to freedom. Anger and grief wage a war inside me, neither side winning, just tearing me apart bit by bit.

Stopping suddenly, I swallow and stare at the clothes scattered all around me. There is no order, only chaos, and that's not good enough.

Reaching up, I grab a big suitcase from the top shelf of the wardrobe and sling it on the bed. Opening it, I push aside the memories of the last time we used this, a getaway before Mia was born and Nicole needed all the comforts from home. With a grimace, I bend down and start to meticulously fold and stack the clothes in the case. It's not fair to hand this over to the charity shop in a pile of messy, creased items for them to sort through. Once the clothes from the wardrobe are done, I turn to the drawers, but she took everything from there. Cleaned it out completely. Her bedside cabinet still has a few bits. I open the drawer and rear back from the scent coating the paperback book. I toss that in the suitcase, along with the reading light and the hand cream. Shaking my head, I take the hand cream back out and march to the window. I open it up and throw the half-used tube as far into the back garden as I can. I don't want it anywhere near me. The smell of it had turned me off, and now it makes me feel sick.

All her toiletries went with her, so the en-suite is empty save for a few of my bits.

Once the suitcase is packed, I zip it up with a finality that's supposed to feel liberating. But I just feel fucking empty. The last remaining physical remnants of Nicole are bagged up, ready to be dumped like yesterday's rubbish. It's fitting, seeing as that is how she made me feel.

"Bitch," I mutter and lug the case off the bed.

Standing back, I survey the room. It feels different without her stuff. Cleaner, maybe? Or just emptier. That's it. It's missing the chaos that Nicole always brought into my life. A bloody tornado of emotions and passion that left devastation in its wake.

The ache in my chest that seems to have set up permanent residency since she left, thuds. Not just because she was an omega to my alpha, but because I loved her beyond reason or sanity.

Loved her.

Not anymore. Maybe if she hadn't walked out on her baby, I would still love her, but she made sure I would hate her, and I do. With every breath that I take, I hate her, and I wish her nothing but pain and suffering.

Then my shoulders slump.

I was never a bitter, twisted man. I've never been the life of the party like Liam, preferring to keep to myself as much as possible and not really liking other people all that much, but I was never like *this*. I would never have even thought to wish someone in pain. She has brought that out in me, and I don't like it. I don't want to be that man.

But right now, I don't know how to get back to the man I was.

Sighing, I leave the bedroom and walk down the landing, pausing at the nursery where Liam is still with Mia.

"Hey," I mutter.

"Hey," he says, looking up. "You good?"

"Yeah. All done." I make a rude gesture to the suitcase, making Liam snicker briefly.

"Is that everything?"

"Yeah."

"You sure?"

"I said yes," I snap and then shake my head. "Sorry."

"Don't apologise, man. I know this must've been tough. But you've done the right thing. I'll take it away right now. Keys?"

"In the blue bowl by the door."

He nods and glances back at Mia, who is sleeping in the cot, before slapping me on the back and heading downstairs with the case.

I go instantly to Mia and feel her forehead. She is still hot, but she doesn't feel as fevered as before. "I'm sorry, sweet girl. You will have to forget her scent and that she ever existed. If she ever comes back, she won't get a chance to know you. At least not until you are old enough to make that decision for yourself. Until then, I will protect you with my last breath, and I will not give her another shot at this. *If* she even regrets her decision enough to come back." Deep down, I know she won't. She was always selfish and a bit of a narcissist, if I'm being honest. Clarity through distance and all that bollocks. Henry tried to tell me she was a red flag at the beginning, but I didn't listen.

Part of me wishes I had, but then that part is drowned out by the fact I wouldn't have the most precious thing in the world to me if I had. So, I'll take this hit for Mia, for both of us, and vow to never, *ever* to be put in a position to be used again.

The ache in my chest tightens as my words hang in the air, a promise to little Mia, who's oblivious to the world's heartaches. Turning away from the cot, I take a deep breath and steady myself, knowing that my strength is what will keep us both safe now.

Brushing Mia's cheek with the back of my hand, I make sure the monitor is turned on, even though I never turn it off. I feel the silence of the room wrap around me like a cocoon. It's suffocating and liberating all at once. She seems to be resting easier now that she's had her bottle, so I'll leave her in peace for a bit, or I'll just want to hold her until the pain goes away.

Closing the nursery door quietly, I head downstairs, suddenly remembering Zara's purr and my unprecedented reaction. It makes me stop midway, hesitating, undecided if I should turn back to my room and hide or go down there and pretend it didn't happen. One thing I know for sure is that we won't be discussing it—now or ever.

Chapter 24

Zara

I hear Ben coming down the stairs. Liam has just left with a big suitcase but didn't say where he was going. I wonder if he's moving back out, but he didn't really give me or Henry the chance to ask.

Feeling the tension rolling off me like waves, I try to focus on something else—anything to distract me from the tight ball of anxiety in my gut. As I hear Ben's footsteps descending, memories of that purr, his growl and the heat that followed flood back, taunting me with sensations I didn't even know I could feel, is eating away at me. It was wrong on so many levels, it's making my head spin. The thought of a spinning head, makes the lump throb again and I stifle my groan.

Henry casts a glance at me, raising his eyebrow. "You okay?"

"Yeah, fine," I mutter as Ben strides into the lounge where I'm laid out on the couch and Henry is in the armchair nearby flicking through a TV magazine. Slowly, I lift my gaze and lock eyes with Ben.

His eyes are a stormy blue, the kind that looks like they've seen too much and yet are always searching for something more. His gaze lingers on me longer than necessary, and I can feel the weight of his thoughts, but he breaks away first, clearing his throat.

"Everything okay upstairs?" Henry asks, breaking the silence. His voice is casual but there's an undercurrent of concern; we've all been feeling the strain lately.

Ben nods, making his way to the other armchair, opposite mine. "Mia's sleeping. Her fever is down a bit."

"That's good to hear," I reply, trying to inject some warmth into my voice despite the awkwardness lingering in the air. "I'll go up in a bit and try to feed her."

"Liam managed," Ben croaks out. "He's got the Midas touch."

"Oh, nice," I murmur, wishing I'd seen that.

We both know we're skirting around what

happened earlier. That purr. The growl. The reaction it sparked in him was unmistakable, and now that I'm over the shock of banging my head so badly, I know slick is dampening my pussy even just looking at him now.

"So, was that her stuff Liam took?" Henry sets down the magazine now, looking over at Ben with a gaze that I want to say is hard, but is difficult to tell.

"Yeah," Ben says gruffly. "It's done." There's finality in his voice that tells me he doesn't want to dig deeper into the topic.

Henry nods knowingly as I process that information. He's only just got rid of her stuff? Why now? What does that mean? Did it have anything to do with me? Fuck. Fuck.

I'm brought out of my spiral by Henry rising and he claps Ben on the shoulder. "Right, I'm going to make us some tea. Zara?"

I nod at Henry. "Please."

The moment Henry leaves the room, the atmosphere shifts again; it's like we're both holding our breaths without quite knowing why.

"Zara..." Ben starts, his voice trailing off as though he's about to say something he might regret. He clears his throat, giving me a look that's filled with confusion, hesitation, and something else I can't quite put my finger on. Then his gaze moves up and he finally sees the bump on my head.

"Shit," he says and moves forward, leaning over the back of the couch to get a better look. "Are you okay? Was that the door?"

"Yes, and yes," I reply with a reassuring smile, glad we are skirting around the other issue. I have literally no idea where to even start with that.

"Shit," he says again and then reaches out to lightly brush my hair away from the bump, his touch sending a blazing trail of heat all through my body. I gulp at the soft touch, and my insides turn to liquid.

Then, I freeze.

He steps back, sensing the sudden frosty atmosphere, but it's not him. It's me. This bruise on my head is worse than what I would've expected. At least for this time of the season.

I gulp and slump down further into the couch. I always bruise more easily the closer I get to my heat. During my heat, I'm as delicate as a peach, but it's unusual for me to react so badly to, an admittedly hard, bump to the head. What does this mean now? Am I going into my heat early? Is Liam's presence messing with my seasons? Is, dare I think it, Ben?

Fuck. Fuck.

"I'll be upstairs with Mia," I blurt out and dart off

the couch, aiming for the stairs before Ben has even uttered a word.

"Oh, okay," I hear him call out as I hit the top and I breathe out, leaning against the wall.

"What is going on?" I mutter and then jump as my phone buzzes in my back pocket of my jeans. Dragging it out, I stare at it with a frown.

No Caller ID

Blinking rapidly, I think back to when I swapped the SIM cards, knowing I did it correctly and didn't mistakenly put the old one back in. I know I didn't.

Did I?

Mia's squawk interrupts my panic, and I shove the unanswered phone back into my pocket as I push the door to the nursery open gently and pick Mia up, offering her comfort as well as myself.

There is no way Eddie could've found my new number. No way, so I'm being paranoid. It'll be some scammer trying to get my card details or my PIN numbers off me.

Busying myself with the baby, I push it to the back of my mind to deal with later. Right now, Mia needs attention and she is making it known she is not a happy girl. I check her temperature, still too high, and set about trying to make her more comfortable.

As Mia settles against my chest, her tiny breaths becoming more even, I feel that tightness in my heart easing. She smells like baby powder and warm milk, a comforting scent that makes it easier to forget the rest of the world.

After a few moments of rocking her gently, I lay her down in her crib with all the tenderness of a bubble floating onto a blade of grass. She looks so peaceful, and I smile softly.

Taking a deep breath, I start to make my way back downstairs. I can hear Henry clattering around in the kitchen and Ben's low voice joining in with some comment that brings forth a hearty chuckle from Henry.

Stepping into the kitchen, Henry glances up from where he's pouring boiling water into mugs. "Just in time."

I manage a smile and nod as I slide into one of the stools. Ben is leaning against the counter now, arms folded over his chest, avoiding my gaze. Good, because I just can't right now.

"Thanks," I say as Henry places a steaming mug in front of me. The warmth from the cup seeps into my hands, and it feels like liquid comfort sliding through my fingers. With a grateful sigh, I take a careful sip, letting the familiar taste of the tea ground me back into the present moment.

As I sit there, sipping my tea and trying not to think about No Caller IDs or unexplained early heats, I'm suddenly aware of the silence that has descended upon the kitchen. It's as if Henry and Ben are both waiting for something to happen, something to break the tension that's so thick you could spread it on toast. Did Ben tell Henry about the incident that shall not be named in the nursery earlier? I feel my cheeks heat up, and then I notice the marked shuffle back of the two alphas as my scent intensifies, and I try to cool myself down with thoughts of Eddie. That's like being doused in arctic water.

Liam's return interrupts the tension as he bursts back into the house like a rainbow after a downpour.

He comes to a halt in the kitchen doorway. "What?" he asks, looking at each of us.

His eyes land on me for a beat longer than the others, clearly sensing the disarray of scents and the awkward energy in the room. He blinks innocently, the corners of his lips curling into a playful smile.

"Looks like I walked into a right drama," Liam says as he ambles over to us, grabbing an apple from the fruit bowl and tossing it casually into the air before catching it.

I roll my eyes but can't help a half-smile, despite everything. "No drama here. All peace."

He takes a bite out of his apple, crunching loudly in the silence. "It's just been one of those days."

"You could say that again."

Liam walks closer to inspect my injury. He reaches out tentatively as if asking permission which I nod to, and then his fingers gently probe around the bump. "How's the egg?"

"Fine. Not quite so throbby."

"Good," he murmurs.

I smile and pull my phone out of my back pocket to check the time and then lay it on the island in front of me. "I'd better get dinner started."

"No, we'll just get something from the chippy," Ben says as Henry makes this strangled noise and shakes his head.

"Stick to the basics," he mutters. "I'll help with dinner."

"Thanks," I say with a smile and move around to see what we can make. Turns out we don't have much except the fixings for a pasta. "I'll have to go shopping tomorrow," I say.

"Liam and I will go after work," Ben says. "You've got Mia, and I don't really want her going out around the shops if she's not feeling well."

"Okay," I say. "I'll make a list."

My phone buzzes again and makes a dull thud against the wood as it vibrates.

"Want me to get that?" Liam asks, indicating to me chopping onions on the other side of the kitchen.

"Sure," I say with a smile, and then I freeze. I'd

forgotten all about the call earlier. "Actually, just leave it…"

Too late.

Liam has the phone to his ear, saying, "Hello?"

Chapter 25

Liam

"Who the fuck is this?" a deep voice growls at me over the line.

I frown and pull the phone away to glare at it before slamming it back to my ear. "Who the fuck is *this*?"

"Hang up," I hear Zara hiss at me from where she's still slicing onions, but I'm already caught up in the confrontation, and this pillock has wound me up the wrong way.

"Listen here, pal," I say firmly into the phone, "if you're looking for trouble, you've called the right number."

Zara looks like she's about to bolt across the room and grab the phone out of my hand. Ben and Henry have gone dead quiet, their attention shifting between the phone and Zara's increasingly agitated movements.

There's a pause on the line, and then the voice returns, dripping with malice. "You tell Zara that Eddie isn't done with her yet. She can run, she can block me, she can change her number, but she can't fucking hide."

My blood runs cold, and I feel anger boiling up inside me like a kettle set to scream. "You fucking what?" I growl, ready to throw down with this asshole, but the line goes dead.

I lower the phone slowly and meet Zara's gaze, her face pale. Her eyes are wide, her hands have stopped moving, and a half-chopped onion has been forgotten on the cutting board.

I feel Ben's presence before he actually speaks, his tone urgent with concern. "What the hell was that?"

Zara, fear on her face, takes a shaky breath and looks like she might crumble right there in the kitchen, so I do what my alpha instincts are yelling at me to do. I cover for her.

"Some dickhead ringing the wrong number."

Zara gulps, and our eyes meet. There's a silent understanding between us.

Ben and Henry look sceptical, but they don't push it. They decide to let it lie, for now.

"I'll set the table," Ben says after a moment.

"Thanks," Zara says, her voice steadier than her hands as she goes back to chopping.

I keep my eye on her as she finishes the onions and slides them into a pan, wishing I could do something more to help her, something to take that fear away from her eyes, but I'm at a loss. Instead, I focus on putting together a salad with a bit too much vigour than is probably necessary.

After Zara manages to whip up a delicious-smelling pasta and sit down to eat, she is quieter than usual.

"What a day," I murmur.

"Yeah," Ben agrees, finishing up. "I'm knackered. I'm going to bed. I'll feed Mia before I crash."

"Okay," Zara says quietly.

"Guess that's my cue to beat it," Henry says, giving me a lingering stare which speaks volumes. He wants answers about that phone call. But then, so do I, and until I can talk to Zara, no one is getting any.

Henry gets up and claps me on the shoulder. "Catch you in the morning."

I nod as he heads out, leaving just Zara and me with the remnants of dinner and a heavy silence. I clear my throat, trying to cut through the tension that's hanging between us like a sodden towel.

"Look, Zara," I start, keeping my voice low, "about earlier —"

She jumps in before I can finish. "Who was it?"

"Some fucker named Eddie. Real piece of work."

"Figured. How did he find my new number?"

I shrug. "You want to tell me who he is?"

Zara clenches her jaw, looking down at her hands, which are fiddling with the edge of the tablecloth. "My ex. I left him the day I came here. It was only days ago, but it seems like a lifetime already."

"I see. Clearly, he didn't want to lose you."

"He didn't want to lose his control over me, you mean," she says bitterly, and I narrow my eyes as this douche canoe is getting worse by the minute.

I watch as Zara takes a deep breath, trying to steady herself. Her bravery is like a light in the dark, and I admire her strength. But right now, she looks so vulnerable, her guard down, and for a second, I just want to reach out and hold her.

"Please don't tell Ben. He will freak if he thinks some psycho is tracking me down."

"And so he should."

"I know, but... Fuck!"

"What?" I ask, startled by her sudden expletive.

"My email!"

"I don't follow."

"He contacted me through a Facetime audio,

didn't he? Through my email address. Fuck! Zara, how could you be so fucking stupid?" She lowers her head to the table, and I wince as she bangs her bump.

"Okay, so he hasn't stalked you and found out your new number," I mutter, trying to keep up with this ever-changing scene. "He's just threatening you into thinking that."

"What did he say?" she mumbles, not lifting her head.

"You tell Zara that Eddie isn't done with her yet. She can run, she can block me, she can change her number, but she can't fucking hide."

"Wonderful," she grits out. "Just fucking great."

"You do know that if he even steps foot near this house, Ben will go ballistic on his ass. Mia is in this house. Does he know about this ex?"

"No!"

"You need to tell him so he can be prepared."

"Fuck!"

"Yep."

"I have to be a grown-up, don't I?"

"I'm afraid so." I rise and go over to her, crouching next to her. She lifts her head, but I don't see fear or panic in her eyes. Just a growing determination not to let this asshole beat her.

"I don't think he would hurt anyone," she says. "He never hurt me, physically, at least. I don't think he has the guts. He's a gaslighting narcissist who found me in a moment of pure grief and vulnerability. I lost my parents in a car crash a bit ago."

"You don't need to explain anything to me," I start.

"Yeah, I do. I don't want you to think I ran out on a maniac who would come here and hurt Mia. It wasn't like that. He is all words."

"Well, you don't know that for sure."

"Fuck."

"Listen, Zara, words can be just as damaging, and this Eddie bloke has gotten into your head enough to shake you up like this."

She exhales sharply, nodding in agreement. "You're right. It's just, I thought I'd left him and all that shit behind."

"You have," I reassure her, but my mind is racing with ways to ensure Eddie stays the hell away from her. "But now we need to make sure he's got no way back in. You'll need to get a new email account, and like it or not, you're going to have to tell Ben about this."

Zara grimaces at the thought, biting her lip with anxiety. "Is he going to be big mad?"

"Nah," I lie, but she snorts as she can see straight through me. "Ben's bark is worse than his bite, except when it comes to protecting his family.

He'll want to know so he can keep Mia *and you* safe."

She sighs deeply, tapping her fingers on the table. I watch as she seems to be mentally preparing herself for the conversation ahead with Ben.

"Yeah, you're right. I need to tell him," she finally says, her voice carrying a new layer of resolve. "I'll tell him in the morning."

"I'll be here for you," I add firmly. "If Eddie does show up here, he will realise pretty quickly that he made a big fucking mistake."

Zara gives me a small smile and reaches out to cup my face. She leans forward and presses her forehead to mine, drawing my scent into her lungs. "Thank you, Liam," she murmurs before she drops her mouth to mine, and gives me a soft, sweet kiss that fills me with a sudden rush of protectiveness. I've been trying to keep a lid on these feelings for Zara ever since she arrived. I've been trying not to push too hard even though I can't get her out of my mind, but her lips on mine blow the damn thing right off. I deepen the kiss, and she mewls softly into my mouth.

Pulling back with every ounce of inner strength I have, I shake my head. "Not yet."

"No," she agrees. "Not yet."

Chapter 26

Zara

I draw back from Liam, my heart pounding. He stands up, and I watch him stride toward the kitchen, clearly needing to put some space between us. I don't blame him. Our scents have filled the air, mingling nicely together, and it makes me want to follow him and kiss him again.

But I don't.

First things first, I need to change my email address and make sure all my accounts are locked down tighter than Fort Knox. Then, come morning, I'll have to sit Ben down and tell him everything.

I grab my phone and start the process of creating a new email account, picking something random and not at all connected to my name or previous addresses. Once that's done, it's a giant pain in the ass to get it connected to my phone as the other one gets wiped.

By the time I'm finished, the clock is ticking towards Mia's feeding time, and I need to get my head down for a bit before I'm up again.

I trudge upstairs and collapse into bed, but sleep is elusive. My mind runs laps around Eddie's message, the startling kiss with Liam, and the impending talk with Ben. How do you tell someone that an ex might be psycho enough to track you down? Something tells me 'over tea and biscuits' isn't going to cut it.

Mia wakes before I can fall asleep, so I drag the throw blanket and my pillow off the bed and walk quietly into the nursery, putting the stuff on the chair before I pick her up and see to her needs. She is still hot, so when I settle her back down, I stay, pulling the chair up close and sticking my hand through the cot bars to keep my hand nearby. Curling up, I fall asleep quickly now, exhausted by this day that has thrown up too many variables for me to be comfortable with.

***

When morning comes, and Mia is rising, I'm stiff as a board, and my arm is still stuck through the cot bars. I remove my arm, smiling at Mia as she turns towards me before I stand and stretch.

"Hey, baby. How're you feeling today?"

I gently press my hand to her forehead. She's still hot but not as bad as yesterday. I grab the thermometer and check her. It's 38.5 degrees, so bad, but coming down. That's a plus.

As I potter about, changing and feeding her, I hear a noise coming from the back garden. Frowning, I settle Mia back in her cot and go to the window to stare out.

Ben is standing in the middle of the garden, staring at something in his hand. He doesn't move. He doesn't do anything.

Turning away, I check on Mia, who seems happy to be changed and fed and back in her cot, so I grab the baby monitor and clip it to my pj bottoms. Returning to my room for some flip flops, I make my way downstairs and to the kitchen. The back door is still open, and it's a bit chilly. I wrap my arms around myself as I go out, pulling the door closed behind me. If he hears me, he doesn't turn around.

Crossing over the damp grass, my feet get wet and cold, but I don't care. Something is wrong.

"Ben?" I ask softly.

He doesn't answer me.

"Everything okay?"

"Fine," he croaks. "Go back inside."

Twisting my lips, I debate whether to leave him

or press further. Whatever is in his hand has set off a downward spiral.

"I'm here if you want to talk. I don't judge, and I'm a great listener."

"Zara... just go back inside."

"No," I say with a huff and walk up next to him. "I don't think I will."

He turns to face me. He is haggard, and the bite on his neck is ugly, red and oozing blood. It is nasty. His mating bite.

"Oh, Ben," I murmur and reach out instinctively to cup his face. He leans into my palm and lets out a choked sob that rips its way through me and brings tears to my eyes.

He turns to me, sobbing, holding onto me as he bends himself practically in half to press the top of his head to my chest. Wrapping my arms around him, I stroke his hair and make a shushing noise as I would to a baby.

"I wish I could take this pain away from you," I murmur as he leans so far into me, I stumble. He grips the sides of my top with his hands, throwing us both off balance, so I grab him and sink to the wet grass with him. He curls up, his head on my lap as I comfort him, feeling helpless and lost. There is no way I can bring up Eddie now. But it's eating me alive. I don't know what I was thinking, but Ben needs to know.

Now is not that time, though. Hearing the back door open, I look over to see Liam hovering. I shake my head as he sees us, and his face goes sober.

Liam doesn't move towards us but doesn't go away either, clearly sensing the raw emotion that's gripped Ben. He looks at me, eyes asking a thousand questions, but I give him a small shake of my head again. Not now. He nods slightly.

Ben's sobs gradually subside to sniffles as he clings to me like a lifeline. It breaks my heart to see him like this, so vulnerable and shattered. His fingers grip my top less fiercely now, and his breathing starts to even out. He lifts his head from my lap, wiping his face with the back of his hand.

"Sorry," he mumbles, looking embarrassed and lost.

"Don't be," I say softly, giving him an encouraging squeeze. "We all have our moments, and I'm here for you."

He nods, swallowing hard as he tries to piece himself back together in front of me. I help him to sit up properly on the damp grass before standing up and offering both my hands to pull him to his feet. His legs are unsteady for a moment before he finds his balance again.

He has something in his hand that digs into my palm. A small tube of something. He glares at it and scowls so fiercely, I think he's going to break his skull. With a growl so loud and fierce, it rumbles the ground under our feet, he turns and hurls the tube back towards the house.

I watch helplessly as it hurtles towards Liam, who is still half asleep and not sharp enough to duck.

It smacks him square on the forehead.

"Oof!" he exclaims as I stifle my inappropriate giggle. "What did I ever do to you, man?" He rubs his forehead as I hide my smile behind my hand.

"Get rid of that," Ben grits out. "And sorry. Didn't know you were loitering."

"Not loitering," Liam points out huffily as he bends to pick up the tube. "Hovering to make sure you were okay."

"Get rid of that, and I'll be fine."

Liam glances at it and then opens the top, giving it a sniff before rearing back. "God, that's potent. What the hell is it?"

"Nicole's fucking hand cream. Get it out of my sight."

Ben stalks back to the house, and Liam quickly steps aside to let him in. I feel a bit raw and exposed after that. Ben has dismissed me without a second thought but I can't let that affect me. He is in so much pain. The mating bond knows it's been rejected fully now, and there's no going back. Ben is going to have to ride it out, and all we can do is be here for him when it gets too much to handle on his own.

Liam's expression softens as he watches Ben storm back inside, the hand cream now squeezed in his fist like it's responsible for all the world's ills. He chucks the tube in the wheelie bin by the back door and follows Ben's path with quieter steps.

I take a moment, staring at the space where Ben disappeared, feeling the dampness of the grass seep around my flip-flops. My heart aches for him, but I also think there's something more I should be doing—something other than just standing here.

Sighing, I follow them back inside, leaving the cool morning air for the warmth of the kitchen.

Ben is nowhere to be seen when I enter. Liam is washing his hands at the sink. He dries them on a tea towel and crosses over to me, wrapping his arms around me. I cling to him, and the world suddenly feels not right again, but not wrong either. I lean against him, hearing his heart beat in his chest, a steady rhythm that soothes me.

"I need to talk to him about Eddie," I murmur, biting my lip.

Liam leans against the counter and crosses his

arms. "Maybe give it a bit, yeah? Let him get his head together first."

"Yeah." But when will that be? I can't take any chances that Eddie is on his way right now and will be beating the door down. Shaking my head, I pull away from Liam reluctantly. "No, he needs to know now." Before Liam can stop me, I bolt up the stairs and march down the landing to the end, where I knock firmly on the door, hoping he's not already in the shower and can't hear me.

"Go away," he says. "Unless Mia needs me."

"Mia is fine," I say calmly. "But I need to talk to you."

"I don't want to talk."

"It's not about you, if that helps. It's about me, and that phone call Liam took yesterday from my phone."

Silence, and then the door opens. Ben glares down at me, now a different man from the one outside. "Oh?" he almost growls, and I panic. Maybe this was a stupid time to come to him.

"Uhm," I fluster, and I see his nose pinch as my scent hits him in the face. "Maybe, I'll come back."

"Who was it?" he grits out, his tone pinning me in place.

"An alpha named Eddie Mowbray. He is my ex. I left him the day I came up here. He is not a nice man, and I wanted to get away from him. It's one reason I was so happy when I got this job. It was a fresh start."

He glares at me down his nose and my mouth goes dry. "What did he want?"

"He wants me back. But it's not like that, I don't think. He was a gaslighting narcissist who preyed on me while I was weak." *Why am I telling him all of this?*

The change in his expression shocks me. He goes from pissed off and annoyed to understanding and almost resigned. "I know what that's like," he murmurs.

"So, you aren't mad?" I venture after a pause.

He frowns. "Why would I be mad?"

"In case he tracks me down..."

His gaze goes hard again, and I gulp. "Is that a possibility? He knows where you are?"

"I don't think so. There's no way he *could* know. I was dumb with my phone, and that's how he got through to me. But that's been resolved. But I needed you to know so you can be prepared if he *does* show up."

"He steps one foot near you; I will rip him to shreds," he growls so ferociously that it takes everything I have not to step back from him. "Mia," he says, his scowl deepening again. "I meant Mia."

Blinking rapidly, I nod my head like an idiot. "Of course," I murmur.

He lets out a huff and slams the door in my face.

"Great work, Zara. That went really well."

I trudge back down the stairs, feeling like I've just walked through a tornado. Liam's in the lounge, sitting on the sofa, fiddling with Mia's soft toy, lost in thought. My heart twinges at the sight of him looking so serious.

"Everything okay?" he asks without looking up, his voice laced with genuine concern.

I slump down beside him and let out a long breath. "I think so. I told Ben about Eddie."

Liam's head snaps up, his brow furrowed. "And?"

"He said he'd tear Eddie apart if he came anywhere near Mia," I say with a half-smile.

"Sounds like Ben."

"Yeah." I rub my face.

Liam sets the toy aside and pulls me into a one-armed hug. I nestle against him, feeling the comfort I desperately need after offering the same to Ben. This is a circle of hurt and comfort. I just hope we can get over the hurt and move forward. Ben especially. Eddie means nothing to me. I wouldn't piss on him if he were on fire, as the saying goes, but his call has still left me a bit shaken and raw. The scent of summer rain washes over me, and I look up into Liam's face, his cute, smiling face, and everything clicks into place. This is an alpha I can rely on, who won't hurt me or try to control me. Slick gushes out of my pussy suddenly, and Liam catches the scent, his grip tightening on me.

"Zara," he murmurs, but I don't let him finish. I crawl onto his lap and cup his face, kissing him deeply, bruising his lips with the promise of more. He groans into my mouth, his hands sliding down to grip my hips, bringing me closer until I can feel his cock stiffen. We're a tangle of need and reassurance, of comfort sought and given.

His fingers edge under the hem of my top, tracing patterns on my skin that leave trails of heat in their wake.

I grind my pussy against him, and he growls softly, a low rumble from his chest that vibrates through my hands. The purr that escapes me is swallowed up by his mouth on mine.

"Fuck," he pants and pulls away. "So, is that a yes for a date?"

His quizzical expression makes me burst out laughing, and I nod. "Yes. Yes, I'll go out with you. But maybe we don't tell Ben right now."

"Good idea. He's grouchy enough."

My heart sinks again, "With good reason."

"Yeah," he agrees, lifting me up to place me next to him on the couch. "You'd better go over there before I ravage you."

I giggle and rise. "You go shower first. You need to get moving for work, and I need to check on Mia."

He nods but doesn't move, watching my every move as I saunter as sexily as I can in wet flip flops and damp pjs up the stairs to check on the baby.

Chapter 27

Benjamin

I'm pacing my bedroom, my hands running through my hair, tugging in frustration. Zara's confession has me wound up tight, but not because I fear for my daughter's safety or Zara's, for that matter. It's because of my slip-up.

Fuck.

Fuck. What a fucking idiot thing to say.

I can still smell Zara's mild fear over telling me about her ex calling mingled with her natural scent, even after she left. It is confusing me in ways that I don't want to be confused.

I'm about to start another lap of my room when there's a firm knock at the door. "Come in," I grunt, trying not to sound as aggressive as I feel. It's not Zara, her knock is softer than that.

The door cracks open, and Liam pokes his head

through, looking like he might be walking into a lion's den—which isn't far from the truth at the moment.

"Everything alright?" He steps into the room but keeps a safe distance.

I stop pacing and stare at him with a deep sigh. "Zara just told me about that fucking ex of hers who rang yesterday."

Liam's face hardens. "Yeah, he sounds like a real asshole."

"Exactly," I say flatly.

"Are you mad?"

"Why would I be mad?"

"Because she didn't tell you?"

"Why would she have had to tell me? Her past is none of my business unless it becomes part of her present. It did, and she told me. Nothing else to be said."

Liam gives me an impressed nod. "Okay, you're taking it better than I thought you would."

"Look, after the morning I've had already, this was nothing."

"Yeah, about that... you okay?"

My shoulders slump, and I sit heavily on the bed. "Without her scent here, the mating is rapidly unravelling. It's getting worse. The pain, the longing, the need."

"Yeah, I figured it would get worse before it got better, but it *will* get better."

"I know, but when?" I flop back to the bed, hands over my face.

"Can't answer that, I'm afraid."

Liam crosses the room and sits at the edge of the bed. "You've got to stay strong, mate. For Mia."

"Yeah, I know. It's just a fucking mess in my head right now."

He chuckles. "We're all a mess sometimes. But you're one of the strongest alphas I know. You and Henry. You're both solid."

I sit up, resting my elbows on my knees. "Being strong doesn't mean shit if you can't protect the ones you love."

"And you will. You are," he insists.

There's a pause, and then Liam's expression shifts to something more hesitant, almost sheepish. "Mind if I ask you something personal?"

A laugh bursts out of me despite myself. "Would it stop you if I said yes?"

He snorts. "Nope. Do you have feelings for Zara?"

Sitting up, I glare at him. "What? No, of course not."

"You growled at her after she purred at you."

"So what? It was a fraught day. Emotions were high."

"You sure about that?"

"Yes," I growl. "Where are you going with this?"

He shrugs. "I like her."

He blinks.

I blink back.

"As in romantically?" I croak, not enjoying the feeling one bit that he has the hots for my nanny.

"Yeah. She's gorgeous, sweet, kind, funny, so freakin' cute, and she is so good with Mia and you."

"Wow, okay," I murmur, trying to process that. I find myself shifting on the bed, discomfort spreading through my chest. Why do I feel like I'm being sucker punched? It's not like I have a claim on Zara. She's free to date whoever she wants, including Liam.

But fuck. The thought of her with someone pisses me off more than I want to admit.

"You're not gonna go all alpha on me and forbid it, are you?" Liam asks, watching me closely.

"No," I say quickly, almost too quickly. "No, of course not. You're both adults."

"Good," he nods, relief evident in his eyes. "Because I asked her out."

My gut twists unpleasantly. "And?"

"She said yes."

I force a smile because that's what you do for your mates, right? You smile and nod and give them a pat on the back, even if inside, you're clawing at walls and snarling like a bloody idiot.

"Great," I manage to say. "That's... great. But don't fuck it up, please, Liam. She *is* so good with Mia; I can't lose her." My desperation seeps out, and he frowns.

"You sure it's just Mia you want her for?"

"Don't," I grunt, standing up and pointing at him. "Don't."

He holds his hands up. "Look, all I'm saying is if you figure out that growl meant more than you're letting on, I'm not stepping back. There's room for more than one alpha, if Zara wants that, of course."

"Are you fucking joking right now?"

He looks at me seriously, shaking his head. "No joke. You know, as well as I do, that sometimes things get complicated."

I let out a frustrated huff, pacing back and forth again. "Yeah, but this is *Zara* we're talking about. My *nanny*."

"So you're worried about it being a cliché?"

"What? Fuck off, will you?"

"Your words say one thing, but your face is giving off a whole other vibe, mate," he prods.

"No! I mean—fuck." I stop pacing and face him,

realising that he's seen right through me. "She purred at me first. It was a shocked reaction. Nothing more."

"But now you're jealous," Liam says.

I want to hurl him out of the window like I did that tube of hand cream yesterday. What is he doing to me?

But deep down, lurking where it doesn't have a right to be, there's no point denying it; the tightness in my chest confirms it.

Liam stands up, laying a reassuring hand on my shoulder. "Look, you don't need to do or say anything else. Your actions speak louder right now. She is under our skin and we both know it. Are you ready for it? No, probably not. Is that going to stop you? Yeah, probably. You're Ben Scott, brooder of the century. Will I still date her? Fuck, yeah. Will I be open to you also dating her if you decide that's in your best interest? More than open. Just let that simmer for a while. No one is going anywhere, yeah?"

"I don't want it to be weird," I reply.

"Why would it be weird?"

I shrug half-heartedly.

"Thinking, not acting right now."

"I'm sick of thinking," I admit with a grimace.

"So, you want to act?"

"Fuck off and let me have a shower. I already owe Alan for bolting out yesterday. I can't be late today."

"Good point. Shower and move your ass."

My mind races as Liam leaves the room. The possibility of Zara being with someone else, with *Liam*, has lit a fire under me—a fire I didn't even know was there until now. It's not just jealousy; it's a realisation that maybe there's something more I feel for her than just her being the nanny.

Maybe.

Chapter 28

Zara

As I'm laying out my clothes for the day on my bed, there is a knock on the door. Crossing over to it, I open it and stare at Liam, wet from the shower, a white towel slung around his hips.

"Uhm," I say, putting my hand up. "I agreed to a date, not a jump in the sack."

"More's the pity," he says with that wicked smile. "But I know. I just wanted you to know I told Ben about us."

All the blood drains from my face. "What?"

Liam's smile widens, not missing a beat. "I told him I asked you out, and you said yes. Just wanted to keep everything out in the open, no secrets."

I feel my heart rate picking up. "And how did he take it?"

He shrugs, that grin still plastered on his face as if he knows something I don't. "He took it like Ben takes anything that surprises him; he brooded."

"Oh, God," I mutter, suddenly worried about what this means for my job. I love this job; I love Mia already. I can't lose her. "This isn't going to be a problem for me working here, is it?"

"No way," Liam quickly reassures me. "Ben wouldn't hold it against you. He's too decent for that." He pauses for a moment, as if considering his next words carefully. "But I think there might be more going on in that head of his than he's willing to admit."

My stomach does a little flip at the thought. Ben is... well, he's Ben. Gorgeous, rugged, and a great father to Mia, knows how to growl at an omega when she's purred in his face like a fool. Fuck, a burp would've been the better option. But he's also my employer and I've always been strictly professional—until last night when things got a bit blurry with all the purring.

"Don't worry about Ben," Liam says, snapping me back to the present. "Worry about what you're going to wear on our date, because I plan to impress."

I laugh despite the nervous flutter in my belly. "You already have," I admit.

Liam winks at me before stepping back.

"Tonight, I'm going to show you how much I want this."

"Tonight?" I frown. "What about Mia?"

"Ben will be here."

Well, good point, but it's short notice.

"Okay, I guess," I murmur and watch as he walks away, hot, wet and sexy as hell. Fanning myself a little, I grab my towel and my dressing gown and head for the shower. I need it after that little encounter. It's not just to get myself in gear but to cool down, literally. My thoughts are racing, not just about Liam, the kiss, and him telling Ben about us, but also about Ben. His breakdown this morning, me telling him about Eddie and his reaction to that. Not to mention the purr and growl situation.

Ugh! I'm driving myself crazy.

As I step into the steamy water, I shake it all off and focus. I'm here for Mia, not to be off gallivanting with Liam, nor to be thinking about Ben in any other capacity than Mia's dad.

The water cascades down my back, soothing my nerves. I've got to keep things in perspective. But my thoughts won't stay focused. I mean, it's one date with Liam, who happens to be incredibly charming and hot—that's all. Yet, there's this niggle at the back of my brain about Ben and his brooding silences.

I turn off the shower, step out, and wrap

myself in my towel and dressing gown. The mirror is fogged up, but as I wipe it clear, I see my reflection staring back at me—my face flushed from the heat and maybe from something else, too.

I hear Mia stirring on the baby monitor, which makes me move. She's going to need her bottle soon, and that's my cue to leave all these confusing thoughts behind for now.

I get dressed quickly, making sure I choose an outfit that is practical for looking after Mia.

I find Ben in the nursery, reluctant to leave, it seems. He is staring at his daughter in his arms and looks up, annoyed when I come in.

"Work," I say gently and hold my arms out for the baby.

He glares at me and refuses to hand her over. But I glare back, and just as I'm about to fold like a cheap tent and drop my omega gaze from his alpha domination, he sighs and hands her over.

"I know you don't want to go, but she's on the mend. I'll send hourly updates, check her temperature and keep you informed. Okay?"

"Fine," he glowers and marches off without so much as a goodbye, have a nice day.

So I decide to be a dick and shout after him, "Bye! Hope you have a lovely day!"

His answering grunt makes me chuckle, and I kiss Mia's head. "Your daddy is a real grouch."

She babbles back at me, which I take as agreement, and set about our little routine which is comforting and fills me with a deep joy just to be here doing what I love and falling deeper in love with this baby girl who has captured my heart.

After settling Mia down for her morning nap, I'm left alone with my thoughts again, and they stubbornly drift back to the two men in my life. Liam with his laid-back charm and easy smile, and Ben with his brooding intensity and fierce love for his daughter. I don't have much time to ponder, though, as my phone pings with a message from Liam:

Got anything specific you need from the shop?

I reply back: *Food.*

To which he sends a laughing face emoji and then: *Don't blame us then if we arrive with beer and bread.*

Shaking my head, I know he's joking. Ben has been fending for himself, so he knows what he needs to buy.

The rest of the day passes in a blur of baby giggles, nappy changes, and bottle feeding. Her temperature stays at a steady 38.5, which is worrying but not an emergency, so I keep texting "no change" to Ben. He replies with that fucking thumbs up emoji which everyone knows is the condescending symbol for fuck you.

So, I leave him to it. I'm not digging deeper into his feelings after this morning. That was plenty for one day.

By late afternoon, I start to get anxious about this date with Liam and leaving Ben here with Mia. It seems cheeky and a bit rude.

You're allowed a life, though.

Well, yeah, but something doesn't feel right about this, and I pick up the phone to cancel with Liam.

But then something else stops me and I chew my lip as I shove my phone back in my pocket.

After making sure Mia is safe and sleeping, I head downstairs. The front door opens, and the guys stroll in, beaming like they did something amazing.

"Food!" Liam announces.

"Great. You want a medal?"

He snickers as Ben gives me a narrow-eyed stare. "What an ungrateful response for the hunter-gatherers." His lips turn up into a smirk, and I giggle.

"Is that how you see yourselves? Tackling the aisles at the supermarket?"

"You don't know what it's like out there for two single alphas doing the weekly shop," Liam says with a laugh. "Dodging omegas like they're sabre-toothed tigers."

"Yeah, I bet," I chortle as I take a couple of bags Ben hands me, glad that his mood has lightened considerably. I guess bonding time with Liam outside of work has been good for him. Maybe they should go out tonight instead?

"But why dodge?" I ask lightly, cursing myself and my runaway mouth. *What am I doing?*

Liam's eyes find mine with a curious stare. Ben, on the other hand, snorts in disgust.

"Huge pass," he grumbles and stalks past me to the kitchen.

"Well, it was fun while it lasted," I say with a sigh.

"Back to that question," Liam says, ignoring me. "You don't want me to dodge?"

I do! I do! But I shouldn't want you to.

I shrug nonchalantly and turn away from him.

"Whoa," he says, grasping my arm lightly to halt my progress to the kitchen. "What's brought that on?" He searches my eyes earnestly. "Have you changed your mind about our date?"

"It's just a date," I murmur. "You are free to do what you want."

"Is that what you think?" he asks with a frown

that worries me I've made a really serious error in judgement here.

Ya think, bitch? Even my brain is shaking its metaphorical head at me.

I hesitate because this tiny moment feels like the cusp of something significant. It's not just about a date; it's about what it represents. Liam's looking at me like he's trying to read the headlines of my soul, and I'm suddenly conscious that I might be broadcasting all sorts of signals I hadn't intended to.

"Look," I find myself saying, "this is coming out all wrong. But there's a lot going on, yeah? Mia's ill, Ben's going through his thing, and I've been caught in the middle of all this."

Liam nods slowly. "I get it," he says, releasing my arm gently, respecting my space. "So, do you want to cancel?"

I'm on the verge of saying yes, but looking into his soulful green eyes that are portraying a genuine fear that I might say yes, I gulp. "No," I say more firmly than I feel. "But let's keep it low-key tonight."

His eyes light up. "Well, it's a good thing you said that because low-key and I are old friends. I've got just the thing."

"Okay," I say and head into the kitchen where Ben is putting away the groceries with that methodical nature of his that tells me he likes order even when his world is spinning out of control around him.

"I'll finish up. You go and get changed and see Mia."

He nods and, without saying a word, heads upstairs.

I crack on with putting away the rest of the shopping, sliding vegetables into baskets and stacking yogurts into the fridge. As I work, my mind wanders, and I think about tonight with Liam—our attempt at a low-key date is what can only be described as an abnormal situation. But what is normal anyway? I feel like I've lost the plot on that one.

Chapter 29

Zara

"Go and get ready," Liam says to me, coming into the kitchen with another bag.

"Here, I'll put that away first," I say, reaching for it.

"I've got it. You go up."

"What about Ben's dinner?"

"All sorted, just go or you will give an alpha a complex."

Giggling, I nod. "Fine, I'm going. What do I wear?"

"Warm and comfy."

"I can do that." Relieved that this is going to be a low-key date like he said, I head upstairs to my room to get ready. Pulling on some black jeans and a long-sleeved black tee, I put on my socks and a black jumper, grabbing my boots and a coat from the wardrobe.

Once downstairs, I sit on the bottom step and put my boots on, then rise to slip into my coat. Hearing a noise from the kitchen, I enter and see Liam heading out the back door.

Following him curiously, I step out onto the back lawn, my feet sinking a bit into the soft grass, watching as Liam, all smiles and casual grace, unfolds a blanket with one hand. He's got a basket beside him and my heart clenches with more feeling than I used to for this sweet, kind alpha. The sight of it all, so unexpected and charming, makes me stop in my tracks.

"Surprise," he says, looking up at me with those eyes that seem to twinkle with some secret joke between us.

"Is this for us?"

"Yep, I thought we could use some fresh air and good food while staying close to home." He pats the blanket like it's an invitation I can't refuse.

My heart skips a little with excitement. He's put together a picnic right here on the lawn, where we can still keep an eye on the house—and, by extension, Ben and Mia.

"This is so thoughtful of you," I say, and I mean it. It's not every day someone plans something so considerate. It's just a simple spread on the grass, but it feels like so much more because he's taken them into account, too.

"Come on, then. Have a seat." He gestures to the blanket, now spread wide, with plates and cups set neatly around a mysterious, covered dish in the centre.

"Okay." I smile, walking over and carefully taking my place on the blanket. The grass is cool under the fabric, the dying sun warm on my skin in this small patch of the garden before it disappears. It's perfect picnic weather, and just like that, I'm buzzing with happiness at the surprise, at the thought he's put into this, and at the evening that stretches ahead.

Liam sets out all sorts of goodies, but I snicker at the pre-packed sarnies.

"Hey, I was on a short timescale," he says, not offended in the least.

"Oh, I know, and this is perfect, absolutely perfect. Ham and cheese," I add, picking up a boxed sandwich.

"Same as you made me that first day you arrived."

"Seems like a lifetime ago."

"A lot has happened," he agrees, taking it from me to open and lay out neatly on the blanket.

"Yeah." I look back at the house and wonder if Ben is watching this. And if he is, what does he make of it? Does he realise Liam thought about him and Mia?

"Fizzy water?" He hands me a paper cup. I'd been too busy lost in my thoughts to hear him open the green bottle propped up next to him.

"Careful, or you might spoil me," I tell him, accepting the cup.

"Too late, I'm afraid. That ship has sailed," Liam replies, raising his cup in a mock toast. "To spoiling Zara, long may it continue."

Our cups come together, and I can't contain the laughter that bubbles up inside. It feels good to sit here with him, sharing food and silly jokes under the open sky. For a moment, everything else fades away, and it's just us, basking in the simplicity of a picnic and the complexity of our growing connection.

Liam flicks a grape towards me, his aim perfect as it lands right in my palm. I pop it into my mouth and chew thoughtfully while he stretches out on the blanket, looking relaxed yet somehow serious all of a sudden.

"I really like you," he murmurs.

"I really like you too."

He smiles, almost sadly. "I've never really liked anyone before."

"I find that hard to believe."

"My dating history's been, well, let's just say, less than stellar."

I tilt my head, curious. "Oh? How so?"

He shrugs, taking a sip of his drink. "I guess I've never found someone who made settling down seem worth it, and then there's what happened with Ben and Nicole, which I thought had put me off for life ever wanting to settle down and mate."

"I can imagine," I murmur.

He grimaces. "No, you really can't. She was a piece of work. Narcissistic, you know? Always needed to be the centre of attention." He shakes his head, his usual lightness fading for a moment. "She didn't just mess with Ben's head—she tried to wedge herself between all of us. Me, Ben, Henry. We were tight, and she couldn't stand it. She wanted to isolate Ben, have him depend only on her. She hated his parents and pushed them away. It was a nightmare. But Ben didn't see it."

"It's rough, but he wouldn't, though. Not unless he wanted to." I *know*. I lived it.

"Rough doesn't quite cover it," he says, acknowledging my other words by reaching out and taking my hand to give it a squeeze. He doesn't remove it, but laces our fingers together. "I—I hate to say this, and I've never said it to Ben, and nor would I, but I think she only decided to have Mia as a way to keep control over Ben. That's why she bolted so soon after. She wasn't cut out for it, and she cut her losses."

"That's sick," I mutter. "*If* it's true. You don't know that for sure."

"I can pretty much guarantee," he growls. "Don't give her the benefit of the doubt, Zara. She was a bitch, and I'm glad she's gone. I feel if she hadn't left when she did, Henry and I would've staged an intervention."

"You're good friends," I murmur with a smile.

"We try. But this went off the rails. I was talking about me, but watching Nicole destroy Ben put me off. It's something that I guess I needed you to know."

"I'm not like her," I start with a frown.

"Fuck, no. I wasn't saying you were. You are the opposite of her, the Anti-Nicole. You are perfect, sweet, kind, loving. You are an omega through and through. I always wondered if Nicole had alpha tendencies."

"It's been known to happen."

"You have changed my outlook. I can see there is good in relationships when there is give and take." His gaze simmers into mine.

"You've really been dating the wrong people," I giggle, but then sigh. "Not that I have a leg to stand on."

"Yeah, the infamous Eddie. Have I mentioned what a toolkit he is?"

I laugh. "Once or twice, but feel free to say it again and be more scathing about it." I lean forward, a blade of grass between my fingers, twisting it as I gather my thoughts. "He had this way of making me doubt myself, like everything was always my fault. If he turned up late, somehow, I'd got the time wrong. If he forgot something, I must've never told him."

Liam shifts closer, resting on one elbow, his gaze fixed on me.

"He loved to play mind games. And the worst part? For a long time, I fell for it. Thought I was going mad."

He reaches out, his hand brushing mine lightly. It's a small gesture, but it sends warmth spiralling through me. "You're not mad, Zara. He was just an asshole."

I meet his eyes then, seeing the sincerity shining there. It's as if he's handing me a piece of his heart, asking me to trust it won't break in my hands. "Yeah, he is. I was grieving when I met him. My parents died in a car crash about a year ago. Drunk driver. He found me at my worst and maybe assumed I was naturally like that. Sad and weepy and a total basket case. He thought he'd lucked out, but he didn't get I was mourning, and when that deep pain of losing them healed a bit, I started to get myself back. I've never been a pushover. I like to please people, but I know when I'm being taken advantage of. Or I did. Eddie lured me in and made me feel comforted at first, but then the cracks started to show, you know?"

"Yeah." His expression is soft and open, like he's peeling back layers of himself to show me he understands. "No one should make you feel less than you are. Especially not some cowardly alpha who's not worth your time."

"I guess we've both seen our fair share of rubbish relationships, haven't we?" I muse, feeling the weight of the past ease off my shoulders.

"Looks like it," he agrees, his smile kind. "But you're here now, and you're amazing, Zara. Don't forget that."

"Right back at you," I say with a grin, shaking off the seriousness of our conversation.

I scoot closer to Liam, our sides touching. His arm finds its way around my shoulders, pulling me in for a hug that feels like home. I breathe him in, his scent mingling with the fresh air around us.

I pull back slightly, meeting Liam's gaze. He waits, patient and attentive.

"It's odd, isn't it? How life throws these curveballs at you," I start, fiddling with the hem of his coat.

"Here I am, meant to be focusing on my job, looking after Mia, and then there's this thing between us."

He studies me for a second, his eyes searching mine. "It's natural, Zara. Feelings don't tend to check your employment contract before showing up, do they?"

I let out a small laugh, despite the seriousness of our conversation. "No, I suppose they don't. But it's complicated, isn't it? I mean, Ben's been great to me, and Mia is a darling. I love her so much already. I can't mess this up."

Liam nods, his hand squeezing mine gently. "It is complicated. But whatever you're feeling, it's okay, Zara. We'll figure it out, won't we?"

"I hope so because right now, sitting here with you, it feels right." My cheeks warm at the admission, and I'm grateful for the fading light that might hide my blush.

"Feels right to me, too," he says, the corner of his mouth lifting in a half-smile that sets my heart racing in a way I can't ignore. We stay like that, close but not quite touching, as the sky shifts from dark blue to hues of pink and orange. It's beautiful, yet I can't stop thinking about the pull I feel towards him, magnetic and undeniable.

"We'll take things slow. No pressure, no grand

gestures. Just whatever feels natural." His gaze is steady and reassuring as he speaks again.

"Thanks. I appreciate the thoughtfulness."

We lean in, and the whispering breeze seems to hush, waiting. I'm teetering on the edge of something unknown, thrilling.

"Zara," he murmurs. His voice has this gravity that pulls at me.

"Yeah?" It comes out breathy, my usual chatter lost somewhere in the wind.

"Whatever happens..." He trails off, but there's an intensity in his gaze that tells me he's as tangled up in this moment as I am.

I nod because it's all I can manage right now. The 'what-ifs' swirl around us like the leaves above. What if I'm reading this all wrong? What if this changes everything with Ben and Mia?

"I don't want to rush you, or..."

"Or?" I prompt.

"Or muck this up."

"Neither do I," I murmur back, feeling the weight of my words. They hang there, mingling with the twilight.

We stay like that, hands clasped, the world shrinking to just the two of us and the quiet hum of the evening. But as much as I feel happy to be here with Liam, and I'm glad we took this step, my heart doesn't feel full. I cast a glance back at the house, towards Ben, and see him staring at us from Mia's nursery window. We lock gazes for a moment before he backs away, and I know then that I'm as lost to him as I am to the alpha in my arms.

How on earth am I going to navigate my tangled emotions for both the man beside me and the one who's entrusted me with his most precious possession?

Chapter 30

Henry

I wake up with the sun peeking through my blinds, with a warmth in my chest that has lingered there since I took care of Zara's head the other day. She's been on my mind more than I care to admit lately. It's like every little thing she does just makes me want to know her better. I want to get her a gift. Something special, to show her how wonderful I think she is and how great she is with Mia and also with Ben.

Tossing the sheets aside, I get up and ready, smiling as I think about how she might react. I mean, what do you even get someone who's as unique as Zara? Flowers seem a bit cliché, chocolates too impersonal. No, it needs to be something that says, 'I've been paying attention to you and all that you do'.

I head out before the shops open; it's just a short, brisk walk into the village. The town is waking up when I arrive, shops lifting their shutters, and the smell of freshly baked bread wafting from the bakery.

The first shop I duck into smells of lavender and beeswax. It's a boutique full of handmade bits and bobs. My stomach does weird flips at the lavender scent. My alpha responds to it, knowing the same scent drifts over Zara's skin like a gentle summer breeze.

What would she like?

There's this buzz in my veins as I touch a knitted hat, then a set of colourful coasters. I imagine her using them, a cup of tea in hand, that relaxed smile on her face. But no, it's still not quite right. It has to be something that she wouldn't expect but will instantly love. A gift that'll make her eyes light up, that'll maybe get me one of those smiles where it lingers just a moment longer than necessary.

Not finding the perfect item, I step back out, squinting as the morning light reflects off the windows. I wander further down the street, hands in my pockets, taking my time. There's no rush, not when it comes to Zara. I'll know the perfect gift when I see it, and I'm determined to find it today. It's one of the perks of making your own hours; you get to go on impromptu shopping trips for omegas you barely know, but, in your heart, feels like you've known her forever.

I push open the door to a small, cosy shop that looks like it's been lifted straight from a storybook, all warm light and inviting displays. My eyes land on a shelf, soft blankets piled high, their colours whispering of comfort and home. This is it, I think as I walk over and run my fingers through one, feeling the plush texture.

"Looking for something in particular?" The shop assistant's voice is friendly, not too pushy.

"Something special," I reply, and my mind paints a picture of Zara curled up on her couch at Ben's, a book in her lap, a cup of tea close by. A blanket, a really nice one, could be part of that. Something she'd wrap around herself and feel cared for and, dare I hope, nest in when the time comes.

I pick up a blanket that's the colour of dusk, soft blues and gentle greys melding together. It's large enough to envelop her completely, and the fabric feels like a cloud might if you could touch one. That's what I want for Zara – to give her a slice of a dream.

"Would you like to get that one?" The assistant appears at my elbow again, her own arms cradling a stack of neatly folded textiles.

"Yeah, this one." My voice is steady, but inside, there's a whole circus going on.

As I bundle up the blanket, a simple brown paper package tied with string, it feels like I'm wrapping a piece of my heart along with it. I pay and leave the shop, hands tight around the package. It's just a gift, but somehow, it's also a confession, a tangible bit of care that I'm not sure I'm ready to admit out loud.

Walking back toward home, the light weight of the blanket is reassuring against my side, but my chest tightens with every step. What if she doesn't see it as just a kind gesture? What if she reads into it, sees the things I'm only just admitting to myself? Like how her laughter makes my day brighter, or the way it nearly broke me to leave her the other day?

I need to calm down, take a breath. It's just a blanket. But it's special because it's for Zara, and she's special *because* she's Zara.

I'm nearly home now, and the nerves are bubbling up like a fountain. I remind myself it's okay to feel this way, to be unsure because feelings like these aren't meant to be clear-cut. They're messy, beautiful, and terrifying all at once.

As I walk up the driveway to where my car is parked, I pull out my keys and decide to drop this off now, or I may never do it. Liam and Ben will be at work by now, so it'll be just Zara and me.

Driving the short distance to Ben's, my palms sweating and my heart pumping wildly, I pull into the driveway and stop for a second, taking stock of this situation. Have I been hasty? Is this inappropriate? Blinking, I look down at the package on the passenger seat and inhale deeply.

Slowly exhaling, I snatch it up and climb out of the car.

Knocking in case the doorbell wakes Mia, I wait.

My hand is a little shaky, but I manage to keep a smile on my face when Zara opens the door. She looks surprised to see me there, but it's a happy surprise, her eyes lighting up and casting all sorts of warmth my way.

"Hey, Henry," she greets me, leaning against the doorframe. "What brings you here?" Her voice has a lilt that suggests she's genuinely pleased to see me.

I hold out the package towards her. "I saw this and thought of you," I say, trying not to stumble over the words. My heart thumps a mad rhythm in my chest as I add, "I hope you like it."

Her eyes drop to the brown paper package, then back to mine. She reaches out, taking it gently and cradling it as if it's something precious. That alone is enough to uncoil some of the tension in my chest.

"For me?"

I nod like an idiot.

"Come in." She steps back to let me pass and

then closes the door. She pads into the lounge, and I follow her, trailing in the wake of her luscious scent.

Zara sits and carefully unties the string and unfolds the paper. When she sees the blanket, her breath catches softly, and that smile I hoped for spreads across her face—a sunrise of joy that hits me square in the chest. It's better than I imagined.

"It's beautiful," she whispers, running her fingers over the fabric. "Henry... this is too much."

I shove my hands into my pockets, suddenly unsure what to do with them. "It's just a blanket," I say, even though we both know it's more than that.

She unfolds it, running her hands over the fabric. "Thank you. This is so thoughtful." She stands up, and I brace myself, unsure of what's coming.

Then she hugs me, quick and tight, and something in me unclenches. She gets it. She gets that this isn't just any old blanket but a piece of me given to her in soft woven threads.

"It's nothing," I manage to get out, though we both know it's everything but nothing.

"Nothing?" She laughs, and it's music to my ears. "This is one of the nicest things anyone's done for me."

I try to play it cool, shrugging casually like it was some random find. "Well, I'm glad you like it. It seemed perfect for you."

Zara's eyes meet mine, and there's a moment where everything seems to still, where the only thing I'm aware of is her gaze locked on mine, heavy with something unspoken. "I'll cherish it," she says softly.

The intensity of the moment makes me want to look away, but I can't; it's like she's seeing right through me. Then she breaks the spell with a smile and a playful nudge of her elbow into my ribs. "You're going to make someone a very good mate one day, Henry."

The words are teasing, but they light a fire in my belly that I've been trying hard to ignore. Zara walks over to the couch, draping the blanket across the back and smoothing it down with pride. She pats it fondly before turning back toward me.

"So, what's been going on with you besides blanket shopping?" she asks with genuine interest as we both sit down on the couch.

"Not much," I say. "Just thinking about making some changes." Staring into her forest green eyes, I know that the decision I had already made but was waiting to get everything properly into place is about to be moved forward. As much as I want to tell myself this is for Ben's benefit and he could do with the financial ease, I'm kidding myself. I feel left out with Liam here getting cosy with Zara, and I want to be a part of that as well. I want to explore this natural attraction I have to her and see if it's real or just wishful thinking and my sense of wanting to settle down.

"What kind of changes?" she asks, but then Mia cries through the baby monitor, drawing her to her feet. "Sorry, duty calls."

"Of course," I murmur and watch her go. "I'll see you later."

I pull out my phone and text a message to the estate agent I know, enquiring about listing my place. It's a solid house with good bones and great views; it'll rent out in no time, and the extra cash here will ease things for Ben even more before he finds himself in a mountain of debt with no way out.

But as much as this is about helping a mate, it's also selfish. I want to be near Zara, see her more often, and learn the little things that make her laugh, or the quiet moments when she thinks no one's watching. I want to be part of her world, woven into the fabric of her days.

The agent replies almost immediately, enthusiastic about the prospect. This is the first step towards something new, something that feels a lot like hope for the future. My future.

Chapter 31

Henry

After leaving Zara, I head to the office to try to concentrate on work, but all I can think about is Zara's arms wrapped around me. Knowing that I have to push forward with my plan, I decide it's time to clear this with Ben before I go any further.

The drive is short, nothing is too far away in this part of the country, and I push open the door to Ben's office building.

It's nearing lunchtime, so he should be able to take a break and talk with me. Stepping into the lobby, I feel like I'm walking into a beehive. The place is alive, with people zipping past me left and right. They're all caught up in their own worlds, clutching papers and tapping away on their phones.

The air hums with chatter, and there's incoming

calls that echoes off the walls. Everyone here moves with purpose like they've got important places to be and even more important things to do.

Colleagues are huddled in pairs or groups, some leaning over desks while others stand in doorways. They talk fast, their words spilling out in quick bursts as if every second counts double. I watch them, feeling a bit out of place with my jeans and casual shirt amidst their sea of suits and ties. Again, a perk of working for myself. But I brush it off; I'm not here for them. I'm here for Ben.

My heart thumps a steady beat, not too fast, but enough to remind me of what's at stake. This chat with Ben is going to change things between us, hopefully for the better. I shove my hands into my pockets, trying to appear nonchalant as I navigate through the maze of activity, making my way to where I know he'll be.

"Excuse me," I mutter as I edge past a couple of people deep in conversation. They barely glance at me, too caught up in whatever problem-solving they're doing. I finally catch sight of him, tucked away at his desk.

"Hey," I mutter as I walk up to him. He's hunched over a blueprint, a pencil behind his ear. He's so engrossed in his work, he doesn't notice me until I'm standing right in front of his desk. I clear my throat, and Ben's head snaps up, his eyes wide with surprise.

"Henry. What brings you here? Is it Mia?"

"No, Mia and Zara are both fine, as far as I know." I mean, I don't know for sure, so I can't insist. "But can we have a chat about something?"

He blinks at me, then nods. "Sure. The meeting room is empty right now." He stands up, stretching to his full height, and I follow him like a shadow.

We slip through a door labelled 'Conference Room B', shutting out the clamour of the office behind us. The room is stark, just a long table and chairs, but it's private. Ben gestures towards a chair, his eyes questioning as he sits across from me.

"Everything alright, Henry?"

I shuffle my feet, the carpet beneath somehow too solid and too flimsy all at once. "Look, Ben. I'm going to be frank. Your situation is not good. There are no places to cut back, and even with Liam helping out, it's a lot. You know? With Mia and Zara."

He frowns and crosses his arms, perching on the edge of the table. "Yeah, I figured." He heaves a sigh. "So what do I do?"

"Make it a three-income household."

"Huh?" His frown deepens. "You mean, you?"

"Yep."

He's quiet for a beat, considering, and I hold my breath. He's not dismissing it out of hand, which has to be a good sign. There's a flicker of something like relief in his eyes, but it's gone before I can be sure.

"You sure about this?" He searches my eyes.

"Very sure. I've put out feelers for the house, and the estate agent already has a queue of people gagging to get into the area. I can rent it out in no time."

"But what about, you know?" He knows I'm thinking about the future, but what he doesn't know is that I want that future to be with Zara. If she decides she wants me, and even if she wants Liam or Ben, or both, or even some rando I don't know, I don't care. I just want her to want me.

"The future?"

"Yeah."

"I'm focusing on the present right now."

"I hate that it's come to this," he groans. "Maybe I should move?"

"That is an expense you simply cannot afford right now. As easy as it sounds and as tempting as it sounds to release some of your income back to yourself, it's not as cut and dried as that."

"Figured."

"So, is that a yes?"

"Yeah," he grins. "Thanks, Henry. You and Liam

are..." He chokes up, and I blink back the sudden tears.

"Don't be a pillock. We're friends, more than that. We're family."

"Yeah, we are," he says. "So, when were you thinking of moving in? Zara panicked when Liam moved in, so maybe we need to give her notice?"

"Today," I say with a shrug, not eager to drag this out while Liam gets closer to Zara. "She'll be fine. I love to clean, I'm tidy as fuck, plus I can cook. She'll be happy I'm there," I say with a snort.

Ben chuckles. "Well, if you're so sure, you can be the one to tell her."

"Ohh, big bad alpha scared of the tiny omega nanny."

"Hey, she is fierce. I wouldn't want to get on her bad side," he snickers.

Going mock-serious, I chew my lip. "Maybe I'll just slip into the household, and she won't even notice I've actually moved in."

"You could... if you think that will work," Ben says, shaking his head, still smiling. He rises and slaps his hand on my shoulder. "I guess I'll see you back at home."

"You'll tell Liam?" I ask. "I didn't see him out there."

"He had to go do a visit. Yeah, I'll tell him."

Nodding, we leave the office and part ways. I can already see Ben's shoulders a little lighter. He isn't as defeated as he looked earlier. I'm glad that I made that happen, and I know this will work out. Zara is just the icing on the cake.

I swing by my house to pick up a few essentials; I'm not doing the full move today, that will take days, but it's enough to get me started, while I get the agents on the phone to tell them to start the ball rolling. I haul out a big holdall and pack toiletries, a couple of changes of clothes, my work stuff and a couple of books to keep me going.

As I pack, a feeling of contentment settles over me. I just hope that Zara feels the same way as I do about this move, but one thing I know is that she can't refute it if she knows it's to help Ben out. The rest will come.

Chapter 32

Zara

After my second cool shower of the day, while Mia is napping, I blow out a breath as I stare at my still-flushed face in the mirror on the dressing table in my bedroom.

"What the hell is this?" I murmur, only because I'm trying to convince myself it's anything but what it is. But I'm a twenty-three-year-old omega who has known exactly what she was since her first heat five years ago. I'm in my pre-heat. This isn't due for another three fucking weeks.

These alphas are messing with my biology, and it has fucked me off on a scale of where one is good, and ten is bad; this is a million.

"Alpha assholes," I moan. "Fucking alpha-holes. That's what you all are."

Dropping my face into my hands, I gulp and

decide to play dumb for a day or so. Maybe it's a false start from all the emotions, and my active heat won't actually appear yet. There is no point in getting Susan to uproot her life on the off chance that this is the real deal. Not yet, anyway.

I pinch my nose as I can smell the scent of lavender wafting about. The guys are going to know.

Sprinting down the stairs and into the living room, frantically lighting the vanilla-scented candles I've spotted and spraying air freshener like there's no tomorrow, I'm desperate to mask my natural scent. My body betrays me as my pre-heat starts to kick it up a notch, a searing warmth spreading throughout me that I am not yet ready to reveal to Liam and Ben.

The washing machine beeps to announce it has finished its cycle of Mia's baby clothes, so I gratefully abandon the stench in the lounge for the kitchen and empty the washer into the basket. The day is warm, and a soft breeze is blowing, so I bypass the dryer and head out to the back garden to peg out.

When I'm done, I give the rotary line a spin, feeling like a kid, but it brings a smile to my face to see the clothes waving about in the breeze. Heading back inside, I hear a noise through the baby monitor, so I head upstairs to see to Mia.

I freeze on the spot, my heart doing somersaults when I see that it wasn't Mia who alerted the sensitive monitor. It's Henry. He's standing in the spare bedroom, the one right at the top of the stairs, surrounded by a sea of boxes and bags. He looks up, his gaze locking onto mine with that familiar, easy smile.

"Hey, Zara," he says, as if it's the most natural thing in the world to be here, moving into the spare room without a word of warning.

These alphas are fucking me off with this! Not that Ben owes me *any* explanation. This is his house, and I work in it; I just also happen to live in it by the nature of the job.

"Hi, Henry. You're moving in too?"

"Yep. The more incomes, the merrier."

I nod, getting it instantly. Ben needs this, so who am I to grumble?

The thought of adding another alpha to this already heady situation sends a shiver down my spine. I should feel cornered, but instead, I feel a strange thrill at the prospect.

"Guess we're going to have to work up a shower schedule," I murmur.

"I'm easy. Most days, anyway," he says as Mia wakes up now, and I need to tend to her. He waves me off without another word, and I leave him to it, heading into the nursery. Mia is still not well and doesn't even wait for her bottle before she dozes back off. All the talking must've woken her up.

Making sure she's settled, I retreat to my sanctuary. My room needs to be a place where I can keep my thoughts straight, especially now. Without even a second thought about what I'm doing, I gather my nesting materials. Throwing the duvet on the floor in the darkest corner of the room, I look around. The blanket Henry gave me is first - it's soft, plush, and the most comforting thing I own. I pile on more blankets, each one adding another layer of security. Pillows come next, fluffy and inviting, creating a fortress of comfort around me.

As I arrange and rearrange the blankets, making sure every corner feels just right, there's a sense of pride swelling within me. This is my space, my haven, and no matter how messed up the world gets, this nest is mine to control, to find solace in. It's soft and warm, a shield against the world and the unexpected turns it seems to enjoy throwing my way.

I'm fluffing up the last of the pillows when his scent hits me, like a clean shirt pulled straight from the line on a sunny day after being washed in bergamot washing powder. It's unmistakable, its citrusy edge cutting through the floral haze in my room.

I sit there for a moment, pillow in hand, as Henry's

scent wraps around me. It's like he's here, in this room, not just moving his stuff into the spare bedroom down the hall. I try to shake my head clear, to focus on the nest I've been so carefully constructing, but it's no good. The more I try to concentrate on arranging the blankets just right, the more I become aware of his presence—like he's a ghost haunting the edges of my senses.

A river of lava runs through my core. I'm not sure if it's from excitement or something else. There's no denying it anymore. In my pre-heat state, Henry's scent is getting to me, weaving its way through my defences, stirring things inside that I'm not ready to face.

And then, without warning, my heat slams into me.

It's like being plunged into too-hot, deep water without a chance to take a breath. My heart beats rapidly, thudding against my ribs so fiercely it makes me dizzy. The cramps in my womb make me gasp for the breath that isn't there, and that deep ache pulses to life between my legs, insistent and demanding attention, needing a knot.

"Fuck," I rasp, clutching the pillow tighter. I press my thighs together, trying to quell the sudden, maddening throb and gush of slick that has soaked my knickers. It's no use, though. Every cell in my body seems to be vibrating, responding to the invisible call of Henry's scent.

My mind races, thoughts scattering like leaves in the wind, all of them trailing back to him. The crisp bergamot, the clean freshness of linen—it's everywhere, suffusing the air, filling my lungs, making it hard to think about anything else. But it's not just that. I glance out the window to see if the rain has started and is hitting the warm ground outside. It hasn't. It's as sunny as it was a few minutes ago.

"Liam," I moan softly and drop to the floor as Ben's scent of fresh pinecones hits the back of my nose. All of a sudden, the scents have surrounded me, are taunting me, haunting me, even.

"Breathe," I mutter, trying to find even a sliver of control. I take a deep lungful of air, gasping for breath, but it's a big mistake. Their scents cling to my senses, potent and intoxicating, sending a clear message to my body that's getting harder and harder to ignore.

Crawling to my nest, stripping my clothes off as I go, I sink into it, hot, fuzzy-headed and aching, surrounded by my fortress of softness, yet feeling entirely vulnerable.

"Zara?" Henry's voice cuts through the haze of my heat.

I open my mouth to speak, but it is too dry.

"Mia!" I suddenly croak, ripping the word from my throat.

"What?" Henry asks, pounding on the door at my panic. "Zara, are you okay?"

I try to answer, but I can't. I need to get to my phone to ring Susan to come over and make sure Mia is taken care of.

Sitting up, the room spins, and I let out a low moan as I sink back.

Two minutes. I need two minutes.

"Zara?" Henry knocks again. "Zara, you're worrying me. I'm coming in."

"No, wait!" I call out in panic, scrambling with the blankets to cover up my red-hot naked body.

He steps into the sanctuary of my room. My breath hitches as his scent intensifies, wrapping around me like a warm blanket. There's no hiding now; he knows.

Henry stops as if he's walked into a brick wall as my scent hits him in the face as much as his is doing to me.

"Stay there," I croak.

"Zara..." His voice trails off, and when I dare to look up, I see the understanding in his eyes, the raw edge of his restraint. He's like a statue, every muscle taut as if he's fighting his natural instincts with everything he's got.

"Sorry, I—I thought you were..." He trails off, unable to tear his eyes away from me.

"Please, just stay there," I plead, gesturing at the imaginary line he mustn't cross. We're playing with fire here, and neither of us has a drop of water to spare.

"Okay," he nods, but he doesn't move back. Instead, he stands firm, like he's the only thing keeping the world from spinning off its axis. Our eyes meet and every nerve ending in my body sparks to life. He's so close, too close, and all I want is to close that gap.

"Zara," he breathes out, and it's like he's saying more than just my name. It's a question, a plea, a temptation all rolled into one.

"Don't," I whisper fiercely because if he says anything else, I don't know if I'll be able to stop myself from leaping across this chasm of desire.

He clenches his jaw, eyes darkening, but he respects my wish. "I'm here if you need me," he says, an unsaid offer hanging between us, charged with the potential to shatter our carefully constructed boundaries.

He steps back, and my body cries out for him. I don't even know why. I barely know him, and yet his unexpected presence has literally thrown me into my heat.

"Mia," I murmur. "I can't…"

"Don't worry about Mia," he mutters. "Can I get you anything?"

I shake my head, hoping he knows to ring Ben because I can't talk anymore. I'm too far gone now.

Henry leaves quietly, and closing my eyes, I picture his face, the unresolved tension swirling between us. We're both caught up in this; steps dictated by rules we're struggling to abide by.

Chapter 33

Henry

My head is a mess, and it feels like my body is on fire, but not in the usual way. It's Zara. Her heat is kicking up a storm, and I'm caught smack in the middle of it.

I've called Ben but had to leave a message, so fuck knows if he is on his way back here or not yet.

I try to concentrate on my work, going over the spreadsheets, but the scent of her heat wafts through the house, thick and sweet as syrup. It's like the air itself is saturated with her need.

I pick up the softest moans that slice straight through my soul. I know she's burning up, skin probably flushed with that tell tale rosy glow of an omega in full heat.

She's trying to be quiet, but each little whimper

she lets slip is a siren call to every alpha instinct I've got.

A part of me wants to storm right up there, offer whatever relief I can, this time not taking no for an answer. She has thrown me into my rut with her heat. I can help her. But another part, the sensible part, reminds me that this isn't just about biology. It's Zara, the gorgeous omega who has been throwing me off balance since the day we met.

I pace downstairs, restless, glad that Mia is still asleep. Every nerve in me is on edge, and it's all because of Zara. I can hear her upstairs, the sound of her discomfort seeping around me. It's making a mess of my concentration. She needs help – that much is clear.

Bollocks to this.

I stop pacing, running a hand through my hair. Offering myself to her isn't something I take lightly. But neither is standing by while she's up there needing someone, and I'm down here doing fuck all about it.

It's not just about easing her heat; it's about showing her I care, that I want to support her, be there for her – in whatever way she needs.

I care about her. A lot. The feelings bubbling up inside me lately are proof enough of that. They've been growing, evolving into something that feels both terrifying and brilliant.

I shuffle up the stairs and down the hallway, my mind a whirl of concern and nerve. Each step feels like I'm walking a tightrope between overstepping boundaries and offering genuine help. The scent that wafts from under Zara's door is a mix of sweet desperation and that lavender and honey scent that is uniquely hers.

Before I can make another move, Mia starts crying, and I gulp. Glancing at Zara's door, she is in no fit state to see to the baby. Ben is nowhere to be found, so it's up to me. Steeling myself, I push open the nursery door to see Mia kicking and wailing. Glancing around, I see all the bottle stuff on a table down the side of the room, along with some machine that looks like it's meant to help.

"Okay, Henry. You are a smart man. You've got this." I walk over to the table and pick up the tub of formula, reading the instructions so I know what I'm doing.

So far, so good.

Scooping out the required amount, I glare at the machine. Luckily, the instructions are tucked underneath it, probably because Ben was as clueless as I am right now. Giving it a quick read while Mia screams the house down around me, I don't let it rush me. I'm steady and set about pushing the buttons and doing what the booklet tells me to. What seems like a lot of time later, what with all the wailing for me to hurry the fuck up, I'm armed, prepared and ready for action. I scoop Mia up and sit in the big armchair next to her cot, cradling her gently as I press the bottle to her lips. She knows exactly what to do as she latches on, suckling like a fiend.

"Thank fuck!" Zara shouts from next door. "You good?"

Chuckling, I shout back, "Yeah. Are you?"

"Bit lucid. I can help if you need me."

My heart thumps a couple of times. Lucid means she got her knot. I lick my lips at the thought of her using one of those knotty dildos to ease herself.

"No," I croak, and then clear my throat. "No, we're okay. You rest."

"Change her nappy."

I stare at Mia for a second before I gulp. "Yeah, okay."

"You don't sound so sure." I can hear the giggle in her weary tone.

"I'm on it like a car bonnet," I retort and then shake my head at myself. *What the fuck was that?*

"Okay," she snorts. "Call me if you need me."

"No, we're good. You rest."

She goes quiet, and I know it's because while the

dildo will give her a bit of relief, it's not enough. Her body knows the difference.

I quickly finish feeding Mia, burping her like a pro—or at least, that's how I'm trying to come off. She gives a few contented sighs, and I feel like the king of the world for a moment. But then reality hits. It's nappy-changing time. I lay Mia down on the changing table and gather my wits. "Right, Henry, let's get this over with," I mutter.

With a surprising amount of grace – considering I'm an alpha who has never done this before - I manage the whole process without much fuss. I see how the wet one comes off, and it's plain how the fresh one goes on.

"Easy peasy, lemon squeezy. Just glad it was a number one," I coo to her, feeling like an idiot.

However, Mia is clean and happy, so my work here is done. For now. Laying her back down in her cot, she looks up at me as if I'm her personal hero before her eyes close and she's asleep.

That's when it hits me again; Zara's need is like a heavy weight in my chest—heavier now that my focus is no longer on tending to the baby.

I step out of the nursery, pause in the hallway, and take a deep breath. Zara's scent is overwhelming. It seeps under the door like an invitation or a challenge. A part of me wants to kick down that door and take care of her needs as only an alpha could.

But that's a gross violation. She is in no fit state to accept my help without it falling under dubious circumstances. If she asks, that's one thing; if I offer again now, that's a whole other bag I'm not willing to open.

Luckily, I'm saved from the torment as I hear a car pull up outside, and I make my way back downstairs, glad I'm not alone in the house anymore with an omega in heat and a baby who is going to need more care than I'm capable of at some point.

Chapter 34

Benjamin

I step into the house, and the scent all around me hits me like a train at full speed. It's thick, heady, and I know right off that Zara's in heat, even if I hadn't received the message from Henry that sent us careening back here like our asses were on fire.

My gut twists in a knot of unease. I quickly glance at Liam, who stands beside me with a tight jaw and fierce, dark eyes.

"Finally," Henry greets us. "I've done what I can with Mia. She's okay for now—fed, changed, sleeping."

I nod, not sure what to say, my mind is too full of Zara's scent and the anxiety knotting up tighter inside me.

Liam's growl is low, almost lost beneath the sound of our breathing. I cast him a sidelong look, seeing the strain on his face, the way he's fighting himself. It's like we're both on the edge, ready to tumble over, and it's all because of Zara.

"Right, I'll go and check on her," I trail off, unsure where to put myself. I can feel the pull, that undeniable urge drawing me towards her, and I know Liam feels it, too. He's barely holding it in, his fingers curling into fists at his sides.

I quickly race up the stairs, holding my breath as if that's going to help, and push my way into Mia's nursery, closing the door quietly and exhaling loudly. I did not expect an omega's heat to affect me in any way whatsoever. This was not a thing I was concerned about by having an omega nanny in my house.

But it's like trying to hold on to water; the urge to go to Zara, to soothe her, to claim her, is overwhelming and earth-shattering—as in, the ground drops away beneath me at this realisation.

"Shh, little one," I whisper to Mia, even though she's not the one needing reassurance. It's me. I'm the one on the razor's edge, fighting every natural impulse that screams at me to be the alpha I am. But Mia needs me now. My duty, my role—it's here, ensuring this little girl is safe and secure, and that's exactly what I'm going to do. Mia's eyes flutter open, and her little fingers curl around mine for a moment before she yawns, her eyes closing again. I take her temperature and it's dropping again.

Relief floods me she is on the mend from whatever caused her fever.

"Night, love," I whisper. There's a mobile of stars and moons above her cot; I give it a gentle tap, and it starts to turn, twinkling softly. The lullaby that tinkles out is soothing, maybe for both of us, because right now, I need all the calm I can get.

Stepping out of the nursery, I close the door with a quiet click and pause, pressing my back to the cool hallway wall. It's time to face what I've been dodging since stepping through the front door. Zara's room is just steps away.

Her scent is everywhere: thick in the air, sweet and spicy and utterly intoxicating. It's like it seeps straight into my veins, setting them alight with this heat, this craving that's so foreign yet so potent.

But then the mating bite gives me a complete bitch slap, pulsing and bleeding so much, I can feel it sticking to my shirt collar. My guts turn over, and I make it back into my bedroom to lean over the toilet to throw up the entire contents of my stomach, sweating and rasping for breath.

"Fuck. You!" I choke out as I slump to the bathroom floor and reach up to flush the toilet.

After a few moments of just breathing, I manage to haul myself up. The reflection staring back at me from the bathroom mirror looks like a wild man, with dishevelled hair and eyes that look more beast than human. I splash cold water on my face, trying to wash away the urge that's clawing at my insides. Pulling at my tie and loosening my collar, I peel the ruined white cotton away from my neck with a grimace.

But then something inside me snaps. Literally.

There's a loud crack that I feel down to my soul, and I stumble back, tripping over my own feet and hitting the deck hard as I land on my ass, half in, half out of the bathroom.

"Jesus," I groan and lie back, putting my hands over my face. "It's gone."

Gone.

Removed.

Broken.

Whatever word you want to use to describe the mating bond I had with Nicole, use it because I'm fucking free.

"I hope that hurt you as much as it did me, you bitch," I spit out and turn over onto my side to curl up as the pain, the dull ache that has been heavy on every cell in my body, finally lets up.

I lie there for a moment, taking deep breaths, trying to process this new reality. My head is spinning; it's like I'm relieved and empty all at the same time. Suddenly, the scent of Zara becomes even more potent, filling the absence where that painful connection to Nicole used to be.

"Fucking hell," I mutter as I slowly push myself up from the floor. There's a part of me that wants to stay here on the cold tile, away from everything else. But that's not me. I'm done hiding.

As I stand up, every muscle in my body screams at me to go to Zara. It feels right – natural even. It's scary how quickly the pull has shifted, how it's no longer a bond but an instinct that tells me where I need to be.

But something stops me.

Zara.

She has no idea what has just happened to me. She has no idea how I feel about her and how I know with every inch of my soul that her heat has snapped the bond like it was nothing. If I go to her now, I'm putting her in a situation she isn't expecting and isn't ready for.

So, I strip off, knowing the shirt is ruined, but

chuck it in the laundry basket anyway, and turn on the shower, letting it run cool before I step in and try to douse the alpha instincts in me to go to the omega in heat only two rooms away and make her take my knot until she can't think of anything else.

Chapter 35

Liam

Wild horses couldn't stop me from climbing the stairs slowly, ignoring Henry as he tells me not to do it. He doesn't know the connection we have. He doesn't know that I can help her if she will let me. Stopping outside Zara's room, I inhale sharply.

"Zara?"

After a few seconds, she gasps. "Liam?"

I push the door open, and the scent hits me like a cargo plane.

Zara's heat is like nothing else I've experienced before. No omega has affected me this way. Without a shadow of a doubt, I know she has brought my rut on early. Very early. There is nothing else for it. She is my fated mate, and while I know this now, she doesn't. At least, I don't think she does.

I'd planned to take my time with her, to go at the pace she's comfortable with. But right now, every bit of me is screaming to toss those plans out the window.

"Zara?" My voice doesn't sound like mine, it's thick with something raw and unfiltered.

My eyes fixate on her, huddled in her nest of crumpled blankets and pillows. She's entangled in it, gasping for air, her body glistening with sweat and slick. Every fibre of my being awakens, urging me to go to her. I know she needs a knot, and I'm consumed by the urge to be the one who offers it.

"Hey," I say, softer this time, stepping closer. Her eyes flutter open, glazed with discomfort and need, and I know I'm already too deep in this to back out now. I want to be the one she turns to, the one who can ease her through this.

Dropping to my knees so as not to overwhelm her, I shed my suit jacket and tie. Crawling to her slow enough that she can stop my approach with one word, I wait for it. But it doesn't come.

My gaze flicks to the side, catching sight of the dildo lying haphazardly next to her, covered in her slick. The growl that escapes me is something I can't stop, even if I wanted to. It's a clear sign she's tried to take the edge off herself, and something inside me flares up, a primal urge I can't ignore. My heart races with a need that aligns perfectly with hers.

"Zara," I breathe out. She doesn't seem to hear me, or maybe she can't focus on anything but the overwhelming sensations crashing over her.

Feeling the carpet under my palms as I edge towards her. Every inch I get closer, her scent wraps tighter around me, drawing me in, urging me on. I'm crawling, slow and deliberate, because part of me knows I should be careful even if every part of me wants to quickly rush to her side, despite any consequences.

"Hey, princess," I say again, trying to keep my voice steady. The urgency in the room is thick, matching the pace of her breaths, and by instinct, my movements echo that rhythm. I'm close now, so close I can feel the heat coming off her in waves. My mind's racing, but there's a strange clarity in what I want, what I need to do.

"Liam," she whispers.

"I'm here," I whisper as I finally reach the edge of her nest. My heart's going a mile a minute, but I'm here now, right where I need to be.

Zara's skin glows with a flush that spreads across her cheeks and down her neck, a rosy warmth that tells of her inner fire. Her hair is a wild cascade around her shoulders, strands sticking to her damp forehead. Despite her dishevelled appearance, there is a mesmerising beauty to her. The chaotic state she's in makes my primal alpha instincts roar loudly.

"Zara," I say softly in comparison to the raging inside me. My voice is filled with an emotion I can't quite name, but it feels a lot like a longing mixed with fierce protectiveness.

She shifts slightly, and the movement draws my gaze to the way her chest rises and falls rapidly. I'm captivated by her, every sense attuned to the woman in front of me. It's as if my world has narrowed to this moment, to her need calling out to mine. She is a goddess, and my cock is so hard staring at her nakedness, but I know, despite this, I would walk away if she told me to get lost.

"Will you allow me to help you?" I murmur, hoping that with everything I've got, she will say 'yes.' It's not just a question; it's an offer laid bare, a promise of relief. "I'm here, Zara. I can help."

Her eyes flicker to mine, and even through the haze of her heat, I see the raw edge of hope. I'm offering not just satisfaction but solace, and I mean every word. Whatever she needs, I'm here to give.

"How?" she murmurs, her voice rough with need.

Smiling softly, I say, trying not to sound smug, "You've brought on my rut."

Her eyes go wide, green pools of surprise and then a purr escapes her that sets my nerves on fire.

I growl back at her, louder than I intended because I didn't want to frighten her with my intensity, but she's anything but scared.

"Come over," she whispers, holding her hand up weakly as she invites me into her nest.

There's no hesitation left in me. That's all the permission my instincts need. I'm ready to be what she needs, to ease this unbearable heat clawing at her insides.

Stripping off the rest of my clothes, I give her a nod to tell her I'm entering her nest now; she smiles back, eagerness splayed over her features. She is about to get what she is craving, and I feel like a fucking god that I'm the one that's going to give it to her.

As I crawl onto the soft mound of blankets, I marvel at how our bodies align and how everything at this moment feels right. Her skin is hot to the touch, a heat that only serves to drive my desire. It's just the two of us, and the electric charge between us could light up the whole of the Lake District.

"Are you sure?" My voice is a husky whisper,

seeking consent one more time because it's as crucial as breathing in this delicate situation. The last thing I want is to steamroll over her wishes. But every inch of me prays she won't send me away.

"Yes, Liam, please," Zara gasps out, her hand threading through my hair and pulling me closer.

I lean down, pressing a gentle kiss against her forehead before trailing lower to capture her lips. The kiss is sweet torture, and it's intoxicating. Our tongues twist together, setting off fireworks behind my closed eyelids.

I trail my kisses down her neck, carefully avoiding leaving any marks. It's an alpha instinct to claim your mate with a physical sign of possession. My body craves to do it, but I resist until she gives her consent and is ready for that level of commitment, which definitely isn't now in the middle of her heat.

Her nails dig into my shoulders as she arches up into me. "Please, Liam. I need you now."

As much as I'd love to linger, I'm not letting her down. Nestling between her thighs which she spreads wide for me, I grab my cock and tease her clit gently, unable to stop myself from covering the tip in her slick.

"Fucking hell," I grunt as I slide into her pussy,

hearing the sound of her slick coating me and pooling out underneath her.

She gasps, a sharp intake of breath that melds into a moan as I bury myself deep inside her. The world outside her nest could be falling apart for all I care because right now, nothing matters except the way Zara's pussy clenches around my cock, and the look of pure ecstasy on her face. Her body is a perfect fit, like she's been made for me, and the thought sends a bolt of possessive pleasure through me.

Setting a rhythm that has us both gasping for air, every thrust is met with a whimper or a cry from Zara. She matches me move for move.

"More," she breathes out, her voice tight with desire.

I give it to her, picking up the pace until I'm pounding into her with all the pent-up need my rut had blessed me with. Her perfect small breasts bounce with every movement, and I can't resist leaning down to take one of her nipples into my mouth.

Zara's hands are in my hair again, tugging slightly, trying to pull me even closer. Her body tightens, and she convulses intensely, her mouth open in a silent scream. It's my cue to give her what she really wants, and I don't make her wait. The knot at the base of my cock, designed to lock our bodies together, bulges as I shoot my cum into deep into her and she lets out a strangled moan which turns to a purr when I growl. Her pussy clutches my knot tightly, almost painfully, clamping down around me like she is possessed.

"Fuck, princess. Good girl. You make my knot so fucking huge with your gorgeous pussy, your slick coating me. Fuck, princess. You feel so fucking tight."

She gasps, her glazed-over eyes widening at my praise.

Her breath comes out in ragged bursts now, and her grip on my hair loosens as the intensity of her orgasm starts to wane. She's still purring, a sound that vibrates straight into my soul, making me feel like the luckiest bastard on earth.

I'm knotted inside her, both of us locked in the most intimate embrace possible, and I can't bring myself to care about anything other than the omega beneath me. Her green eyes have softened, the raw need replaced with a dazed satisfaction that fills me with pride. I've done that; I've taken care of her.

"Fuck, Liam," she whispers after catching her breath, "That was so much more than I expected."

"I know," I murmur in her ear. "We're meant to be." I say it lightly in case she scoffs at me and rejects me as nothing more than a cock with a knot, but she doesn't. She doesn't say anything, though.

I brush a sweaty strand of hair from her face and smile.

We're silent for a moment, our breathing the only sound in the room. It's comfortable, this quiet between us. It feels like we're the only two people in the world right now.

Eventually, the tightness around my knot lessens slightly, and I can feel our connection starting to ease. But I don't pull away yet; I stay nestled between her thighs, savouring the afterglow that wraps around us like a blanket.

Her fingers trace idle patterns on my back, and it's bliss. Despite the craziness of our rut and heat-induced tumble, there's a sense of rightness that settles deep in my soul. She has to feel it. She has to. It's like all my life, I've been waiting to fit with someone just like this.

Zara yawns then, a small, exhausted sound that makes her seem impossibly more adorable. "Stay," she mumbles, the word slurring slightly with her weariness and the aftershocks still coursing through her body.

I don't need telling twice. "I'm not going anywhere," I reply, my voice laced with a contentment that's new to me. I'm used to caring for the omegas during their heat, but this is different. Zara isn't just another omega; she's mine in a way that has nothing to do with biology or instinct and everything to do with the way my heart races at her smile.

Her response is a contented sigh, and slowly, her breathing evens out, but before she drifts off to sleep, she murmurs, "Meant to be."

Chapter 36

Zara

Waking up with a start, I feel cool. Still hot from my heat, but the warmth of Liam's body next to mine is gone. Sitting up, I feel weird, like I should be succumbing to my heat urges again, but I'm not. Glancing around, I frown. It's still light out but getting dark, which means I haven't been out for very long. Wondering where Liam went, I don't have long to wonder when he taps lightly on the door and pushes it open, carrying a tray of sandwiches and a bottle of water.

"Hey, princess. Thought you might be hungry," Liam says, his voice carrying that gentle tone that makes my stomach flip in the best possible way. I smile at the sight of him caring for me like this.

"Do I even want to know what Ben and Henry

have to say about this?" I ask, hiding my face behind my hands as he kneels and places the tray and himself on the edge of my nest, respecting my nesting boundaries.

He frowns slightly. "I wouldn't know. I didn't see either of them. I assume they're holed up in their rooms, trying not to pounce on you."

"That's sweet," I murmur, my cheeks flushing at the thought of all that pouncing. It's not a horrible thought. In fact, it's one that the omega inside me decides she likes. A lot. Clearing my throat, I reach for a sandwich.

"How are you feeling?"

"Better now," I admit. "Thank you. But it's a bit odd."

"What do you mean?" he asks with concern.

"It feels like the heat is receding slightly. I mean, more so than would be usual after a knot."

"Oh?" He arches an eyebrow and bites into a sandwich.

I do the same, just for something to do that doesn't feel awkward after my confession.

"I've heard of that happening," he says after a few chews and a swallow. "Not often, but it can happen under certain circumstances."

Snorting, I ask, "So what? You're the omega expert now?"

He chuckles. "I've had my fair share of ruts, princess. I learn stuff."

My jaw tightens at the mention of him rutting with other omegas. Not that I can say anything about it, but the green-eyed monster is trying to rear its stupid head, and I can't push it back down.

He sees my mood change and smiles darkly. "Oh, jealous, are you?"

"No," I spit out and then shove the sandwich into my mouth again to avoid more conversation. That doesn't stop him, though.

"You are, and I love it, but you have absolutely nothing to worry about, Zara." His face goes serious. "I meant what I said about us and that we're meant to be. I feel it. Do you?"

"I wouldn't be jealous if I didn't," I murmur, looking away.

"Don't be jealous," he murmurs. "They were nothing compared to you, to this. I'm not jealous of your past alphas because I know they didn't get *this* with you."

"Well, aren't you so bloody perfect, then?" I ask with an embarrassed giggle.

He laughs, too. "Not even close. I just know what this is."

We lock gazes, and I return his smile. "Me too. But I'm still confused about the heat."

"Maybe it was fate trying to give us a jump-start," he says.

"Maybe. Or maybe she will come back and give me another round, this one worse than the last."

"Maybe. But I'm here for you if she does."

"Thank you, Liam," I say sincerely and scoot a bit closer to him over the soaking wet blankets.

He reaches out to brush a lock of hair behind my ear, and his touch sends a thrill shooting through me. "No need to thank me, princess." His lips twitch into a half-smile, and I notice how his eyes linger on mine, warm and affectionate. "I've run you a bath," he adds.

"Oh, really? An omega could get used to this treatment."

"Please do."

Suddenly, I remember my responsibilities and exclaim, "Mia!"

"Ben's got her, I assume. She's not in the nursery."

Nodding, I feel terrible. Here's me thinking only of myself when I'm supposed to be here for her. "Okay. I'll have a bath and then see if I feel up to going to find Ben to have a conversation with him, that's going to be awkward as fuck."

"Nah,' Liam shrugs. "I think you'll find that conversation will go along just fine."

Shooting him a curious stare, I breathe in and keep eating until my hunger is satisfied. I pause, assessing if my heat is about to demand another knot, but I feel like I've gone back a step to my pre-heat, making me wonder if the entire active heat wasn't that at all, just really bad pre-heat. Oh, who knows? It's confusing and exhausting. I want that bath, to tidy up my nest, and then to have that talk with Ben.

Finishing my sandwich, I rise, feeling the room tilt slightly. Liam is on his feet in an instant and catches my arm, steady as a rock. "Easy does it, love. Your body's been through the wringer."

I nod, taking a deep breath. "Yeah, thanks." He throws my dressing gown over my naked body and supports me as we walk to the bathroom.

"It's cooler because I thought you'd be hot," he murmurs, looking unsure all of a sudden.

"It's perfect," I tell him as he helps me step into the lukewarm water, and I sink down gratefully.

He leaves with a grin and a promise to check in on me in a bit, closing the door behind him.

It's blissful, and I close my eyes for just a moment. But thoughts of Ben worm their way into my mind, and they're not unpleasant ones either.

After a good soak that leaves me feeling more human and less like an overheated mess, I wrap myself in a fluffy towel and head back to the bedroom. Getting dressed in joggers and a tee, feeling even less like my heat was only hours ago, I get to work on my nest, pulling off the soaked blankets and replacing some of them with fresh ones. I want to wash the one Henry gave me and replace it in my nest.

Grabbing the laundry bag, I shove it inside and creep out of my room and down the hallway to the stairs. As I pass Henry's room, I speed up a bit and take the stairs quickly, ducking into the kitchen. I shove the blankets and my clothes into the washer and set it on a delicate cycle.

"Hey," Ben says from behind me, startling me into straightening up.

I spin around as if I've been caught with my hand in the cookie jar. "Heyyyy."

Cringing at my tone, even more so when he smirks, I plaster a smile on my face.

"Everything okay?" he asks.

"Yep. Just doing some washing."

"I can see that. But your heat..." He trails off, looking as confused as I feel.

Feeling my cheeks flush, I shrug lightly, trying to sound nonchalant. "Oh, you know how it is. It seemed like it was the real deal, but it's calmed down now. At least for the time being."

Ben searches my eyes, "So, are you on a heat

hiatus, then?"

"It looks like it," I reply, tucking a strand of hair behind my ear. "I'm not even sure what that was all about."

He steps closer, lowering his voice to a conspiratorial whisper. "You and Liam—"

"Yeah," I interrupt him before he can go any further. "Things have progressed. Is that okay?"

He frowns. "Why are you asking me that?"

I shrug. "It just feels like something I need to set straight. I'm here for Mia and you, not to be falling into something with Liam."

"People fall. There's not much you can do about that." The way he says that sends a tingle of desire over my skin.

"Oh?" I murmur, practically drowning in his gaze. Something seems different with him. He seems freer, lighter, like something has shifted inside him. My eyes automatically drop to his neck. It's crazy how I didn't notice it immediately, as it is right there, unhidden by the collar of his black tee.

It hasn't healed up entirely, but it looks a thousand times better than the last time I saw it, just this morning. Moving on instinct, I step into his space and brush my fingers lightly over the side of his neck. "This looks better."

"It feels better. The bond has snapped," he blurts

out, staring down at me, his blue eyes sharp and stormy at the same time.

"Snapped," I murmur, shifting my gaze down to his mouth before it shoots back up to his eyes.

"Snapped."

"Are you okay?"

"Better than."

"Good."

The tension is simmering between us. I want him to drop his mouth to mine, to kiss me.

His breath hitches, and he closes the gap. His lips press gently against mine, carefully at first, as if he's testing the waters, but then it's all heat and hunger. My arms wrap around his neck, pulling him closer, feeling the hard lines of his body against mine.

I'm melting into him like I was made for this moment. Our tongues tangle, and his hands slip down to grasp my hips, bringing me flush against him. I can feel every inch of him, rock solid and wanting, just like I am.

Finally, we break apart for air, gasping slightly. His forehead rests against mine, and our eyes meet, holding everything words can't express.

Mia shrieks from the lounge, demanding attention and the moment is lost.

Ben steps back hastily as if he is now the one

with his hand in the cookie jar, and without another word, he darts off, leaving me alone and more than slightly confused.

Chapter 37

Benjamin

Bolting out of the kitchen like I've just nicked the crown jewels from the Tower of London, my heart's racing faster than a greyhound on its best day. My legs can't carry me fast enough to Mia in the lounge.

I scoop her up with all the agility of a professional baby juggler, bouncing her slightly as she wails in my ear.

"There's my girl," I murmur, trying to anchor myself with her innocence and pure joy. It's grounding, it's necessary because, hell, what just happened in the kitchen?

My gut twists at the thought of our kiss. That wasn't supposed to happen. Not now. Definitely not now when everything's so complicated. But it was like being hit by lightning, electric and wild and impossible not to feel down to my soul.

I settle Mia in the crook of my arm as I sit and attempt to give her a bottle. She's refusing again, which is worrying on top of everything else, but her temperature is steady, so I'm trying not to panic. Her sleepy eyes watch me like she knows something's up. It's as if she can feel the turmoil building inside me, and now it has reached its peak.

"Daddy's got himself into a bit of a mess," I tell her, even if she can't understand. She just yawns, making me want to protect her from all the world's chaos.

But what about protecting myself? Right now, I feel like I'm dangling off the edge of a cliff by my fingertips. The bond breaking was sudden, but at the same time, I felt it should've happened ages ago. It was supposed to be permanent, eternal, but then again, so was Nicole. I shake my head, trying to rid myself of these thoughts as I watch Mia wiggling about, but not in distress.

I've got to sort myself out. I'm a dad. A single dad. My whole world has shifted from under me, and it's freeing in a way I hadn't imagined, but it's terrifying, too, because there's no road map for what comes next.

Liam swings open the door, exuding easy charm

and careless grace. His grin widens as he spots us, but his eyes dart to me with an unspoken question.

"Everything alright?" he asks as he ambles over.

I manage a nod. "Yeah, just peachy." My voice is more strained than I'd like.

He doesn't look convinced but doesn't push it, turning his attention to Mia instead, stroking her cheek with the back of his finger gently. "Want me to try?" he asks, indicating the bottle.

"Sure," I murmur. "You're riding a high. Go with it."

He snickers and takes her from me, settling himself comfortably in the chair as I pass him the bottle.

Watching them together eases some of the tension in my chest. This feels normal; this feels safe.

But there's nothing normal or safe about the way my pulse still hums from that kiss with Zara in the kitchen. The memory teases at my mind - her body against mine, her soft lips, the intensity in her eyes that matched mine. It scares me because it felt so right despite being so wrong.

It has to be wrong. Doesn't it? It's too soon for any of this.

But I can't push the thought of the mating bond breaking when Zara was in her heat. It's too much of a coincidence. Isn't it?

I glance back at Liam as he manages to get Mia to suckle on her bottle. I don't begrudge him the triumphant smile. Who cares who feeds her as long as she drinks?

"I kissed her," I blurt out, full of unwanted exclamations today, it seems.

Liam raises an eyebrow. "Zara?"

"Obviously," I growl, frustrated.

"And how was it?"

We stare at each other.

"That's it? That's all you have to say after you've given her your knot."

"You know about that."

"This is my fucking house. I know what goes on in it."

Liam shrugs, looking as unconcerned as his words would suggest. "I told you, this doesn't bother me. If Zara wants us both, then I'm cool with it."

But his words, meant to be reassuring, only grip my insides tighter. I know Liam's easy going nature, but this isn't just about what Zara wants. It's about what I want too and if I'm honest, I haven't got a clue.

Watching Mia, completely absorbed in her own little world of her bottle and Uncle Liam, I see her simplicity. My life – our lives – have just turned into something that resembles a lopsided Rubik's Cube and I'm not sure there's a solution where all the colours match up.

"Liam, it's not that easy," I finally admit, my voice low. "My bond with Nicole broke earlier, because of Zara. Her heat—"

"I know. It brought on your rut. Same as me. It's how I was able to help her. And weirdly, I did help her. Her heat was brought to the front to deal with all these underlying issues. Fate's a bitch like that. But it's not just about me; you and Henry are involved as well. He bought her a blanket, which she put in her nest. I could smell his scent all over it. She wanted him close by with her. She's caught in the middle of three alphas, but as far as I'm concerned, she doesn't have to choose."

"Agreed," Henry says, coming into the room. "She really had the blanket in her nest?"

"Yeah," Liam says, looking up with a smile. "You moving in here was the tipping point. Her pre-heat bubbled over. I think it's back under control for now, but her full heat will be back in a few days, and you two either need to shit or get off the pot, as that saying goes."

"God, that's disgusting," I groan.

"But you get my drift, yeah?"

"I don't even know where I stand with her," Henry murmurs.

"Then go and find out."

"How do you know so much about omegas and their heats?" I ask, annoyed that he seems to be this expert all of a sudden.

He gives me a smug grin worthy of Jeremy Clarkson. "I've made it my business to know. I'm not a selfish dick."

Henry hesitates at the door, looking as though he's about to go into battle rather than into the kitchen to have a heart-to-heart. I don't blame him. Zara is a whirlwind – one that's got us all twisted up inside.

I don't even really know how to process the fact that he has basically duped me into letting him stay here so he could move in on Zara. I know I'm being unfair and ungrateful. Henry and Liam are both doing me a massive favour that I wouldn't even have asked, and yet they offered. I shouldn't be such a cock about it. Zara isn't mine, so she is free to do whatever she likes with whoever she likes.

I watch him leave, his shoulders squared in determination, or maybe it's resignation – it's hard to tell sometimes with Henry. Meanwhile, Mia finishes her bottle, and Liam entertains her with peek-a-boo with a muslin square, completely at ease despite the emotional tornado he's just casually stirred up.

Mia gurgles happily, and I'm momentarily

distracted by the pure joy on her face. It's infectious, and for a fraction of a second, I forget the havoc of our lives. But then it all comes flooding back.

I shake my head; it's too much to deal with right now. "How can you be so calm about this?" I ask, turning to Liam, who's now got Mia over his shoulder to burp her.

Liam shrugs, "Life's too short to get worked up over things you can't change. Besides, Zara makes me happy. And if she's happy with Henry, or you, or all of us, then that's what counts. We're all adults. We can make this work if we want to."

I know he's right in theory, but it doesn't stop my gut from twisting into knots – and not the good kind. Still, looking at him being so effective with Mia, so unfazed by everything, a part of me starts wondering if maybe I'm the one making this more complicated than it has to be.

Chapter 38

Henry

I step out of the room, pulling the door shut behind me, feeling like I'm walking on a tightrope with no safety net below. Liam's words ring in my ears, 'shit or get off the pot.' Charming. But he isn't wrong.

As I head slowly to the kitchen, each step feels heavier than the last. It's like I'm carrying the weight of this whole mess on my shoulders. What am I going to say to Zara without scaring her away?

Hesitating when I reach the open doorway, my heart pounds so hard I can practically hear it in my ears. This isn't just about sex or heats or ruts; this is about something more, something deeper, and it scares the living daylights out of me because it's so sudden. But I don't just want her for now—I want her for all the times to come, good and bad.

Taking a deep breath, I finally step through the door.

Zara's sitting on a stool staring out of the window, a mug of tea in her hands. She looks up at me with those big eyes of hers, and for a moment, we just stare at each other.

"Hey," I manage to choke out.

"Hey yourself," she replies with a bright smile as she puts down her tea on the island. "What's up?"

Right, straight to the point, then. I shuffle awkwardly from one foot to the other. "We need to talk. It's about... well, it's about us."

Her smile fades a little as she stares at me. "Yeah, I've been thinking a lot about us, too."

Diving in at the deep end, I need to hear it from Zara. "Liam mentioned you had the blanket I bought you in your nest."

Zara nods slowly. "I wanted—no, needed—your scent close. It hit me hard when you were across the landing, and I just... it's hard to explain."

"Try?" I croak.

She smiles again. "I was already in an early pre-heat. I think being so close to Liam and maybe Ben, I don't know. Then you came in, and it pushed me over the edge. But it's receded a bit now. It's still there, but it reverted back to a pre-heat as opposed to an active one. It's odd, and I don't really understand it."

I nod slowly, taking all that in. My scent drove her into her heat. Sure, the other alphas were involved as well, but it was me being here that pushed her.

Exhaling slowly, I feel like we're dancing around the edges of what we really need to discuss. "Look, Zara. I care about you a lot. More than I thought possible in such a short amount of time. But I guess that means something."

There's something raw and vulnerable in her gaze when she searches my eyes. "I care about you too," she whispers.

"So what do we do?" I ask. The question hangs between us like a challenge.

Zara shifts on the stool, and I'm close enough to catch her subtle scent, which is intoxicating.

"We try," she says simply. "We talk, we communicate, and we take this one day at a time. Because I want to explore this. It *does* mean something. This – whatever this is – with you, with Liam, maybe Ben, it means something."

We're all in this tangled mess together, and for some reason, that thought brings a wave of relief crashing over me.

Reaching over the island that separates us, I grasp her fingers lightly. "Yeah," I agree. "One day at a time."

She squeezes my hand gently, as if sealing our new pact. "So, did you get settled in?"

Chuckling at the change of topic, I nod. "Yeah. There is still a lot to get from my place. It has to be cleared out for the renters, obviously. I'll have to put a bunch of stuff in storage."

She nods. "Did you get the washing in?"

I glance outside. "Yeah, folded and put away."

"You are handy, aren't you?"

"I cook as well." I can't resist the brag.

Her eyebrows go up. "Oh, that was a bad move, Henry. You just sealed your fate."

Snorting, I glance at the clock. It's late now, but I don't think anyone has eaten yet. "I'll get some soup on. I saw some tins in the cupboard earlier."

"You're a rockstar."

"It's tinned soup. I can do better given half the chance," I snicker, giving her a look.

She giggles. "Still, saves me doing it."

We're both laughing as I turn to the cupboard and take out some tins. The simple domesticity of the moment isn't lost on me. It feels natural, like we've been doing this for years rather than minutes. I grab a pot and get to work, finding comfort in the routine of preparing a meal.

The door opens again, and Liam walks in with Mia in his arms, looking a little frazzled but managing a smile. "She finally decided that sleep was for losers," he says, rocking her gently.

"Hey, you." Zara gets up to coo at the baby, and I watch them, this strange family we're becoming. The warmth that swells in my chest is unexpected, but not unwelcome.

"Soup's on," I announce after a few minutes, setting bowls on the island. "Where's Ben?"

"Sleeping on the couch. It's been a rough day. I think the bond breaking has done him in emotionally as well as physically."

"His bond broke?" I ask as I stir.

"Yeah. Zara's heat was the thing that did it."

Zara's small gasp alerts me that she didn't know that. I turn to her, but her eyes are locked on Liam, and his on her.

"Oh," she murmurs and automatically reaches for Mia as she lets out a soft cry. "I'll go and settle her in the cot."

She flees, leaving me and Liam to stare at each other.

"Talk go okay?" Liam asks.

"I think so. One day at a time."

"Best way."

Nodding, I turn around and keep stirring, feeling like the soup is a metaphor for our lives.

Chapter 39

Zara

Carrying Mia upstairs as I leave the kitchen after my hesitant talk with Henry, I'm a bit overwhelmed and bewildered, but in a good way. The air feels clearer somehow like we've opened the windows and let the stale doubts out.

Henry's honesty is refreshing, and his willingness to communicate gives me hope. The conversation we just had didn't solve everything, but it's a start – a promise of trying – and that's what matters right now.

I can't seem to wrap my head around being with more than one alpha. How does that work? Will there be jealousy? Liam doesn't seem too bothered, and neither did Henry. Does that mean they don't really care enough to be jealous? Is this all going to blow up in my face when it goes sideways?

I glance around the nursery, a sanctuary from whatever awaits on the outside.

Liam steps in behind me, his smile tentative but warm. "Hey," he says as he closes the door behind him, as I settle Mia in her cot.

"Hey," I whisper, biting my lip slightly.

"You okay? How are you feeling with the heat that has backtracked."

I giggle. "Okay, I guess. Pre-heat is simmering, so something went totally out of whack there for a while."

"I told you earlier, it's fate."

"Yeah. About that..."

"Uh-oh."

"No, it's good, I promise. I just need a hot minute to take all this in. Ben and I kissed earlier, and I don't know what that means. He bolted before we could say anything. Well, Mia needed him, so that's unfair, but we still left things hanging."

"So why are you sitting here and not with him talking about it?"

"I don't know if he wants to talk about it."

"He does."

"How do you know?"

"He's confused, he needs to know what's going on."

"Yeah, that makes two of us. Also, he's sleeping, I'll leave him."

"He's awake. The smell of soup woke him." Liam's hand finds mine, just as Henry's had earlier, and he gives it a reassuring squeeze. "Zara," he says, his voice laced with that gentle certainty that always seems to help me find my footing. "You've got to be honest with him – with all of us. You can't leave things unsaid; it'll only make the confusion worse."

I nod, knowing he's right. Honesty is the cornerstone of this, whatever it is.

"Besides," Liam continues, "Ben wants you. He might not have said it out loud yet, but it's obvious. He wouldn't have kissed you if he didn't feel something strong."

My heart does a little flip at his words, and I wonder about the possibilities. "It's just hard to believe that all of this is happening."

Liam chuckles softly, his thumb stroking over my knuckles in a comforting rhythm. "Yeah, I know. But believe it, because we're all feeling it."

We exchange a soft smile as I lead him out of the nursery. We're far from figuring everything out, but there's a sense of unity between us that feels like the strongest foundation we could hope for.

"Come on then," he says decisively. "Let's go find

Ben and sort this out. No more hiding or running away."

I nod. The air feels different now, charged with a nervous energy that's not entirely unpleasant. It's the feeling of standing on the edge of something new, something that could be brilliant if we just have the courage to jump in together.

As we walk down the stairs towards the living room, I can feel my pulse racing.

We reach the living room, where Ben and Henry are waiting for us. Ben's eyes lock onto mine as soon as we enter, and there's a silent question in them that makes everything else fade away.

"Zara," he starts, his voice steady but with an undercurrent of something I can't quite place. "We need to talk about what happened earlier."

I take a deep breath and step forward. "We do," I agree, holding his gaze.

"We'll leave you to it. Come and find us and soup when you're ready," Henry murmurs as he and Liam leave us alone.

Ben runs a hand through his hair. "What did that kiss mean to you?" he asks bluntly.

My stomach churns with butterflies—the good kind—but it's time for honesty. "It meant that there's something between us, something I can't ignore any longer. I like you, Ben, more than I've admitted until now."

His eyes soften, and he takes a step closer, closing the distance between us. "I like you too, Zara. A lot. That kiss was impulsive, but it felt right. It still does."

"So what now?"

His expression is earnest. "I'm not going anywhere if that's what you're asking. But we all need to be on the same page here."

"I want to try," I say finally, voice steady despite the tremor I feel inside. "But I'm scared this is too soon for you."

"Me too," Ben replies quietly.

"Which?" I ask, wrinkling up my nose in my confusion at his reply.

"Both."

His admission sends a rush of relief through me. It's not just me who's scared. Henry and Liam seem so nonchalant about it, but inside I'm terrified.

"So, which part are you going to listen to?"

He searches my eyes for a long time. So long, in fact, that I think he's going to tell me to get lost.

"I want to move forward," he says eventually as I wring my hands with anxiety coursing through me. "But I can't push the hurt aside. I was burned. Badly."

"I know," I whisper.

"And I don't want to rush or mess things up," he continues, his voice laced with vulnerability. "I like you, Zara. But I've got Mia to put first. I need to take this slow. Can we do that? Take it day by day?"

He's standing so close now, and his honesty makes my heart ache in a way that feels both terrifying and exhilarating. I nod, getting him completely. The man's been through enough to make anyone cautious, and the fact that he's willing to try speaks volumes.

"Yes, we can take it slow," I assure him, my voice stronger than I feel. "I want you to feel safe and comfortable with how things progress."

Ben exhales a shaky breath and pulls me in for a hug. His arms around me are like a promise of safety, and I let myself melt into his embrace. It's warm and secure – a sharp difference to the flurry of emotions that have been chasing each other around inside my head.

"Thank you, Zara," he murmurs into my hair. "For understanding."

We stay like that for what feels like an eternity, but it probably only lasts a few minutes. Eventually, we pull apart just enough to look at each other.

"But there is this thing that's looming," I murmur.

"I know," he says and runs his hand through his

hair again, a sign I've come to associate with him being nervous.

"What are we going to do about it? I can move out, go to a hotel—"

"No!" he says vehemently. "You are not going to a hotel where any old fucker could break in and take advantage of you."

Raising an eyebrow at the protective streak that came flying out of nowhere, I suppress my smile.

"You will stay here, and we will just have to see what happens," he relents.

"Can you do that, though? If you submit to your alpha instincts, can you take me without being all in?" I have to ask. I have to because so much depends on his answer.

He frowns fiercely. "I'm all in, Zara. I just need—"

I blink.

"Are you all in?" he asks, glaring at me.

"Yes. I'm all in. I adore Mia. I couldn't love her more if she were my own child, and you... you're more than any omega has a right to ask for."

"Don't say things like that," he rasps. "I'm not ready to hear those things."

"Tough, because you need to know your worth, Ben. She has torn your soul out, and you have lost faith in yourself. But I see you, and I'm going to be here every day making sure you know how much I care about you." I reach up and cup his face.

His eyes hold mine, and there's a shimmer of what could be tears, but I know Ben; he's not one to let them fall easily. He nods, takes a deep breath, and leans into my touch.

"You're too good to me," he murmurs.

"No, she was terrible to you. I'm going to show you again what love looks like, but I need you to let me, Ben. Don't back away. I won't hurt you, and I won't hurt Mia, ever. This is real now, and reality can be scarier than any confrontation of feelings."

"Thank you," he murmurs, and there's something like hope lighting up his face now. It's beautiful, and it makes everything feel worth it.

"Let's get some soup and some sleep," I say after a beat.

"Sounds like a plan."

We head into the kitchen, not touching but close. I'm still worried about the choice he's going to make when my heat hits in a couple of days, but I'm not going to push him or even ask him again. He will do whatever he's going to do, and I'll be there for him regardless.

Chapter 40

Zara

The tomato and basil aroma fills the kitchen, soothing my jangled nerves. Ben is in the dining room, setting the table, and each clink of cutlery is a reminder that our little unit is functioning and that there's normalcy in the chaos of our emotions.

Henry dishes up the soup, and Liam brings over the tray of bread and butter, which looks like slices of pure heaven.

"This is simple, but so fucking good," I say with a smile at Henry, who beams.

"You ain't seen nothing yet," he says.

Smiling, we join Ben in the dining room and sit down to bowls of the steaming soup.

"So, how was work today?" I ask, forcing casualness into my tone. It's important to keep things light, to not let the weight of what's looming dampen every interaction.

Liam chuckles softly. "Same old, same old. Though Gareth managed to spill coffee on his pants and spent half the day looking like he'd had an accident."

I giggle at the image. "Poor bloke. Could he not have used the hand dryer in the loo?"

"Paper towels, so he was shit out of luck," Ben says, trying to sound casual, but I can see the tension in his eyes.

We find comfort in the domestic simplicity of sharing a meal. As we eat, a peaceful silence envelops us. It's not awkward or strained, but rather a moment of stillness before the impending storm, which we all know is my heat. I can already feel the hot soup flushing my skin as my pre-heat simmers under the surface.

Henry leans back, watching me with a keen yet gentle gaze. "Are you feeling alright?" he inquires, his voice laced with concern but not pushing too hard. He seems to have mastered the skill of knowing just how far to prod without it being too much.

I nod. "Yeah, just a little warm is all. Now that I'm not distracted, it's hitting me again."

Liam reaches across the table and hands me a

glass of water. "Here, this might help cool you down a bit."

I take a few sips, grateful for the cold liquid soothing my throat. The truth is, the heat is like an itch I can't scratch yet, an anticipatory buzz under my skin that's powerful and exhilarating.

We finish our meal with light banter, but I can tell the alphas are glancing at each other when they think I'm not looking. They're worried about how things will go when my heat arrives in full force. But for now, they're doing their best to keep things normal.

After dinner is cleared away and the dishwasher hums in the background, we hover awkwardly.

"I guess, I'll head up. Mia will be waking soon," I murmur.

Ben nods, looking like he wants to say something but can't quite find the words. "I'll come with you, give her a cuddle before she goes back down."

"Okay," I murmur, having hoped I could make a great escape from the strain I can feel building as my scent gets more potent around these alphas.

We make our way upstairs, the creak of each step punctuating the silence that has settled between us. As we enter Mia's nursery, the soft glow of the nightlight casts dancing shadows across the room. Mia stirs in her crib, her little fists clenched as if she's dreaming about gripping something tightly.

I pick her up gently, cradling her in my arms as she nuzzles into my chest, still half-asleep. Ben stands next to me, his hand lightly touching Mia's back, his expression softening with every tiny sigh she makes.

"She's precious," he whispers, his gaze not leaving Mia. "Thanks for being here for both of us, Zara."

I look up at him, seeing the vulnerability behind his strength. "I wouldn't want to be anywhere else."

We stand like that for a while, lost in the tranquillity of the moment. Eventually, Mia has had enough of waiting for her bottle and grunts in annoyance. Chuckling softly, Ben goes to prep while I sit in the armchair, getting her comfortable.

Ben hands me the bottle and I take it, placing it to Mia's lips. She latches on and soon is suckling, fast asleep in that wondrous way that babies have.

Ben crouches next to us, his scent filling my senses as he watches us.

"I think I'd like to try to be more for you," he says hesitantly. "For us. It scares the shit out of me, but I don't want to run anymore."

My heart does a little leap at his words. "There's

no need to rush forward, Ben. I'm not going anywhere."

"I know," Ben says with a nod. "But look at you."

I stare into his eyes, filled with tears, but happy ones, as he shakes his head slightly. "You are more a mother to her than *she* ever was. She adores you, and I know you love her. What more could I ask for?"

"Someone to love you?"

He pauses. "Yeah, that too."

We sit in silence, the only sound is Mia's contented feeding, her little body warm against my chest. It feels like we're a complete picture, a puzzle that's slowly fitting together. Ben's vulnerability is beautiful and terrifying all at once. It's a new layer to our relationship, one filled with the promise of what could be.

Ben's smile is tentative but genuine. He reaches out to stroke Mia's cheek and then surprises me by lifting his hand to cup my face. "I guess I've been a right prat, haven't I? Running scared when what I want is right here."

I nod. "It's okay to be scared. It just means that what you stand to lose or gain matters."

He sighs, his shoulders relaxing as he accepts my words. "I will be there for you," he says firmly.

"And I'll be here when you're ready," I assure him. "No pressure."

"No, Zara," he says, shaking his head as I misunderstand. "I will be there for you during your heat if you'll have me."

"I'd like that," I murmur, feeling my cheeks heat up.

Mia finishes her bottle, and I set it aside, burping her gently before laying her back in her cot. She snuggles into her blanket, and I smile at the peace she embodies.

As we leave the nursery, Ben's hand finds mine, a silent thank you and a promise all at once. He pulls me closer and kisses the top of my head. "Get some sleep."

"You too," I murmur, and we part ways, my heart thumping loudly. This day has been bizarre, but I'm sure fate is having a fucking party right now. My crazy heat that wasn't a heat has drawn us all together in an effort to endure when my heat does hit for real, we all know where we stand.

Who the fuck would've thought that was possible?

Before today, I'd have said no, but now, I'm a believer. I slip into my room and collapse into my nest, missing my blanket from Henry, which is still in the dryer. A soft knock on the door alerts me to Henry's presence on the other side.

"Yeah?" I call out.

The door opens, and Henry peeks around, carrying my blanket fresh from the dryer, warmth radiating from it like a hug waiting to happen. He's barefoot, dressed in black joggers and a white tee, his blond hair tousled and gorgeous.

"I figured you'd be missing this," he says, draping the blanket over me. The scent of laundry detergent mixes with his own unique aroma, and it's comforting. "Or hoped, rather."

"I was, but I was too lazy to move to get it. Thank you. You're going to spoil me, aren't you?"

Henry shrugs as he hovers on the edge of my nest. "Someone has to. You take care of everyone else."

Sitting up, I reach out and grab his hand, giving it a squeeze. Henry's an alpha through and through, but he doesn't need to strut around proving it like Eddie used to. He has that quiet confidence in every move he makes, and it's suddenly sexy as fuck as he stares down at me, those blue eyes full of heat and something akin to awe.

He squeezes back, his thumb rubbing circles on the back of my hand.

"Can I stay? Just for a bit?" Henry's voice is low, a touch of uncertainty threading through his usual confidence.

"Yeah, of course," I murmur. "Join me?" The idea

of having him nearby is comforting in ways I'm only just starting to understand. He doesn't wait for another invitation; he eases down beside me in my nest, his body a strong line of warmth against my side.

"Are you okay?" he asks, his voice laced with genuine concern. He knows how close I am to my heat, and the tension that comes with it is almost tangible.

"Yeah, just tired," I admit, fighting off a yawn with little success. "It's been a long day."

He nods in understanding, then his eyes soften even more, if that's possible. "That it has. Sleep now, sweetheart. I'll see to Mia when she wakes."

"Could you be more perfect?" I mutter as sleep is beckoning me.

"Only for you." He kisses the top of my head.

I smile, feeling the tension bleed out of my body.

With him by my side, I feel a sense of calm wash over me, easing my worries about the impending heat that awaits us.

Henry's hand continues its gentle caress until I'm teetering on the edge of sleep, his steady breathing syncing with mine.

"What about you, though?" I mumble, half-asleep. "Don't you need to rest, too?"

"I will," he whispers back, "but right now, I've got you."

Chapter 41

Benjamin

Once inside my room, I flop onto the bed and stare up at the ceiling. There's a part of me that's terrified about the heat. Not because of what it means physically—that part is basic instinct, something we alphas are born ready for—but because of what it represents emotionally. Zara needs someone she can trust implicitly, someone who'll be there for her every step of the way without fucking it up.

I mean it with everything I've got that I'm going to be there for her, and she accepted my offer, so this is a good thing. Nicole is behind me, and Zara is in front of me. A whole world of possibilities is just waiting to happen.

Knowing I can be this for Zara and Mia, and even for myself, has a sort of peace settling over me.

This is right. It's perfect, and I know now that Nicole was a means to an end for me. She gave me Mia, which brought Zara into my life. It's funny how fate works, but I truly believe this was fate at play—from the very beginning.

Turning over, I sigh—a slow release of breath that takes all the anger and pain away with it and leaves me restful. It's been a long time since I went to sleep properly without being dragged under by sheer exhaustion, unable to sleep because of the pain and needing to be there for Mia.

Making a mental note to ring my mum tomorrow to see if she will have Mia for a couple of days when Zara's heat hits full-on, I think that's best. It breaks my heart to have to part with her for a couple of days, but three alphas in rut with an omega in heat is no place for a baby.

Settling deeper into my pillows, I let my mind stray further. It's been a hell of a ride these past few months, but as I shut my eyes, the last thing I think about is Zara's smile, the way her entire face lights up when she's genuinely happy. It's a beautiful sight, and one that I need to see more often.

Sleep comes easier than usual tonight. Maybe it's because, for the first time in a long time, I feel like things are finally clicking into place.

But whatever it is, I drift off with the promise of

tomorrow tingling in my veins—a future where Zara's scent fills my senses, not just during her heat but every day after that.

A future.

As dreams start to weave through my consciousness, they're full of laughter, the warmth of bodies nestled close, and the sweet tang of satisfaction that comes from knowing you're exactly where you're supposed to be.

It's a new day tomorrow—a day closer to Zara's heat and all the challenges that come with it. But for tonight, at least, everything is perfect in its place.

***

When I wake up, it feels like I've slept for a week and am groggy with it. I'm in the exact same position I was when I fell asleep. Rubbing my hand over my face, I realise a soft knock at the door woke me.

"Yeah," I call out groggily, getting up and going to the door.

It's Henry and Liam.

"We need to talk," Henry says, fixing me with a glare that catches me off guard.

"What did I do? Or not do?" I ask.

"Get compos mentis and then come downstairs," Liam says.

Raising an eyebrow at this order, I slam the door in their faces and turn to the shower.

The spray of the water is a wake up call, like a slap to the face, but in a good way. Steam fills the shower cubicle as I quickly scrub away the grogginess, trying to figure out what I've missed that's got Henry looking at me like I've betrayed the bloody crown or something.

Dressed in fresh clothes and more awake now, I head downstairs. As I descend, I can hear Liam's laugh and Henry's deeper chuckle. Whatever this is about, it doesn't seem they're too pissed off.

In the kitchen, they're both sitting at the island, mugs of tea in their hands. The morning light pours in through the window, washing over them and for a moment, I feel this surge of something akin to pride.

"What's up?" I ask, grabbing a mug for myself and flicking on the kettle. "Is Mia okay?"

"Mia is fine. I've taken care of her this morning. Zara is sleeping in. I think her heat, her real one, is about to hit any minute," Henry says.

"So then what?"

He and Liam exchange glances. "We have something to ask you. A proposal, as it were," Liam starts, but then looks at Henry.

Henry rolls his eyes and slaps Liam on the shoulder. "Okay, mate, you've chickened out. I've got this."

"Got what?" I snap, getting pissed off as I pour hot water over a tea bag.

"Liam and I are deadly serious about being with Zara. We feel she is our fated mate, and we have discussed at length this morning how that affects us. All of us."

"Okay, and?"

"How do you feel about her?"

Exhaling sharply, I find it's too fucking early for this. "One day at a time is how I feel about her."

"But you're going to be there during her heat?" he presses.

"Yes, we discussed it last night. Can we get to the point of this annoying conversation?"

"We need to know if you see yourself with her, in the future. Long haul," Liam takes over again.

"That's a heavy question and one I can't answer. Yes, I'm attracted to her. Yes, I'll be there for her heat. Yes, there is something between us that is new and exciting. Do I think it's fate?" I pause.

"That's the question of the day." Henry takes a sip of his tea.

"Yeah, I guess I do. Everything happens for a reason." I've said it and confronted it out loud, and it feels good. It feels right.

"So if we are all in this one hundred per cent, perhaps we should make this more formal," Henry says, searching my eyes as he places his tea down and pushes it away.

"What do you mean?"

"Oh, for God's sake, man," Liam exclaims, running his hand through his hair. "You two could beat around the bush all fucking day. We want to make a pack with you as our prime if you'll have us. Okay? There. Ball. Court. You." He points at me and then crosses his arms.

I stare at them both, my mug of tea halfway to my lips. A pack with me as their prime? It's a serious commitment. "You have agreed to this, the two of you?"

"Yep," Henry says. "Look, we know it's fast, I mean, or is it? We've known each other forever. It makes sense. We are all living here, contributing to the household, and raising Mia. Why not make it official?"

I set my mug down with a clink against the countertop. My mind races through every moment we've shared since we could walk. It does make sense in the weird way that our world works. "So, we would be a pack and we would, I assume you're suggesting, we mate with Zara—as a pack?"

"That is what we are suggesting. Eventually. The pack thing needs to come first, and the mating, while Liam and I feel we are ready, has to go at your pace. You've just had your bond broken with *her*. We know rushing into another mating is probably the last thing on your mind, right now..."

"Yeah," I say, but it is half-hearted. The idea of forming a pack with these two idiots and then all of us mating with Zara, giving Mia stability and love from all sides, is not as scary as I thought it would be when they first hit me with this.

"Yeah...?" Liam asks. "You don't sound so sure."

"No, I'm just surprised that the idea isn't making me run a million miles away. If anything, it's rooting me here."

"So, you're in?" Liam clarifies, still looking slightly sceptical, as if he can't believe what he's hearing.

"Yeah," I say more firmly this time. "I'm in. But we do this right. We talk to Zara together. This has to be her call, too."

"Of course," Henry agrees readily.

"We'll do this properly," Liam adds. "We respect her choice no matter what."

It feels like stepping off a cliff and trusting that the water below isn't too shallow. But I know without a single shred of doubt that I'm ready for the plunge.

Light footsteps catch my attention, and suddenly, Zara appears in the doorway, rubbing sleep from her eyes. Her hair is tousled, and a look of confusion crosses her face.

"Why did no one wake me?" she asks, blinking at us. "Has Mia been fed? She's fast asleep, I didn't want to disturb her if someone has seen to her?"

"Mia is perfect," I murmur, staring at her in wonder.

Liam turns to her with a wide grin while Henry gives her a soft smile. "Morning, princess," Liam says. "Tea?"

She nods slowly, still half in dreamland. "Sounds good," she mumbles before yawning widely. Her scent surrounds us, and a low growl escapes me as it does Liam and Henry. We are in our rut together because of Zara, this gorgeous omega who has entered our lives and swept us all off our feet.

"You're just in time," I say gently, "We have something important to discuss with you."

Her eyes flick between us all, a glimmer of wariness mingling with the sleepiness. But then she straightens up a bit, as if bracing herself for whatever we're about to throw at her. "Alright," she says with more vigour than before. "What's going on?"

"We've been talking," Liam begins, his tone unusually earnest for this time of the morning. "About us. About you. And about Mia."

"And?"

Liam's about to go on, but he looks to me, silently passing the baton as the would-be prime alpha of this new pack. I clear my throat, feeling the weight of what I'm about to suggest. "We want to form a pack," I say slowly. "The three of us together—with you, if you want it—as our omega."

Zara blinks rapidly as she processes the words. She looks at Henry and then at Liam before her gaze settles back on me. "A pack?" she repeats softly.

"Yes," I affirm, watching her closely. "We'll take care of Mia as a family, and well... we'd like for you to be part of that family. In your own time, of course, if that is something you know in your soul you want." I can't leave that part to chance. She has to be all in. No wishy-washy agreement because she feels forced into it. I don't think I can take another rejection in this lifetime.

She takes a deep breath in and lets it out slowly, her eyes never leaving mine. "That's quite a proposal for this early in the morning." The corners of her mouth twitch as if she's fighting back a smile or perhaps nerves. "Can I have that tea first?" she asks, only half-joking, gesturing to the kettle with a quirk of her eyebrow. Liam immediately moves to get it done, the universal signal that no matter how tense the situation, a good cuppa can make everything better.

I watch her as Liam prepares her tea, trying to

gauge her reaction beyond the initial shock. She's poised, but I catch the slight tremor in her fingers as she tucks a strand of hair behind her ear.

Once Liam hands her the mug, Zara wraps her hands around it, inhaling the steam before taking a tentative sip. "Okay," she starts, setting the mug down on the island with a little more certainty than before. "You want us to be a pack? So, mating with me?"

"We see you as part of our, well, our everything already," Henry murmurs, knowing she needs to hear from all of us. Not just me. "The three of us are going to form the pack first. That is our thing. But we see a future with you, Zara. It's fate and we want to mate with you, when you and, of course, Ben, are ready for that. Full disclosure, Liam and I are ready for that now."

"Wow, okay," she says, and I see something shift in her expression—a softening around her eyes, maybe even a touch of relief. She takes another long sip of her tea before nodding slowly. "And just where would I fit into this pack? What's expected of me?"

"You'd be at the centre," Liam says quickly. "Our omega. It wouldn't just be about duties or roles; it's about support and about love."

"And no rush on decisions about mating," I add

firmly, knowing she needs to feel free, not pressured. Knowing what little I do about her previous relationship; her free will is more important than anything else right now. "We just want you to know where we stand and make sure you're comfortable and happy with any choices you make before your heat arrives and things get…"

"Heated?" she giggles.

"Yeah." I return her smile, and I see no fear in her gaze. No hesitation. No doubts. She is fucking incredible.

Zara takes another sip of tea, letting the warmth settle inside her before she speaks. Her eyes scan each of us, affection and deep thought dancing in her gaze. "It's a lot to take in," she admits, her voice steady but soft. "I'd be lying if I said I haven't felt something different with you three. Like a pull." She sets the mug back on the island and folds her arms, suddenly looking more determined. "Like it *is* fate that brought me here to all of you."

"So, not to put words in your mouth… we need a yay or nay," Liam says, the worry in his voice echoing around the kitchen that she is going to shove this back in our faces and run.

She smiles. "It's a yay. It's fast, and it's wild, but I know it's right. I feel it in my soul," she glances at me, "and my biology doesn't lie. The three of you together threw me into this heat early. If that isn't fate screaming at me to accept you as my future mates, then I don't know what is."

The tension in the room evaporates like steam from a hot shower when you open the window, and my heart tries to beat its way out of my chest with the force of my relief that she didn't reject me. Us. Liam exhales loudly, the kind of sound you make when you've been holding your breath underwater and finally breaking the surface. Henry looks like someone's just given him the moon.

"Yay," Liam murmurs and draws her to him for a kiss. It's deep, and he clings to her as she does to him.

When they break apart, I clear my throat as Zara slams her hand to her head. "Heat?"

"Yeah," she croaks. "You fuckers are killing me here."

Chuckling, Henry grabs her and scoops her up before she falls off the stool. "Let's get you back to your nest."

"I'm okay. It's not full on yet."

"Yet," I murmur. "I'll call Mum and see if she can take Mia for a couple of days."

"And we'd better call in work," Liam murmurs. "We won't be going anywhere for a few days."

"Alan is going to throw a shit fit," I sigh, but reach for my phone anyway. There are plans to make and things are moving quickly now. There is no time to fuck about second-guessing my decisions. This is happening, and I know it's going to be perfect.

Chapter 42

Liam

I can barely keep my hands to myself as I tap out the message to Alan, leaving Ben to sort out Mia with his mum. I hate that we have to send her away, but it's for the best right now, and it will only be a couple of days before we, at least the alphas of us, can come out of the haze of the rut and Zara's heat long enough to care for her.

"Sorted," I declare after pressing send, stuffing my mobile back into my pocket and moving closer to where Henry is cradling Zara, who looks both exhilarated and a bit overwhelmed by the sudden change in her life's direction.

The atmosphere is charged; we're on the cusp of something new and exciting. It feels like we're all plugged into the same current, buzzing with anticipation.

Zara leans into Henry slightly before reaching out a hand to me. I take it without hesitation, bringing it to my lips to kiss lightly. "I want a shower before things get worse," she says. "Yesterday was weird. It was sudden, and it was fierce, but now that I think about it and know it wasn't the real deal, I can feel the difference bubbling under my skin already."

"Shower, food and rest before things turn, yeah?" I say, letting Henry take her upstairs while I turn back to the kitchen. Henry is better in this area than me, but I know Zara likes sarnies and right now, all she needs is sustenance not a gourmet meal.

"Sorted?" I ask when Ben comes back in the kitchen looking like something struck. This is moving fast, and I take a second to evaluate his temperament.

"Yeah, mum's on her way. She is excited, to say the least."

"Well, she gets granny time, so not surprising."

"More than that. I told her about the pack and Zara. She is thrilled."

"Oh, nice. Scott family approval. Love it."

We share a smile.

"You one hundred per cent sure?" I have to check.

"Yes," he replies with no hesitation. "I'm not letting that bitch hold me back from the best thing that's ever happened to me."

Grinning, I slap him on the shoulder. "That's the spirit."

I start making a stack of sarnies, piling them high with every bit of salad, ham, and cheese I can find. This is nurturing in its simplest and most basic form. Keeping Zara, our omega, fed and happy is top of the list.

The doorbell rings just as I've wrapped the last sandwich in cling film. Ben's already bolting for the door, ready to welcome his mum, who's come to whisk Mia away for some unexpected granny time. I hear his muffled voice, the creak of the door swinging open and then shut again, followed by that soft hum of adult-to-baby babble that tells me Mia's in safe hands.

Heading up stairs, leaving Ben to say goodbye to Mia, Zara's emerged from the shower wrapped in a fluffy towel, her hair damp and her cheeks flushed. She is dazed and in no fit state to be on her feet. Henry's with her, his hands gentle but possessive around her waist.

"Shower good?" I murmur, balancing the tray as I hold open her bedroom door.

Zara nods, her eyes glazed over. "Yeah, it helped."

I place the tray down on the floor near her nest and help her get settled. She is just in a towel which I want to rip off her and devour her, but there will be plenty of time for that later.

Henry darts off and returns to offer Zara one of his t-shirts, which she accepts with a soft smile. He helps her into it, and she sighs contentedly as the scent of one of her alpha's fills her senses.

There's something primal about these moments; we're orbiting around Zara like planets around the sun. I need to give her something of mine. Going back to my room, I look around for something meaningful, and then it hits me. I grab my favourite hoodie - the one I've lived in on lazy Sundays, the one that's soaked up more of my scent than any other piece of clothing. It's comfy and worn in just the right way. Darting back to Zara's room, I see her nibbling on a sandwich, as Henry returns the towel to the bathroom to dry on the rack.

I hold out the hoodie to her. "Will you accept this?"

She gives me a look that could melt iron before she nods enthusiastically. Holding it out for her, she slips her arms into the sleeves. The hoodie swamps her smaller frame, but she looks bloody adorable in it. "Thank you," she whispers, and something flickers in her eyes - gratitude mixed with affection and desire.

Suddenly Ben appears at the door, his expression full of relief and need as he looks over at Zara nestled in garments from both Henry and me. "Mia's with mum," he announces.

Zara's face falls slightly. "Is she okay?"

"Happy as a clam," Ben assures her. With a soft smile, he places a carefully folded rugby shirt on the bed. "For when you miss my scent."

Her smile grows wider as she reaches for his shirt, pressing it to her face for a moment before letting it rest next to her on the pillow.

"Thank you. I needed this. I feel a bit less agitated now that I'm surrounded by your scents."

"We'll leave you to rest now and check on you in a bit."

"Okay," she says with a sleepy smile.

We leave her alone and stare at each other out on the landing. "So now?" I ask.

"Good a time as any," Henry agrees.

We both stare at Ben as this is up to him. As the prime of our soon-to-be-pack, he has to bind us to him with a bite to the wrist.

"Let's do it," he murmurs, and we head back down for this pivotal moment where our lives are going to change irrevocably.

Chapter 43

Benjamin

My blood is rushing through my veins, making me a bit dizzy. With Zara upstairs, wrapped in the scents of her alphas, this feels right in every way.

Henry and Liam are behind me as we enter the living room, where the soft glow of the morning sun spills through the window, giving everything a golden edge. It's peaceful, almost sacred, and I'm suddenly aware of the gravity of what's about to happen.

"Ready?" Henry asks, his voice steady, but I can spot that flicker of anticipation in his eyes.

Liam gives a silent nod enough to tell me he's all in.

"Yeah," I reply, trying to keep my voice from betraying the whirlpool of emotions inside me. "Do we need pomp and ceremony?"

Liam and Henry chuckle. "Nah," Liam says. "That's not us."

"Good," I breathe out.

As they stand before me, I take a deep breath and focus on what they mean to me—partners in this wild adventure that life has thrown us into. They are more than friends; they're the anchors that will keep our omega and our baby safe and our pack balanced.

First, I turn to Henry. "You ready?"

He bares his wrist without hesitation. "Do it."

I place my teeth against his skin with slow, deliberate movements, feeling the warmth and texture of his flesh against my lips. As I apply pressure, there's a slight give and I taste the metallic tang of blood on my tongue. With an almost audible click, the bond solidifies between us, and I feel something shifting deep inside me. A surge of power and responsibility settles over my shoulders like a heavy cloak, but it's a burden I gladly bear. Henry's face is contorted in pain from the bite, but his eyes shine with fierce loyalty and belonging. And I can feel it too - the unbreakable connection that now runs bone-deep between us.

As the moments tick by, I release his wrist from my teeth and slowly lower his arm to his side. In the quiet of the room, the only sound is our synchronised breathing, a reminder of the connection we now share.

"Your turn," I murmur to Liam, turning towards him.

With an unwavering gaze, he steps forward, offering up his wrist without a word. As I sink my teeth into his skin and our bond solidifies, a wave of completeness washes over me. It's as if all the puzzle pieces have finally slotted into place, revealing a clarity and understanding that this is just the beginning.

We stand in silence for a few heartbeats longer, allowing the weight of our new bond to settle in. The atmosphere feels charged with energy, crackling with potential and possibility.

As I reluctantly release Liam from my grip, I extend my arms towards the two alphas in front of me. They eagerly clamp down on my wrists, their sharp teeth piercing through my flesh and completing our pack bond. In that moment, I can feel their thoughts and emotions coursing through me, intertwining with my own. We are now bound together in an unbreakable unity.

With one final burst of energy, they release their bites and let go of my wrists. The intense pain shoots through my body like a bolt of lightning, but amidst the pain, there is a sense of fulfilment and connection. We are one pack, united and ready to face whatever challenges may come our way.

"Fuck me," Liam mutters, his voice low and ragged with emotion. I can see the sweat glistening on his forehead from the intensity of our encounter.

Nervously, I let out a shaky laugh, trying to process the weight of what just happened between us. It was like a dream, but so real at the same time.

"That was perfect," Henry murmurs, his eyes fixed on us. "Do you think Zara feels it somehow?"

I close my eyes, feeling the familiar pull in my gut as my instincts take over. The rut has hit me hard, and I know I need to knot my omega now or risk losing control.

"Maybe," I whisper, my mind foggy with desire and longing.

My body is on autopilot as I start toward the stairs, the need to be with Zara and reinforce the pack bond with the other alphas, completely consuming me. Liam and Henry are close behind, the energy between us crackling with shared urgency.

We reach the door to the bedroom where Zara is resting, and I pause, collecting myself. I can't just burst in like a man possessed; I have to remind myself that this is also about her needs, her comfort.

Gently pushing open the door, I see her stirring,

her expression one of drowsy curiosity. But as her eyes catch mine, they widen slightly, as she can sense the shift in dynamics.

"Everything okay?" she asks, worry lacing her tone.

I swallow hard and offer her a reassuring smile. "More than okay," I say. "We're bonded now—properly. You might feel a bit of it too, maybe?"

She blinks at me for a second before understanding dawns on her face. A slow smile spreads across her lips. "I thought there was something different when I woke up just now. I can feel the equilibrium has changed."

Henry moves forward, sitting on the edge of the nest. "How do you feel about that?" he asks softly.

"Like I'm exactly where I'm meant to be."

I cross the room and kneel by the nest, my hand reaching out to brush a lock of hair from her forehead but not touching her, not until she says.

She tilts her head, giving me silent permission, and my fingers trail gently against her skin. It's electric, the connection humming between us now amplified by the bond I share with Henry and Liam. She takes a deep breath, and I can see her sinking into the sensation, the acknowledgment of our newly forged ties.

"Come here then," she murmurs, her voice a blend of tenderness and need.

As I lean in to kiss her, Henry and Liam join us on either side of the nest, our pack gathered around its heart. Her lips meet mine with an urgency that tells me she feels it too—the rut, the bond, the insatiable need to be claimed.

Our kisses are deep and meaningful as we each take our turn, affirming our commitment to Zara and to each other. The scent of arousal fills the room, a tangible sign of our synchrony that has us all teetering on the brink of something monumental.

"I need this—I need you all," she murmurs.

There's no room for hesitation. We understand the intricacies of our situation.

Slowly, we undress until we are naked in her nest. Any shyness that I thought I might feel isn't there. It is natural, and it is right.

Chapter 44

Zara

I watch them, my alphas, as they strip away their clothes and their inhibitions, standing before me in a show of unity and strength. There's a moment, just one, where I'm utterly still, drinking in the sight. They're gorgeous in their vulnerability, displaying their willingness to be mine as much as I am theirs.

My heart beats faster, my body reacting to the raw masculinity and the want in the air. It's a heady feeling to be the omega at the centre of this circle, both cherished and desired.

Henry kneels first, his blue eyes dark with need as he leans in and brushes his lips against mine. It's a kiss that promises so much more, a prelude to the intense connection we're about to share. Liam follows, his touch is gentler but no less intense. Finally, Ben joins us, and their kisses blend into one seamless tide of desire that leaves me breathless.

Their hands roam over my body with a tenderness that conceals the urgency simmering underneath. I can feel their craving to claim me, echoing mine to be claimed.

Each caress is amplified by the pact they've made. The knowledge that they are bonded with each other fills me with indescribable warmth.

We shift and shuffle until we find positions that allow for closeness and depth. My heat is consuming me now, leaving me dazed and full of a need for a knot from one of my alphas. My gasp is swallowed by Ben's kiss as Liam laps at my slick, pooling in my pussy, ready to take their knots. Our movements become fevered. I feel hands and lips everywhere, sensations blurring as I'm gripped by my alphas and their love.

Their growls mix with my purrs as they move around me, a tangled mass of limbs and heat. It's overwhelming in the best possible way. Their rut is as relentless as my heat, driving us all to the brink of wildness.

"Please," I beg when I can't take the craving any longer. "Please."

Ben is the first alpha to settle between my thighs. His enormous cock is pressing against my pussy, and he growls, low and deep, as he slides inside me, and I coat him with slick.

"Fuck," he grunts and leverages himself over me.

His movements are deliberate and powerful, and it's all I can do to hold on to him as he buries himself deep. The stretch is divine, the fullness exactly what my body cries out for. Liam and Henry don't sit idle; their hands and mouths are on me, stoking the fire that Ben is fuelling.

Henry's lips find mine again, swallowing any sound I might make as Ben thrusts. Liam's hands cup my breasts, his fingers teasing my nipples into hard peaks that ache for attention. It's a sensory overload, but I wouldn't give it up for the world—they are my world.

I feel the coil in my belly tighten, and I know I'm close to shattering into a million pieces under their combined touch.

"Come around my cock so you can feel my knot bulging inside you, Zara."

"Fuck!" That's all the permission I need. My orgasm rips through me with the force of a tidal wave, crashing over every nerve ending as I cry out into Henry's mouth as he covers it to kiss me deeply.

Ben's body stiffens as his climax hits him, his knot swelling to lock us together as he shoots his cum into me with a loud, possessive growl.

"Good girl," Liam murmurs as Ben rolls us to the side. "How do you feel?"

"Good," I murmur, staring into Ben's eyes. "Are you okay?"

"Better than I've ever felt," he whispers. "You are mine, Zara. Ours. We will never let you go."

Cupping his face, I smile. "I'm not going anywhere, I promise."

He nods, accepting my vow as the truth. His gaze holds mine, a silent conversation that speaks of futures and forever. I'm still locked to him, his knot keeping us joined in the most intimate of ways, a physical manifestation of the invisible ties that bind us all together.

I can feel Henry shift behind me, and his hand glides down my spine in slow, assuring strokes. He's a solid presence at my back, grounding me even as I float on the high of the post-orgasmic bliss. A contented sigh escapes my lips as I bask in the afterglow with my alphas surrounding me, their scents potent and stirring my heat back into a clawing need for more.

As Ben's knot begins to recede, he gently pulls

away from me with a soft kiss on my forehead. Henry rolls me onto my back, his eyes tender yet filled with a raw passion that sends me into a deep lust, and then everything is blurry, leaving me completely at their mercy, but I trust them implicitly to take care of me.

Chapter 45

Henry

The moment Ben pulls back, I see the opportunity and take it. There's something primal about being this close to her, about being able to touch her in ways that only we can. It makes my cock stiffen further as I see the slick and cum pooling out of her pussy. The blankets are damp underneath her, so I lift her hips gently and shuffle her around the side. She is lost to her heat now. There won't be much from her end, so it's all down to me to give her my knot and help ease the torment her heat brings to her.

I lower myself onto her, my lips finding hers in a kiss that's soft and sweet. She wraps her arms around me, holding on tight like she never wants to let go. It feels right. Her body is soft and warm under mine, and I move against her, teasing us both.

"Ready for my knot, love?" I ask between kisses.

Her nod is weak, and her eyes are glazed over. My cock is rock hard for her, pressing against her clit, demanding entry. I grip the shaft and rub just the tip against her slick for just a moment. Her hips buck up towards me instinctively, and it takes everything not to slam into her right there.

I push in slowly, savouring the tight heat that envelops me inch by inch. The sensation is nothing short of exquisite. Her gasp turns into a purr, and then she's pulling me deeper into her. I start a slow rhythm, but it doesn't last long; need overtakes patience, and soon we're moving together with emotional urgency.

Each thrust pushes a deeper purr from her as Liam kneels beside us, kissing her softly, allowing her space to breathe, to feel my cock inside her.

Liam's touch is a spark to the fire already consuming us. He runs his fingers through her hair, smoothing it back from her flushed face.

I feel her muscles begin to clamp down on me, and I know she's close again. Her eyes meet mine, and there's a combination of love and lust that almost undoes me.

I growl low in my throat as I feel my climax building. "Let go for me, sweetheart. Come for me so I can give you my knot."

Her body quivers underneath me, her inner walls spasming as she comes hard around me. The pulsing of her pussy is too much, and I can't hold back any longer.

With a final deep thrust, my knot expands at the base of my cock, locking into place just inside her pussy. A low, feral growl escapes me as I cum deep inside her, marking her as ours. Zara's purrs are muffled by Liam's kiss.

As our bodies are joined by my knot, the room fills with the sounds of heavy breathing and soft murmurs of pleasure. The heat from our bodies makes the air almost tangible, thick with desire and satisfaction.

I collapse gently on top of her as Liam moves away, careful not to crush her with my weight, our sweat-slicked bodies pressed together in a perfect embrace. Her legs wrap around me instinctively as we stay connected, our hearts beating in sync.

Ben moves to sit beside us, his hand resting lightly on Zara's foot, his presence just as important as when he was buried deep inside her. Liam is behind her, offering a contented smile and running his fingers down Zara's back when I roll us to the side so that I can collapse entirely. The exertion of rutting with an omega in heat, is more than just sex. It's everything when it's with the omega who is going to be your mate.

We linger like this, wrapped up in each other as time seems to stand still.

"I've got you," Liam whispers to Zara, voice laced with tenderness. "We've all got you."

Time seems irrelevant as we drift off into a blissful haze. Zara's breathing steadies, her chest rising and falling in the rhythm of deep sleep. Ben's gaze meets mine over her head, and we share a silent understanding of the bond that's been strengthened today. Love doesn't just double or triple; it seems to multiply endlessly with each shared moment like this.

Eventually, the physical connection of my knot diminishes, allowing me to gently withdraw from Zara. I miss the warmth immediately.

Drawing the covers up over her, Liam and Ben settle around us, their touches on Zara reassuring and protective. Even in her sleep, she smiles, a gentle curve of her lips that speaks volumes about her trust and happiness.

It's not long before sleep claims me, too—the kind that is deep and peaceful, knowing full well that when we wake up, there will be even more need from Zara to ease her heat. It will grow more intense, but we will be here to keep up with her and give her everything she needs.

I drift on a sea of pure happiness as plans start to form about taking Zara to see the lakes once her heat is over. The thought of picnics and lazy boat rides flit through my mind before darkness takes me completely.

When I wake up, the light from the window is softer, an indication that time has passed, and evening is here. Zara is still nestled between us, a small frown marring her otherwise peaceful face. It's obvious her heat isn't giving her any respite, even in sleep.

I reach out to brush a strand of hair from her face, my movements careful not to wake her. She stirs anyway, her eyes fluttering open, heavy with sleep and desire.

"Hey," I whisper, voice rough from sleep. "Do you feel okay?"

She nods, then winces slightly as another wave of her heat hits her. Ben stirs beside us, his protective alpha instincts immediately coming to the forefront as he senses the change in Zara.

"Tell us what you need," Ben says, his voice tinged with concern.

Zara licks her lips and looks between us. The

scent of her heat is stronger now, wrapping around us like a lavender-infused cloak.

"Knot," she murmurs.

I glance at Liam, who has woken up, too. His green eyes are bright with arousal and concern for our omega.

The word is all the motivation we need. I move away from Zara, as Liam runs his hands gently up her thighs. Ben's already leaning down to capture her lips in a kiss, deep and promising, telling her without words that she's going to be taken care of.

Chapter 46

Liam

I'm doing my best to focus on her, but the way her heat scent wraps around us is like a drug I can't resist. It's all the permission my body needs to spring into action.

I kiss the inside of her thigh as Ben's mouth moves over hers. She makes this little half-whimper, half-purr that goes straight to my dick. It's not just about sex; it's about being what she needs us to be in this moment.

Her hands find my hair and tug gently, guiding me where she wants me. She's asking for reassurance, for the pleasure we can give her to ease the relentless ache of her heat.

I move up her body, pressing a soft kiss to her belly and then between her breasts. She's so fucking responsive, every touch drawing a deeper purr or a shiver from her. It's intoxicating.

Ben pulls back from their kiss and looks at me with that alpha intensity he does so well.

My rut is urging me to claim my omega. Guiding my cock between her spread legs as Ben cups her face tenderly and leans down to whisper something that makes her smile through the pain of her heat. Whatever it is he's said, it's exactly what she needs to hear because she relaxes slightly—a beautiful trust given over to us.

I slide into her slowly, savouring the sensation of being fully sheathed in her soaking wet pussy. The tightness, the slick, her heat—it's exquisite. She purrs softly, her body accepting me, gripping me with her need as I growl possessively back at her.

Each thrust is measured and deep, designed to stoke the fire of her heat even further.

I'm lost in the feeling of being so intimately connected with her again. Zara gasps softly beneath me, and I know I need to be gentle yet steady to give her what she needs.

Ben slides one hand down, finding her clit and rubbing gently in circles that have Zara arching towards us, seeking more contact. She's close to coming undone. Her pussy clenches around my cock, and it drives me insane with the need to follow her over that edge.

Her breath catches with every push, and I can feel my knot starting to swell. Ben's hands never stop moving over her skin, worshipping every inch of her as if she were the rarest treasure.

I set a rhythm that's all give and take, pulling purrs from Zara that drive me. I pound into her, needing to feel more of her, always, just like this. Her slick has soaked my dick, and it's bliss. Pure and utter bliss. The blankets under us are soaked with her slick, and the other alphas cum, but it doesn't stop either of us from chasing that high that comes with my knot.

Ben moves closer, his lips brushing Zara's ear as he whispers assurances that we're here for her, that she's ours, and we're hers—in all the ways that matter. It's not just bodies entwined, but lives and futures, too.

Henry slides in on her other side, reassuring her we are all still here.

As I thrust into her again, my knot expands completely and locks us together. Zara cries out, a mixture of relief and ecstasy washing over her features as another orgasm ripples through her as I dump my cum deep inside her, hoping to impregnate her. It's a wild thought. One I've never been interested in before, but this, with her, is pure, honest, gorgeous. She is forever.

We stay locked like that for a while – joined together in the most intimate way possible. Ben's hand is still on her, now softly caressing her skin as she comes down from her high. Henry is whispering words of affirmation, his touch gentle and adoring on the other side of her. She's surrounded by care and love, and it's exactly what she needs.

Eventually, my knot deflates enough to pull out gently. She winces slightly, but there's a satisfied smile on her lips, and that makes everything worth it. I flop down beside her, spent but fulfilled, watching as Ben leans in for another kiss, sweet and lingering this time.

Henry leans down and kisses her forehead softly before murmuring, "Let's get you cleaned up, sweetheart."

We shuffle around to make space as Ben carefully scoops Zara into his arms and stands with effortless grace. He carries her off towards the bathroom while Henry and I strip the bed of the soaked blankets.

I grab some fresh linen from the cupboard and start making the nest whilst Henry heads to the kitchen for a glass of water for Zara. It's these small gestures of care that knit us even tighter together.

Omegas may be known for their need during heats, but what is less talked about is how much they give back to their alphas in trust and love. She's the heart of our home, and we orbit around her—each of us warmed by her presence. Standing back as I scrutinise my handiwork, I realise that it's not perfect. She will want it the way she wants it, and that's fine. But we're not having her nest in drenched bedding, so it will do until she comes back and organises it herself. After three knots, she should be lucid for a while. Enough to see to her omega needs for nesting and refuelling.

Sitting back as Henry returns, we wait, knowing Ben will take advantage of the alone time with her, and that's also fine. Great, even. He needs this as much as she does, and it warms my heart to see him truly happy for the first time since I can't remember when.

Chapter 47

Zara

As Ben runs the shower for me, I lean into his chest, the warm water a beautiful backdrop. His arms are secure around me, and it's just us in this little bubble of peace. The pain of my heat has subsided for now, replaced by this bone-deep contentment that spreads through me.

"Feeling better?" he asks, his voice low and gentle.

I nod against him, too wrapped up in this moment of tranquillity to speak. It's just Ben and me, and the quiet understanding that what we have has moved well and truly passed being just his nanny and onto something irrevocably more special. Mind you, I knew that the second I purred at him.

Smiling up at him, his towering height making me feel safe and secure in this tiled cubicle, the water cascades over us, washing away the remnants of our earlier activities. His touch is worshipful as he lathers shampoo into my hair, massaging my scalp in a way that has me moaning softly in pleasure.

"There's nothing I wouldn't do for you," he murmurs as he rinses the suds from my hair.

I believe him. In every touch, every look, I feel valued and cherished. With Ben, Henry, and Liam—all my alphas—there's a sense of belonging I've never known before.

He washes my body with the same reverence he showed my hair, his fingers skimming over my skin as if memorising every inch. There's no rush, no urgency; just the steady, loving attention that says I'm his in all the ways that matter. His cock stirs as my hand brushes against him. I grip him loosely, telling him with that one action that I want him right here, right now, and he groans, a mix of surprise and raw need buzzing in the air around us. His eyes darken, and his lips capture mine in a searing kiss, one that is filled with a hunger that is never fully satiated.

His erection presses against me insistent, and I know this is more than just the heat and the rut; it's an affirmation of our connection. Ben lifts me up, my legs wrap around his waist as the water pours over us, an elemental force matching our passion. He enters me slowly, our wet bodies crashing together with the force of it.

It's slower this time, more about emotion than the wildness of before. His thrusts are deliberate and deep, each one pulling a sigh or a moan from my lips.

Ben's hand finds mine against the tile and he laces our fingers together, an anchor in the slippery heat. He kisses me—deeply, thoroughly—as if he can pour every ounce of his feelings into that one act. Maybe he can because I feel it down to my toes, sparking through me like lightning.

"You feel so fucking good," he breathes against my lips.

The walls of the shower echo with the sound of our combined moans, the steam growing thicker around us as our heat builds. There's no holding back —the intensity of the moment strips away all inhibitions.

We hit our climax together, my cry muffled by his shoulder as his name falls repeatedly from my lips. There's nothing but Ben—one of my alphas—and the knowledge that we belong to each other completely.

As we come down from the high, Ben presses his forehead to mine, eyes still closed as he savours the moment, his knot buried deep inside me. "Let's not move for just a minute," he whispers.

"Couldn't even if we wanted to," I giggle softly, content to stay wrapped in his arms—safe, loved, and utterly satisfied.

We finally unravel from each other as Ben's knot diminishes enough to carefully set me down on my feet.

Ben wraps the largest towel around me, tucking it in carefully. Kisses trail up my neck as he secures me within its fluffy embrace. "There," he says softly. "All bundled up."

I smile up at him, feeling like the luckiest omega in the whole Lake District. "Thank you," I murmur.

He simply winks at me and opens the bathroom door. The scent of freshly brewed coffee hits us as we step out.

Liam pops his head out of my room with that cheeky grin. "I've made up your nest with dry sheets, but feel free to undo the whole thing."

"Aww, thanks," I say with a grin, feeling lucid and happy after four knots. I'll need a lot more to come in the next couple of days, but for now, I can put this time to good use. Entering my room, I stare at the nest and shake my head with a laugh. "A for effort and A plus for the thought, but do you mind?" I wave my hand at the neat nest, which is entirely the problem. I want it messy and cosy. "Where's the blanket Henry gave me?"

"It's in the wash," Henry says, coming back into the room with coffee and snacks. "It was sodden." He chuckles.

"I want it back as soon as possible," I murmur, feeling a bit frantic that it's not in my possession. I grab the t-shirt he gave me instead, which I'd ripped off along with Liam's hoodie before the alphas came to find me because I was too hot and put that on, and then Ben's rugby shirt over it. It comes down to my knees, making me giggle as I grab the hoodie and put that on as well. Handing the damp towel back to Ben, I set to work fixing up the nest as best I can without the central part. I remind myself, as the anxiety of being away from it nearly rips me apart, that I'll have it back as soon as it's dry.

Henry watches with an amused twinkle in his eye as I attack the nest with a kind of organised chaos that only I could achieve. The snacks he's brought sit forgotten for a moment as I burrow into my new fortress of comfort, cushions and pillows flying as I arrange them just so.

"Sweetheart, you're going to bury yourself in there," he teases, setting down the tray on the nightstand.

I peek out from my cocoon of bedding. "That's the general idea," I laugh. "But don't worry, I'll come up for air... and food... and knots, naturally."

Liam snorts from the bed where he's made himself at home with a fondness in his gaze that sends a shiver of warmth through me. "I bet you'd surface faster if we dangled the blanket in front of you like bait."

Rolling my eyes, I toss a small pillow at him, which he catches effortlessly. "You know me too well, but yeah, basically."

Ben settles down next to Henry on the floor on the edge of my nest with a contented sigh, both looking at me with affectionate amusement. "Our little omega making her nest," Ben murmurs.

I beam at them, surrounded by softness and love. "My nest wouldn't be complete without my alphas."

Henry leans in first, planting a soft kiss on my lips before passing me a mug of coffee. "We're right here, sweetheart." His voice is as comforting as a warm blanket fresh out of the dryer.

Taking a sip of the coffee, I savour the rich flavour before turning to Liam with expectant eyes.

He gets the hint and slides in closer, offering me a plate of biscuits. "Wouldn't want you to go hungry with all the nest-building."

"You're trying to butter me up for later, aren't you?" I tease, taking one and biting into it with delight.

"Nah," Liam replies smoothly, his eyes twinkling, "Just keeping our omega fuelled and happy."

I relax back into the pillows, munching on the biscuit contentedly. The warmth from the bodies of my alphas envelopes me like a snug embrace, their presence both comforting and invigorating.

Ben reaches out to brush a crumb from my lip and then leans forward to follow it with a gentle kiss. "We'd do anything for you," he whispers against my mouth.

Henry chuckles softly. "I think we can safely say that our little omega is pampered."

I shoot him a mock glare from over the rim of my coffee mug. "And don't you forget it," I say with feigned haughtiness.

Liam's laugh fills the room as he stretches out on the bed, his body relaxed but his gaze still on me with affectionate warmth. It's funny how everything seems brighter when I'm with them—the world outside this room could be falling apart, but right here, everything is perfect.

Chapter 48

Zara

My lucid period fades after about an hour. When Henry disappears and returns with my blanket, which he places over me, all warm and soft from the dryer, I smile and feel the heat drag me under again.

He tucks the blanket around me, inhaling deeply, and the scent of Henry fills my senses along with the other two alphas, and it's gorgeous. It sends a wave of blissful satisfaction tumbling through me. My eyes begin to droop as the heat weaves its magic, lulling me into a state of drowsy contentment.

Ben's hand traces patterns on my back, gentle and soothing, while Liam's fingers entwine with mine, holding them gently. "You're being pulled under again," Ben murmurs.

My eyelids flutter as I fight the urge to curl up in

a ball, wanting to savour every lucid moment with my alphas. But the struggle becomes too much. The cramps start, and every bone in my body aches.

"Please," I murmur, slurring it like I'm drunk, and the only thing that matters is the knots from my alphas.

My voice is soft, barely a whisper, but it has them leaping into action. They move towards me, touching me, caressing me, kissing me all over.

Henry leans in closer, his breath warm against my ear. "You know we're here for you, always ready to give you what you need," he whispers before capturing my lips in a deep and passionate kiss that leaves me breathless.

Liam's fingers graze along my arm before his hand settles on my hip, as I melt into Henry's kiss. His touch is firm but gentle, a silent promise that he'll take care of me. Ben's hands are on the other side—a perfect balance that envelops me completely.

Henry's kiss becomes more insistent, his tongue tangling with mine while Liam and Ben each take a side, their mouths trailing hot kisses down my sides and towards my exposed pussy.

I arch into their touches, craving the connection, the fulfilment only they can provide.

Together, they peel away the layers between us until I'm naked, my breath quickening with anticipation. They surround me; three alphas completely in tune with my body and its needs.

Henry's hand slides down between us, fingers teasing over sensitive skin, making me gasp. "You're so ready for us," he murmurs.

Liam leans back slightly to admire me, his gaze full of adoration. "Our gorgeous omega," he says with a smile.

Ben moves down my body, his lips worshipping every inch of skin as he goes. The heat from his mouth sends sparks of pleasure radiating through me, and I squirm under their combined attention.

With each kiss and touch, the sense of anticipation builds. My alphas know every curve and contour of my body already, navigating me towards ecstasy with expert precision. They are unhurried, yet their movements have an underlying hunger that matches mine.

Liam's hands are firm on my thighs, gently parting them, while Ben's exploration continues its descent until his breath whispers across the most intimate part of me. A gasp escapes me as Henry kisses along my collarbone, his teeth gently grazing the skin, sending another shiver through me.

Their energy is infectious—three alphas completely attuned to our collective desire—and I'm lost in the sensation of being adored by them.

Ben settles between my thighs with a devilish grin before he gives me a taste of his wicked tongue. The sensation is electric and I let out a sound that is half-moan, half-scream, which ends in a feral purr, which excites the alphas around me. A mesh of growls is returned to me and I shiver with the possessiveness coursing through each of us.

Liam captures my mouth in another kiss, swallowing the sounds of my pleasure, his hand intertwining with mine, holding me steady as waves of desire crash over me. I squeeze his hand, anchoring myself to the moment, to him. Ben licks and sucks my clit into his mouth, tasting my slick and devouring me as if it's the only thing that will satisfy him.

Then he rises and enters me slowly—so fucking slowly—and it's both torture and bliss. I tilt my hips up to meet him, urging him deeper without speaking a single word.

Liam's voice is a low groan in my ear. "That's it, princess. Take him in like a good little omega."

His encouragement sends a surge of warmth through me.

With each thrust from Ben, I'm pushed closer and closer to the edge. The room is filled with the sounds of our union—the slick soaking my pussy is covering Ben's cock, making it easy access for him to keep pounding me, to bury himself even deeper.

They move together seamlessly around me and inside me, and I'm at the centre of it all—cherished and worshipped.

"Can you take two of us, princess?" Liam murmurs. "Two knots?"

My eyes, on the verge of closing, snap open. "Wha—?" I ask with shock. That would be something else, but I'm not sure I'm built that way.

He chuckles. "Let's see if she can take two knots," he says to Ben, who looks as shocked as I do.

But then he's all in. He sits back, dragging me onto him, his cock still deep in my pussy. I straddle him, feeling weak and fuzzy as Liam comes up behind me. He cups my breasts as Henry joins us to the side, watching eagerly to see if this is something I can do. I'm not so sure, but the heat is screaming at me that two knots are better than one, so get on with it, already.

Liam pushes me forward slightly and positions his cock at my already stuffed pussy. My mouth drops open as I feel him push himself inside next to Ben's huge cock.

"Fuck," I purr loudly as it feels overwhelming at first, but the slick pouring out of me is easing his way.

My pussy stretches, accommodating them both, and the sensation is like nothing I've ever felt before. It's fullness; it's completion. I purr, a constant sound that makes them react in a way that can only be described as feral, as they start to pound me together.

"Look at you," Henry says, his voice thick with desire. "So fucking perfect for us."

Liam's hands grip my waist, guiding me onto them with each forceful drive. The room is spinning, and I'm lost in the symphony of growls and my purring.

Ben cups the back of my head, pulling me closer to him. He kisses me deeply, hungrily, as if trying to merge our souls into one. The intensity of his kiss almost distracts me from the escalating pleasure building inside me, but not quite.

I can feel their knots starting to swell inside me, that unmistakable pressure that feels like it might rip me wide open. But I don't fucking care. I want it. I *need* it.

"Yes," I manage to breathe out between half moan, half purrs. "Yes, knot me."

"That's it," Liam encourages, his voice strained with effort. "You're taking us so beautifully, princess."

The praise pushes me towards the brink of my climax.

"Are you ready for us?" Ben grunts.

"Yes," I breathe out. I'm panting now, every fibre

of my being focused on the incredible feeling of being claimed by two alphas at once.

My vision blurs as I come hard around them, clenching and releasing in rapid waves that seem to coax their knots to inflate and lock inside me. They both roar, a sound that vibrates through the room like thunder, as they spill their cum into me. The dual sensation of them pulsing in my tight pussy sends aftershocks cascading through my body, and I keep purring, unable to stop the sound that's a siren call to them.

Henry moves closer, his lips claiming mine in a searing kiss that steals what little breath I have left. "You're fucking incredible," he rasps against my mouth. His fingers trace down my body, adding another layer of sensation, but I'm so sensitive now that even his light touch feels like a direct jolt to my core.

The heat and strength of Liam and Ben as they hold me, their bodies still joined with mine in the most primal way possible, is the most incredible feeling. I feel like I'm flying high on a cloud of ecstasy. We're a tangle of limbs and shared satisfaction, riding out the waves of pleasure as they gradually recede.

As we come back to earth, I realise that we're not just connected physically now; something has shifted between us. This new intimacy has bound us together even tighter—if that's possible. We belong to each other completely.

"Mating," I pant. "I want it now." I gaze down into Ben's eyes, needing his permission. I know the other two are already there, but Ben... he is the one who will turn this into a mating or simply three alphas and their future omega.

He gazes back at me with an intensity that makes my mouth go dry. He opens his mouth, but nothing comes out.

Chapter 49

Benjamin

I'm speechless for a second, completely blindsided by the raw honesty in her eyes. There's no way I can deny her—deny us—what we all clearly want. My voice comes out hoarse, emotion clogging my throat. "Yes," I say firmly, locking my gaze with hers. "Mating. I want that, too."

Liam and Henry echo in agreement, their voices a rugged chorus of consent. We're all on the same page now; there's no turning back.

There's an electric charge that zips through us. It's like we've ignited something ancient and powerful—something that transcends the mere physical connection we've just shared.

The knots are still swollen inside her, but that doesn't stop me from reaching up to pull her in for a searing kiss. I feel like an alpha who's just won the lottery without even buying a ticket.

"Our omega," Liam says with a reverence that sends another rush of pride through me.

"Our Zara," Henry murmurs, and his thumb brushes over her lips in a tender gesture.

She smiles down at me with such love and trust that it nearly undoes me. "Our forever," she whispers, the weight of the promise clear in her voice.

It's not just sex now. It's not just heat or temporary pleasure. This is life-changing; it's destiny intertwining our fates.

"Are you sure about this? It's not just your heat—"

She presses her fingers to my lips. "I'm sure. I'm lucid enough right now to want this with every cell in my body. Bite me, Ben. Mate me before Liam and Henry do the same. I want to bite you back and have us entwined forever. I will never leave you and Mia. Never. You are part of my heart and soul. All of you are."

She is saying everything I need to hear. Mia, my precious baby girl who has already lost one mother, cannot go through that again. But I truly believe that Zara is my one. I thought Nicole was. But what we had wasn't *this*. Not by a long shot. It paled in comparison and was weak and feeble. Zara bursting into my life is a revelation, and I'm not going to let fear hold me back.

I cup the back of Zara's neck and draw her close to my mouth. I bare my teeth, grazing them over her jugular.

"I'm ready for eternity with you," she murmurs, and I don't need anything else to convince me this is perfect.

I sink my teeth gently into her flesh, marking her as mine for life. The taste of her is intoxicating; her sweet submission floods through me. My body solidifies the promise with a deep rumble that seems to resonate with the very foundation of the earth.

She gasps, but it's a sound of completion rather than pain. I can feel it—the bond hovering, ready to be completed by her bite to me. It's something more profound than anything I could've imagined. It's like we're not just two people anymore; we're pieces of a picture finally put together to form a whole image.

Liam and Henry are watching us with eyes full of emotions—happiness, relief, and an overwhelming sense of belonging.

As I relinquish my bite, making sure it's gentle, I gaze down at her neck and see the perfect imprint of my teeth, the blood oozing out of the wound but, it's not just a bite; it's a symbol of eternal commitment. A brand that says she's mine, unquestionably and unconditionally.

"Bite me," I murmur, giving her my consent in words.

She nods, her eyes fixed on the bite scar that Nicole gave me.

"Yes," I say firmly. "'Right over the top. I don't want any reminders of her, to you or to me. Claim me completely, take me from her with everything inside you, Zara. Make me yours and only yours."

Her eyes light up at my words. Possession fills her gaze as she leans in and presses her lips over the bite mark.

Her teeth sink in, and a surge of heat floods through me, hotter and more potent than any heat I've felt before. It's like she's searing her claim onto my soul, and I welcome it without hesitation. Her bite is firm but careful, a perfect mirror of what I've given her.

A growl rumbles through me—a primal sound of possession and satisfaction. There's no pain, only a profound sense of rightness as our bond snaps into place, stronger than steel. It's as if all the fragmented parts of me are finally making sense.

When she pulls back, her lips are stained with

my blood, and there's a gleam in her eyes that tells me she knows she's won me over entirely. "You're mine now," she says, her voice low and fierce.

"Forever," I affirm, feeling the weight of the word settle into my chest. It feels like coming home—like I've been wandering aimlessly and have just found my way back to where I belong.

My knot deflates alongside Liam's, but we are nowhere close to be being done yet. Liam grips her long waves in his fist and presses his mouth to her neck from behind. "My turn?"

"Yes," she rasps, and she tilts her head to give Liam better access to the spot he's eyeing. The room is thick with the scent of our mingled arousal, the air charged with the energy of our newly formed bond. I watch, a fierce thrill coursing through me, as Liam leans in and marks her with the same care and reverence I did.

Henry isn't still either; his hands roam over her body with a gentle possessiveness that only an alpha can have towards his omega. His touches are whispers of promises yet to be kept, each one eliciting soft moans from Zara that stoke the fire. I slip out of her pussy as Henry watches, just as I do, both of us filled with a sense of pride and satisfaction at this union we're completing together. There's no jealousy here, just pure, unadulterated love for our omega and for each other.

Liam releases her from the bite, and she pulls herself off his cock to turn to him. "Bite me, princess," he growls, exposing his neck to her.

Zara's hands tremble slightly, not from fear but from the sheer intensity of the moment. Her gaze searches Liam's, and there's a silent understanding that passes between them—a promise of infinite tomorrows. She reaches up, her fingers brushing against the strong column of his throat, feeling his pulse race under her touch.

Her mouth descends on him with a passion that matches the depth of her feelings. When her teeth break the skin, Liam's entire body shudders, a low growl escaping him. His hands find their way into her hair, not to guide or control, but to connect, to feel every inch of this pivotal moment.

The bond between them ignites with an unspoken power, a silent explosion that intertwines their destinies. Zara is lost in the sensation, the taste of Liam's essence on her tongue, and the knowledge that she belongs to these three alphas—to three soulmates who will protect and cherish her for eternity.

Now it's Henry's turn to step forward, his expression one of sheer adoration mixed with an unmistakable alpha presence.

"I have a request," Henry murmurs.

"Okay," Zara whispers. "Hit me with it."

We wait as Henry gathers her to him, his cock ready to impale her and give her what she needs before her period of lucidity recedes.

Chapter 50

Henry

I pull her down onto my cock without any hesitation. She gasps as I fill her sensitive pussy up with an engorged cock, so turned on by everything that has happened.

"Bite me first," I murmur against her lips.

Her sharp intake of breath makes me chuckle slightly. I've shocked her, but I want to be hers, all hers, before I make her mine.

Zara's eyes meet mine, and there's a flicker of surprise that quickly morphs into a fiery determination. She understands what I'm asking, what this means to us both. It's not just about the physical connection; it's about the trust, the mutual surrender to each other.

She lifts her hand and gently traces the outline of my jaw before bringing her lips to mine in a soft kiss that promises so much more. Then she pulls back just enough to look into my eyes before she slowly, deliberately, moves her mouth to my neck. I tilt my head to the side, baring myself completely to her. The room is silent except for our heavy breathing and the beating of our hearts, which seems loud in my ears. When her teeth finally sink into my flesh, it's a sensation that rocks me to the core—a searing heat that floods through me, marking me as Zara's in a way that no one else has ever done.

When she releases me, she smiles up at me, a wicked gleam in her eye as she whispers, "Now you're mine."

"Completely."

I cup the back of her head and kiss her sweetly before I tilt her head to the side.

"Yes," she purrs. "Now."

She grinds down on me, riding me wildly. She trembles in my arms, coming hard around my cock, which makes my knot inflate suddenly inside her as I shoot my load deep into her. I bite down, and she screams, feeling our bond locking into place.

We're lost in each other, nothing else existing beyond the confines of this room where our lives have become irrevocably entwined. Zara's cries are a symphony to my ears, the sound of an omega completely and utterly fulfilled. The way she clings to me, her nails digging slightly into my back, is everything.

As I release her from my mating bite, Liam's voice breaks through the haze of satisfaction that's enveloping me. "Fuck, that was intense," he says, and even his usual playful tone is laced with awe.

The intensity was more than I anticipated, yet exactly what I craved. I wrap my arms around Zara even tighter, if that's possible, revelling in the softness of her skin against mine.

Zara's eyes flutter open after what feels like an eternity. She looks between us all, a dazed but blissful smile spreading across her face.

"You're stuck with us now," I tease gently, brushing a stray lock of hair from her sweat-dampened forehead.

"And that's exactly where I want to be," Zara breathes out, her voice weak but filled with a joy that sends another wave of contentment crashing through me.

Liam, Ben, and I exchange a look over Zara's head, an unspoken understanding that we've all crossed a threshold together. There's no going back from here, not that any of us would want to. Our connection is solidified, strengthened by the trust and the passion we've just shared. Zara sits on my knot, slumped against me, her head resting on my shoulder. I ease her down, so she is lying on her side next to me, joined in this intimate way that has brought me so much joy and peace, I never want to leave.

"Sleep now, sweetheart. We will be here when you wake."

Zara's breath slows and deepens, her body relaxed against mine, the exhaustion of the moment catching up with her. Her eyelids flutter shut, the long lashes casting shadows on her cheeks, and I marvel at how peaceful she looks in the aftermath. She's got a post-mating glow about her, and it makes my chest tighten with emotions I'm still trying to understand.

"Should we stay like this?" Ben asks quietly, his voice filled with concern as he gazes down at Zara's sleeping form.

"Yeah," Liam agrees. "She'll want to wake up with all of us here. Makes it more real, doesn't it?"

I nod, feeling a sense of protectiveness surge through me. I'm acutely aware of the weight of her in my arms, of how right it feels. It's like every piece of my life has suddenly snapped into place with Zara at the centre of it all. My knot deflates, and I pull out of her, dragging the blanket I bought her over her naked body.

The room settles into a comfortable silence as we each find our own way to relax while still being close to Zara. Liam stretches out in the nest beside her, his hand finding its way to hers and intertwining their fingers.

"I'm going to get the first aid kit. See to all these bites before they get infected." Ben says, hovering for a moment before deciding to get up and be practical, which makes Liam and I laugh softly.

"Good thinking, prime alpha," Liam murmurs.

My eyes drift closed for just a moment, but I fight the lure of sleep. I want to be awake when Zara stirs.

Ben returns with a small white box, the contents rattling slightly as he sets it down on the floor beside the bed. He gives us a wry grin and starts cleaning Zara's bites first. I watch him, admiring his gentle touch as he tends to Zara's needs, even when she's unconscious. It's these small acts of care that build the foundation of our relationship—each of us looking out for one another.

She flinches in her sleep but doesn't wake. She nestles further into the nest as Ben turns his attention to Liam, cleaning the wrist bite first and then the neck one.

Liam is still holding Zara's hand, his thumb stroking over her knuckles in a soothing rhythm, and I can tell he's just as captivated by her as I am. He catches my eye for a second and smiles, that cheeky grin that always promises mischief. But there's something else there now, a depth of feeling that wasn't as evident before. This bond has changed us all.

Ben moves closer to me, cleaning the bite mark on my neck and wrist before he starts to do his own.

"Here. I'll do it," I murmur, holding my hand out for the antiseptic wipe.

He smiles and hands it over and I get to work, making sure he is fixed up as he did to us.

We're quiet for a while, each lost in our thoughts. There's a tranquillity that follows the storm of our passions; it's a silence filled with contentment and the weight of what we've become to each other.

"How does it feel?" I ask Ben quietly, curiosity getting the better of me.

"You mean Zara's bite over Nicole's?" he asks with a wry smile. "Like it was meant to be."

"Good," I murmur and sit back.

"So, the bitch is dead?" Liam asks. "Or the last of the bond, at least?"

"It was dead the second I laid eyes on Zara. I just wasn't ready to admit it," he murmurs, eyes on our omega.

Ben's confession resonates in the silence, like the final click of a lock falling into place, and we all feel it. The past, with its pain and complications, doesn't hold sway over us anymore. It's about the now, about Zara, and the life we're building together.

"Yeah," Liam agrees, squeezing Zara's hand gently. "Funny how it takes being knocked over the head with something this good to see what's been missing."

We chuckle at that because it's true; we'd all been missing something vital before Zara turned our world upside down in the best possible way.

"We're truly a pack now," Liam says after a while, his tone one of wonderment. "I mean, I knew we would be. But actually doing it..."

"It's real," I say simply.

"And perfect," Ben adds, his gaze never leaving Zara.

We watch over her as our whole reason for being now sleeps. There are no words needed among us; we just are.

Chapter 51

Zara

I wake up feeling like I'm wrapped in the softest, warmest blanket in the world. But it's not a blanket—it's Liam, Ben, and Henry's arms. My body feels tender and sated, and there is a gentle ache reminding me of what we've just shared. I let out a contented sigh, burrowing deeper into the cosy warmth of the nest.

Opening my eyes, I'm greeted by the sight of my alphas looking back at me with such open affection that it makes my heart feel like it might burst. The room is filled with early morning light now, and from somewhere outside comes the distant sound of birds chirping; it's a beautiful new day.

"Morning," I murmur sleepily.

"Morning, love," Henry responds. "You crashed for hours."

I giggle. "I was worn out."

"How are you feeling?" Ben asks as he strokes a stray lock of hair away from my face.

"Like I've been hit by a truck—in the best possible way."

Liam leans over and plants a soft kiss on my forehead. "We'll take care of you."

"I have no doubt about that."

The room is oddly peaceful, given the storm of emotions and activities from last night. There's no urgency or awkwardness like you might expect after such an intense encounter. It feels natural—like this is how it was always meant to be: the four of us together as one unit.

My brain is still a bit foggy with my heat, but the reality of the situation seeps through. We formed a pack, an unbreakable bond. As I glance at each of them, my heart swells with a feeling I can only describe as complete.

"So, what's for breakfast?" I ask, my stomach growling audibly to punctuate the question. The mood lightens even further.

"Whatever you want, sweetheart," Henry says with a chuckle. "I'm at your service."

"Hmm, pancakes. With loads of chocolate chips and whipped cream," I answer without missing a beat. "If we have any of that."

Liam nods approvingly. "A woman after my own heart."

"I'll go and buy it if I have to," he replies with a small smile.

He gracefully slips out of the nest. As he pads out of the room, his backside catches my eye, and I grin.

Liam catches my gaze following Henry and raises an eyebrow playfully. "Enjoying the view?"

I blush but don't look away. "Absolutely."

They laugh, and there's a teasing twinkle in their eyes that tells me they don't mind one bit.

The conversation turns light and easy as we chat about nothing in particular. The mundane routine of it all solidifies our acceptance and integration into this new way of living.

Before long, Henry returns bearing a tray that smells like heaven. The pancakes are fluffy as clouds and loaded with chocolate chunks, just like I wanted. There's no whipped cream, but that was a long shot anyway.

I'm surrounded by food and love, and it's hard to think of anything better than this. I watch them eat, their eyes occasionally meeting mine with such warmth that I have to look away, overwhelmed by the emotion of it all.

Henry's pancakes are genuinely amazing, and I

tell him so between bites. "You outdid yourself with these," I say earnestly.

He beams at me, looking ridiculously pleased with himself. "Only the best for my omega," he says with a mock bow.

Liam shakes his head, his eyes sparkling with mirth. "You're going to spoil her rotten."

"As she deserves," Ben murmurs.

We finish breakfast in a comfortable silence, sated and content. The dishes can wait; right now, this moment is all about us. Eventually, Liam stretches his long limbs and stands up, taking the tray with him.

"I'll take care of these," he declares, grabbing the plates.

"No, let me help," I start to say, but Henry pulls me back down beside him.

"Liam's got it. You're not moving from this spot," he insists gently but firmly.

I'm about to protest when Ben adds, "Henry's right. You need to rest after last night."

Despite my instinct to argue, I watch as, to my disappointment, Liam pulls on a pair of joggers and picks up the tray to take to the kitchen.

After a minute or so, the doorbell rings, and we stare at each other in surprise. "Are we expecting anyone?" I ask, raising an eyebrow.

"Mum?" Ben murmurs, clearly worried about Mia, which makes me worried now. Ben is already on his feet and pulling on his discarded pants, with Henry following.

"Stay right there," he murmurs as he and Ben leave the room.

Blinking, I purse my lips, hoping it's nothing. My cheeks flush, and my heat is returning after a long rest. I need the alphas back here soon. As I wait, I hear raised voices, and one of them is definitely *not* Ben's mum.

"Eddie," I hiss, hearing my ex's irritating voice filter up the stairs.

I roll my eyes so hard I'm worried they might get stuck that way. What on earth is he doing here? He's supposed to be a closed chapter in my life, a blip, an error in judgment, not someone standing on my doorstep causing a ruckus.

Groaning inwardly, I listen as the voices get louder. There's the sound of a scuffle and then silence. My heart races; what if Eddie's caused trouble? He was always good at stirring the pot and making a bloody mess. In an instant, I'm up and pulling on leggings and Ben's rugby shirt, which is the closest one to me. Heading downstairs, ready to confront Eddie, I see my three alphas in the doorway arguing the toss with this idiot.

"Eddie," I snap. "What the hell are you doing here? How did you even find me?"

The alphas part like the Red Sea as they hear my sharp voice, showing me the form of my previous boyfriend. He is shorter than these three, less muscular, almost weedy.

His arrogance is out in full force as he holds up his phone. "Tracked you. You think I let you wander around London without knowing your every move?"

"Liar," I hiss, knowing that's not true. *Or is it?*

"You did what?" Ben snarls, gripping Eddie by his tee. "You utter fucker."

"How?" I ask again, marching up to him.

"Zara, go upstairs," Henry murmurs. "We've got this."

"No!" I snap, but I'm not angry at Henry. "How?" I turn back to Eddie. "How?"

"Find My Phone. Wasn't difficult to hack into yours. I've been worried sick about you, Zara. You've made me worry, and I find you here with these three assholes. I've had to wait to come to find you. You knew I didn't have the money to come straight away and had to wait. You made me wait and worry—"

"Shut your fucking face before I rearrange it for you," Ben snarls, not having a single second of Eddie's gaslighting.

I step closer, anger simmering in my belly like a

storm about to break. "Worried? You're the last person who should be worried about me," I spit out, disbelief and contempt colouring my words. "You never gave a shit before, so why start now?"

Eddie's gaze flickers to the alphas, a sneer twisting his lips. "Because you're mine, Zara. And you belong in London with me, not here playing house with..." He looks the alphas up and down with evident disdain.

Before he can finish, Henry steps forward, his voice low and dangerous. "She's not a possession, you cock. She's more than you'll ever deserve or understand."

Liam flanks me protectively while Ben still has a fistful of Eddie's shirt. The tension crackles in the air, but then Liam's voice cuts through it all, calm and collected. "Eddie, you need to leave. Now."

Eddie tries to shrug off Ben's grip but fails miserably. "Oh, no. This isn't over," he warns, pointing a finger at us. "Zara is mine."

"It *is* over," I say firmly. "It was over the moment I left you." My heart pounds with defiance as I stare him down.

"You're sadly mistaken there, pal," Liam says, stepping forward and giving Eddie a rough shove away from Ben and further down the path away from the house. He has gone feral, and I gulp. "You see,

Zara is ours. She is our mate, so if you want her, you have to get through us first. Are you up for that?"

Eddie's face pales as he realises the physical difference between him and the wall of muscle that is my alphas. He takes a step back, his mouth opening and closing like a fish out of water.

"No, she's—" Eddie starts, but his voice is wavering now, the cockiness seeping away with each passing second.

"Yeah, I thought not," Liam sneers. "Take your pathetic self out of here and don't ever come back. If you think tracking her was clever, just remember we will do much more than that to protect what's ours."

Eddie's scowl falters. "Fuck this," he spits out, taking a step back. "You think you can just take her away from me? You think I'll just walk away?"

"That's exactly what you're going to do," I interject, my voice steady even though my heart is hammering against my ribs. "Because if you don't, then they'll have to answer your question, won't they?"

Eddie's eyes dart between the three men, clearly reassessing his odds. For a moment, uncertainty flickers across his face. A bead of sweat rolls down his forehead as he realises that these aren't the type of men you mess with—not when it comes to their mate.

"Zara," he tries one last time, aiming for a softer

tone that comes off as insincere and desperate. "Come back with me. We can sort this out."

I shake my head firmly. "There's nothing to sort out. I'm happy now and mated. You need to leave."

Eddie's defiance crumbles as he sees no leeway, no sympathy in my stance or in the eyes of the alphas. With a huff of frustration and a glare that could curdle milk, he turns on his heel and storms off down the path, his retreat a sharp contrast to his earlier bravado.

Ben releases a deep breath and rakes a hand through his hair. "What an absolute tool," he mutters, a look of pure disgust etched on his face. Liam nods in agreement, his protective stance easing now that the threat has dissipated. Henry reaches out to gently touch my arm, a silent offer of comfort.

I let out a long sigh, feeling the adrenaline start to ebb away from my body. The fear and anger that had surged through me now gives way to relief and an overwhelming sense of being loved and protected.

"You guys okay?" I ask, glancing up at each of them in turn. Their gazes soften as they look back at me.

"We're good, Zara," Henry says, his voice gentle but with an undercurrent of steel that suggests he would take on the world for me if he had to.

"As long as you're safe, that's all that matters," Liam adds with a reassuring smile.

Ben wraps his arms around me in a tight hug, lifting me off my feet for a moment. "No one gets to treat you like that," he says fiercely when he puts me down. "You're our omega, our heart."

I smile up at them, feeling incredibly lucky despite the close call. "My alphas," I say softly. The words are simple, but they carry the weight of my gratitude and love.

"Do we have to worry about him coming back?" I murmur.

Henry shakes his head, his gaze firm and reassuring. "He won't be back. He knows he's outmatched, and we made it clear that there will be consequences if he tries anything again."

Liam nods in agreement, his hand finding mine and giving it a comforting squeeze. "We'll keep an eye out just in case, but I doubt he has the balls to show his face around here after today."

"And if he does, we'll kick his ass back to London before he can blink," Ben says.

The air is lighter now, the tension having dissipated with Eddie's retreat. I'm not worried. Eddie would have to be stupider than he looks to come back here now. He expected to find me weak and broken, just like he found me all those months ago. But Liam is right. He is sadly mistaken. I'm not that same woman. Not anymore. I'm more than I ever have been with my three alphas by my side. Ben shuts the door and locks it.

"The thing about bullies like him is they will always back down where there's a bigger bully. He's a coward. We don't need to worry about him."

"So, you consider yourselves big bullies now?" I giggle.

"For you, we will be anything." His dazzling smile is enough for me to leap at him. He catches me and slams me up against the wall, rattling my bones as he drags his cock out of his joggers.

"Mine," Ben growls as he thrusts into me.

"Yours," I purr, slicking up his cock instantly. The pleasure builds rapidly, threatening to consume me whole as my alpha pounds into me, bringing me to a rapid climax before he knots me hard and fierce, plastered against the wall, as my other two alphas watch with heated gazes.

I allow myself to fall into the lull of my heat and place my trust in these men who will do anything for me.

Chapter 52

Zara

Many knots later, my heat passes, and I feel invigorated and renewed. As I tidy up my nest, I smile. Susan is bringing Mia home soon, and I want to be all tidied up and ready to cuddle her and devote my attention to her. I wonder if she will know I'm now her stepmama. Will she have a sense of the family we've created? She's only three months old, but I like to think she would feel the warmth and love that fills our home. Like she can sense that the people who surround her are bound together by a fierce, protective love.

Making my way downstairs, I see Liam and Henry in the open doorway, screwdrivers in hand, while Ben glares at a piece of paper in front of him.

"What are you doing?" I ask with a smirk.

Ben turns to me, and his glare turns into a grin. "Trying to install this doorbell cam. Just in case."

"Trying?"

"It's harder than it looks," Liam grumbles.

"Why didn't you get a wireless one?"

"Because we want it on all the time, not just an app on your phone," Henry grunts.

Fair enough.

"Did you try YouTube? Cuz, you know, I fixed the bathroom door lock after a tutorial."

Three sets of alpha eyes turn to give me annoyed stares. "YouTube?" Liam scoffs. "No. We've got this."

Giggling as I hold my hands up and leave them to it, I go to the kitchen to brew up. I'm sure a nice cuppa will help ease the alpha-ness, and they'll be more amenable.

There's some bustling going on and then a wail as I assume Susan and Mia have arrived.

Hurrying back to the front door, I see Ben holding Mia close, breathing in her little baby scent and a look of adoration on his face.

"Hey, baby," I murmur, going to them and stroking her head. "How is she?"

"Better, her temperature is back to normal," Susan says, pushing past the alphas in the doorway with a curious stare.

"Don't ask," I say with a snicker. "Tea?"

"Love one," she says, and we leave the men and baby to sort out the camera.

I can feel her eyes on me as I make her a cup of tea, and then she clears her throat. "Thank you," she blurts out.

Frowning, I turn to her. "What for?"

"Being you." She flings her arms around me, tears in her eyes.

I return her hug with a smile. "I know this is sudden, but when you know, you know. You know?"

"I know," she says, pulling away and reaching for the kitchen roll to tear a piece off to dab at her eyes. "I'm just so happy Ben has found the right one. I never liked that Nicole," she says under her breath. "We tried to tell him, but he wouldn't listen, and then she got pregnant… You know what? None of that matters now. You're here, and you've made him happy. I can see it in his eyes."

"I won't hurt him," I murmur, knowing she needs to hear that.

"I know you won't. You're a good woman, Zara. A good omega and a wonderful mother to Mia."

Tears prick my eyes at this validation. I smile at Susan, warmth swelling in my chest. "Thank you," I murmur back. "That means a lot coming from you."

With two cups of tea cradled in my hands, with Susan bringing the third, we make our way back to the commotion that is now our front door. The sight that greets me makes me chuckle; Ben is muttering under his breath, holding the instruction manual upside down, while Liam and Henry seem to be having a silent argument over which screw goes where.

"Here," I say, extending the peace offering of a steaming cup towards them. Ben looks up, gratefully accepting the tea and taking a long sip before turning back to the doorbell cam with renewed determination.

"We don't need YouTube," Liam insists again, taking his tea, though his tone holds less conviction this time.

"Didn't say anything," I say before bending down to pick Mia up from where she's gurgling happily in her pram next to the men.

Susan and I exchange smiles and she says, "Well, I'll leave you to it. You look like you've got your hands full." She gives Mia a soft kiss and a tickle under her chin, and then she leaves, shaking her head, her shoulders shaking as she holds back the laugh, I know she's dying to let out because I am too.

Once she's gone, the alphas finally concede defeat – sort of.

"Fine," Henry says, putting down his tea on the

side table. "Let's give it a quick glance, just to check our progress, yeah?"

There's a comical huddle around Liam's phone as they watch and then mimic the steps.

"I knew that," Liam huffs out. "See?" He proves it by showing the alphas what to do... apparently.

I settle on the couch with Mia cradled in my arms, watching these big, tough alphas fumble through instructions designed for mere mortals. I can't help the laughter that bubbles from my lips when Liam drops a screw, and it rolls into oblivion, only to be followed by Henry's cursing as he tries to search for it.

"We're supposed to be good at this," Liam mumbles, almost like he's admitting defeat to the universe.

"You are good at many things," I assure him with a grin. "This is just not one of them."

Ben gives me a mock glare over his shoulder. "Tea and sarcasm, is it? That's what we're getting now?"

"Absolutely," I respond, popping a dummy into Mia's mouth as she starts to fuss. "It's part of the service."

Mia settles down, sucking contentedly as the boys resume their task. They look like some sort of modern art installation – three handsome men in various states of DIY disarray. Finally, there's a triumphant click, and the doorbell cam lights up.

"Ha! Got it!" Ben exclaims. His eyes meet mine, and there's triumph mixed with relief in them.

"Yes, you got it," I say dryly. "YouTube got it."

"Shut up," Liam grins now, shaking his head but there's no annoyance in his eyes, just playful irritation.

Henry stands back, wipes his hands on his jeans as if he's just finished a masterpiece. "Check it every single time, Zara. Every single time. Okay?"

I give him a mock salute. "Got it, boss."

He gives me the finger back, which makes me snort and jostle Mia into wriggling in my arms. "Nice," I say.

He grins as I stand up and take Mia upstairs. She is ready for a bottle and some cuddle time. Ben follows me as I knew he would.

When we get to the top of the stairs, Ben's hand finds the small of my back, a light touch that brings comfort and warmth along with it. I feel him close behind me as we walk into Mia's nursery, the pastel colours and soft fabrics inviting us into a world filled with peace and love.

"Need a hand?" Ben asks, watching me prepare the bottle, his eyes flickering over Mia and then back to me.

"I've got it," I say. "Unless you want to feed her? You must've missed her these last few days."

"More than I thought possible," he murmurs, but doesn't move to take her from me.

He watches us as I sit, his gaze softening when Mia latches onto the bottle with an eager little noise that fill the room with life. She gazes up at me with those big eyes that are just like Ben's, full of trust and innocence.

This moment feels like one of those quiet triumphs that nobody talks about – the simple act of feeding your child while surrounded by love. It's these moments I want to hold on to, to remember when things get chaotic or when doubts creep in at the edges.

Ben seems to understand without a word spoken; he moves closer until he's sitting on the arm of the big, cosy chair, his arm comes around us in a casual embrace – protection, love, support all bundled into one effortless gesture.

"You're amazing, you know that?" he murmurs into my hair, his breath warm against my skin. I can feel his chest vibrate with the timbre of his voice, a soothing rumble that's as comforting as the chair I'm nestled in.

"I'm just feeding Mia," I reply, trying to downplay the moment, but internally I'm basking in his praise.

"That's just it, though, isn't it? You make it seem so simple, so easy. But you're doing everything, Zara. You've single-handedly brought this family together. It was broken, shattered into a million pieces, and you fixed it," Ben says. He presses a kiss to the top of my head, and it feels like a seal over his words – a promise, a recognition.

I laugh softly, shaking my head. "I'm hardly doing it all on my own. I've got you three as my right-hand men."

"Right-hand alpha mates," he corrects me teasingly. "You can't forget that part."

"How could I?" I snort gently, careful not to disturb Mia, who is now half-asleep, her sucking slowing down as she drifts off.

"We try our best," Ben says with mock solemnity, and then his tone shifts to something lighter. "And speaking of trying our best," he continues with a smirk, "I think Liam and Henry have plans for tonight after Mia's down for the night."

"Oh? Do these plans involve more DIY disasters?" I ask with raised eyebrows.

Ben chuckles slowly. "Hopefully not. But perhaps a quiet dinner? Liam found a recipe for a curry that he's convinced he can master. Henry, not so convinced, is there to supervise and hopefully make it edible." He chuckles.

"Sounds perfect," I say, finishing Mia's feeding and gently burping her before laying her in her cot. She's a little slice of heaven, and I swear she understands every word we say. "We all need a quiet night. Good food, a bit of wine, and the best company," I add, feeling the energy in the room lighten.

Ben stands up and stretches his arms above his head. "Should we leave them to it then? Let's see if they can handle dinner without setting off the smoke alarm."

I laugh lightly. "I have faith in Liam's cooking skills—or at least Henry's ability to salvage them."

We make our way downstairs, where Liam and Henry are already arguing.

"It's not rocket science," Liam is saying with a huff, his hands brandishing various spice jars like weapons.

Henry snatches one from him. "Yeah, but it might as well be with you in charge."

It's all banter, though. "I think Liam can handle it," I say, giving him a bright smile before I turn to Henry and add, "It's just that his enthusiasm sometimes outpaces his skill set."

Henry lets out a loud guffaw as Ben tries not to laugh too hard.

I perch on a barstool at the kitchen island, ready to watch the show. Ben pours me a glass of wine and joins me, our knees brushing as he sits on the stool beside mine.

Liam looks over at us with a fierce glare, but the glint in his eyes gives him away. "Watch it, or I'll ban you from the first taste test," he warns, though the smirk on his lips tells me it's an empty threat.

Henry shakes his head, rummaging through the fridge for the chicken. "Just concentrate on not burning down the kitchen, mate."

I sip my wine, feeling content as I watch the two of them bicker and move around each other with an ease that speaks of years of friendship turned into something more meaningful. We are a true pack: friends, lovers, and everything in between.

"We've done well – more than well – and this life we're creating is as real and beautiful as anything I could have ever hoped for," Ben says, taking my hand and kissing my knuckles. "Thank you for coming into our lives and staying even though I'm a bad-tempered asshole."

"You're not really bad-tempered, and there was never any doubt I would stay. I knew you needed me, you and Mia."

We share a smile and the sound of sizzling from the stove as Liam finally starts cooking, which has

Henry darting over to lower the heat. The scene is chaotic but strangely harmonic, like an orchestra warming up before a performance.

As they continue their masterpiece, Liam stirring the curry with Henry directing every move – I lean into Ben, feeling his warmth against my side.

Happiness fills my soul, and I hope that my parents would've approved of this pack we've created and are building on with shared memories and love.

Chapter 53

Benjamin

I watch Zara's eyes sparkling with the kind of love and contentment that seeps out into the room, infecting everyone with a dose of feel-good. I think how lucky I am. How lucky we all are to have her in our lives.

"Henry, mate, you're hovering like a bloody helicopter. Let me breathe, will you?" Liam complains, turning his focus back on the sizzling pan. But he's got that softness in his voice that means he's only half serious.

Henry just raises an eyebrow at him and steps back with a smirk, giving Liam his coveted breathing space. "Just making sure we don't end up with charcoal for dinner."

I lean over to Zara and whisper, "Ten quid says they'll end up with curry on the ceiling." I'm rewarded with her snorting laughter that she tries to stifle with her hand.

We sit in comfortable silence for a moment, watching the chaos in the kitchen unfold. I've come to love these moments. The place was cold and unfeeling with Nicole. Now, we're not just existing together; we're living—a proper family. Mia is safe and loved upstairs and we're about to enjoy a home-cooked meal courtesy of our very own culinary duo.

The smell of spices fills the air, and Liam finally looks like he's got a handle on the curry situation. He gives it a taste and seems pleasantly surprised. "Shit, this is actually good," he says with genuine wonder.

Henry slaps him on the back. "Told you it'd be fine if you actually followed the recipe."

I catch Zara's eye and nod towards the pan. "Looks like I owe you ten quid," I say with a chuckle.

She shakes her head, amusement dancing in her eyes. "Keep your money, love. I'd rather bet on how many times Liam will sneak tastes before it's actually served."

"Okay, you're on," I agree, grateful for the lightness we've cultivated in this house. The tension that used to hang heavy is gone, replaced by laughter, the occasional culinary mishap, and a whole lot of love.

Mia starts fussing over the baby monitor, cutting through our bets and merriment. I stand up from my stool. "I've got her," I say, already moving towards the stairs.

Back upstairs, I pick Mia up from her cot and cradle her against my chest. She quiets almost immediately, big blue eyes staring up at me as if I'm the only thing that matters to her. "Hey there, little one," I whisper, rocking her gently. "It's not just us anymore. You've got an amazing woman downstairs who loves you more than life itself. *That* is what you deserve, my precious girl. You will never know the pain of being without a mum because you have one. A better one. The *best* one anyone could ask for."

Mia gurgles, grabbing onto my finger with her tiny hand, and it's like she understands.

I sway gently back and forth, and murmur, "One day, hopefully soon, you will have a brother or sister and then more after that. Daddy wants this house filled with love for you, sweet girl."

I turn as I hear a noise behind me.

Zara stands there with tears in her eyes and holds up the baby monitor. "Could hear you."

"I know," I reply with a smile.

"You really want more babies?" she asks carefully.

"So many. Are you up for that?"

"With you three? More than up for it. I want it."

I nod, grateful for this omega who has shown me what love is supposed to look like.

Mia's soft breathing syncs with mine until she's calm enough to lay back down. I tuck her in her cot, my heart full to bursting.

We head back downstairs, hand in hand, smiling like idiots in love.

"Just in time," Liam announces as he removes the curry from the heat, his face flushed from both the cooker and pride.

Zara lets go of me and crosses over to him, wrapping her arms around him. "You're perfect, and this is going to be amazing," she murmurs before he swoops down to kiss her.

"Aww, shucks," he chuckles, pulling back. "But leave the praise until after."

"Deal."

Henry starts to set the table, placing a kiss on Zara's forehead as she passes by him. "You okay?" he asks gently.

"Yeah, just overwhelmed, but in a good way," she replies, helping him with the plates.

Liam looks over at us, a knowing twinkle in his eye. "So, what are we celebrating?"

Zara and I exchange a glance, and it's like there's an invisible thread that connects us all. It doesn't need words – it's written in our shared laughter and the ease of our movements around each other.

"We're celebrating family," I say finally, pulling out the chairs for us to sit down. "And what we have now, and what's hopefully coming soon."

Their faces light up with comprehension and joy, as we sit down to eat. The curry is perfect—flavourful and just the right amount of spice. Liam's proud grin is infectious as we heap praise onto him.

"Looks like you've got some competition in the kitchen," Zara teases Henry playfully.

"Oh, I don't mind at all. As long as we're together and happy, that's all that counts," Henry replies, giving her hand a squeeze.

Liam raises his glass. "To family, love, and a future with more little feet padding around."

We all agree, filling the room with the unmistakable sound of a family that's found each other at last.

Epilogue

Zara

Nine months later

My eyes flutter open, and a warmth wraps around me like a snug blanket. The bedroom is all soft glow and quiet, the kind of morning light that sneaks through the edges of the curtains and whispers that today's going to be a good one. I stretch out, arms reaching for the ceiling as I smile.

It's Mia's first birthday today. Nine months have passed since that tiny, wailing bundle turned my world upside down in the best way possible.

I slip out of bed and tiptoe across the room, my senses on high alert. I can hear the rest of the house is awake, but I don't want to make a sound, wanting this little moment to be just me for a few minutes.

The bathroom feels cool compared to the cosy warmth of the duvet I've just left behind. There's no dawdling; I know what I'm here for. I rummage through the cupboard, finding the little box I stashed away for when the time felt right.

The timing is definitely right today. It's Mia's birthday, and here I am, about to find out if she might be getting the news of an upcoming sibling as a gift. I take the test and wait while the minutes tick by.

A nice, long breath escapes me as I glance at the result. My heart does a little skip, filling me with a warmth that even my bed can't provide. It's like all the happiness inside me has bubbled up to the surface, and it can't be contained. But there's no rush to announce it, no desperate need to share—just yet. This moment, it's mine, a tiny secret bubble of joy.

I step out of the bathroom, knowing today's going to be so much more than cake and candles. It's the start of another chapter, another little adventure, and I can't wait to see the looks on my alpha's faces when they hear. But for now, it's just me and this happy little secret, wrapped up in the soft morning light.

I nip down the hall to Mia's room quickly as she is protesting loudly now. A little bubble of laughter escapes me as I push open the door and there she is, all big blue eyes and a mop of curly dark hair, making her look just like her daddy.

"Morning, birthday girl!" I beam at her, my heart swelling up so big it might just lift me off the ground.

She greets me with a toothy grin, reaching out with those tiny hands that somehow grip my heartstrings every single time. "Mama!"

"Gotcha," I say as I scoop her up, peppering her face with soft kisses that make her laugh and squirm in delight. Her happiness, so pure and infectious, fills the room like sunshine, and I whisper against her cheek, "Love you more than all the stars, little one."

Holding her close, I breathe in the scent of baby shampoo and that unique Mia smell, a mix of warmth and innocence that wraps around me like the cosiest blanket. It's moments like this, with her cuddled in my arms, that I know we've built something extraordinary, something full of love and light out of a dark situation.

"Ready for your big day, munchkin?" I ask, nuzzling her nose with mine, and her giggles are the only answer I need.

I shuffle down the stairs with Mia nestled against my shoulder, her little hand playing with a strand of my hair. As we descend, the familiar sounds of morning in our house wrap around us. The clink of crockery and the low rumble of laughter tells me the day has already kicked off in the kitchen.

"Careful, mate, that pan's about had it," Ben's voice carries through the hallway, laced with humour.

"Hey, don't blame the pan, blame Liam," Henry retorts, and I can almost see his cheeky grin from here.

"Both of you, hush, or you'll wake the birthday princess," Liam says, his tone softer but still buoyant with the easy banter they share.

I round the corner into the kitchen, and I see my three alphas, like pillars of strength and love in our home. Ben is at the island, leaning back against it, with a coffee cup in hand, and with that warm, inviting smile that was so rare at first but now shows him for who he really is. His dark hair is still wet from the shower, but those keen eyes miss nothing, especially not his daughter making her grand entrance.

Henry stands by the stove, spatula in hand, wrestling with what smells like a glorious attempt at pancakes. His concentration is pure Henry – precise, thoughtful, always quietly confident even when faced with a rebellious breakfast batter.

Liam is setting the table, the muscles in his forearms flexing as he moves plates and cutlery with care.

He looks up, and his gentle gaze meets mine, filled with an affection that sends a wave of warmth through me.

"Morning," I say, my voice brimming with the happiness that bubbles inside me.

"Happy birthday, Mia," Ben says, walking over to plant a soft kiss on her cheek while Henry and Liam join in, peppering her with birthday affection.

Ben turns to me and gives me a soft kiss on my forehead. He breathes in my scent, and a questioning look crosses his face. I simply smile back at him, not ready to share just yet.

"Look who's ready to take on her first big birthday!" I announce, tilting Mia so she can see her daddies.

Mia responds with excited babbles, reaching out to them. They're wrapped around her little finger, and the sight fills the room with a glow that's better than the brightest sunshine breaking through the Lake District clouds.

"Food's nearly ready," Liam adds, bringing over a freshly brewed pot of coffee to the island. "Grab a seat, princess."

"Thanks," I say, grateful for the normalcy these moments bring, grounding us in the every day even as excitement flutters in my chest like a trapped bird eager to soar.

Settling Mia in her highchair, her little hands clap in anticipation, and I copy her, beaming and bursting with so much love that tears prick my eyes. Handing her a squeaky rubber duck, the kind that makes her eyes light up every time it lets out its funny sound, she takes to it immediately, squeezing it with glee. At the same time, I look over at Ben, Henry, and Liam huddled around the table inhaling food and coffee like it's their last day on earth.

"Sleep well?" Ben asks, his eyes are soft on mine as he passes me a mug of steaming tea.

"Yes, Mia sleeping through finally is like a miracle," I reply, placing the mug down and wringing my hands with a sudden attack of nerves as Henry swaps Mia's duck for a slice of jam on toast cut into squares, and then sits.

"Dada!" Mia shouts out, and Liam goes to her even though we have no idea which Dada she means. They're all Dada, and that's just perfect in my eyes.

"Here, let me help with that." Liam's already on his feet, wiping a smear of strawberry jam from Mia's cheek with the corner of a tea towel.

My gaze flicks between the three of them. My pulse quickens; it's now or never. "Guys, I need to tell you something..." I start, the words teetering on the edge of my lips. They all turn to me, anticipation hanging between us like bunting at a street party.

"Go on," Henry encourages, leaning forward.

I take a deep breath, the news fizzing inside me like a bottle of champers ready to pop. "I have something amazing to tell you all."

"Spill it then," Ben says, his smile encouraging but unwittingly adding weight to the pause before the reveal. He knows. He can tell the difference in my scent. The other two might not be as attuned, but Ben's been through this before.

I'm grinning so wide my cheeks ache, but I don't care. "I'm pregnant," I blurt out, the words rushing out like they've been bottled up for way too long.

Their reactions are immediate and electric. It feels like time slows down for a split second, everything suspended in the air between us.

Liam stands first, knocking his chair back as he does. He wraps me in his big arms, lifting me clear off the ground in one of his bear hugs. The others are quick to join in, pulling us into an all-encompassing and warm group embrace.

"I knew it! We're going to be dads again!" Ben chuckles, his voice thick with emotion, while Henry plants kisses on top of my head, murmurs of joy tumbling from him.

The house is now a riot of laughter and cheers, the earlier calm washed away by a tide of sheer elation. I can barely hear myself think over the excitement, but it doesn't matter. This is what happiness sounds like: chaotic and utterly perfect.

Mia claps her hands in her highchair, joining in the excitement without knowing why. Her little face is lit up with glee. I reckon she senses the love swirling around; it's infectious, after all.

Liam's laughter echoes around the kitchen, and he says, "Looks like the birthday girl is going to be a big sister!" He sets me down gently, but his eyes are dancing with mirth.

We all settle down again, breakfast resuming amid an atmosphere thick with plans for the future and fond recollections of the past year. Mia gurgles happily, oblivious to the fact she's at the heart of this new joy unfolding.

Henry looks across at me with those sincere eyes. "You okay? Not feeling overwhelmed, sick, tired?" he asks.

The concern in his voice is touching; they always look out for me so well. "Nope," I reply confidently. "I've never been better."

The warmth of their joy wraps around me, and I'm floating on a sea of love. It's pure amazement, the way they look at me as if I've hung the stars in the sky. I've never felt so cherished, so absolutely vital.

"Zara," Ben breathes out, his hand resting gently

on my stomach, his eyes alight with visions of our future. "A little miracle."

"Right, we've got loads to sort out," Liam says.

"First things first," Henry starts with that soft smile that always makes my heart do funny things. "We need to make sure you're eating right, Zara. I'll whip up some of those smoothies you love."

"And we'll have to see about Paternity Leave," Ben states.

"Can we not just bask in this for a minute?" I laugh, because leave it to my lovely alphas to skip straight to logistics when I'm still processing the fact that there's a tiny life growing inside me.

"Of course, princess." Liam reaches for my hand, squeezing it gently. "But you know us, always wanting to be ahead of the game."

Rising from the table with a smile, I say. "Right, I'm off to get the birthday girl cleaned up."

My heart does a little skip at the thought of Mia in her party dress for when Susan and Peter come around later after the guys get back from work.

"Need a hand?" Ben offers.

"I've got it," I answer, shaking my head. "You three need to get going."

"Bye, Mama," Liam calls out with a cheeky wink.

Giggling, I scoop up Mia and head upstairs, the soft carpet silent beneath my feet.

I lay Mia down on the changing mat, her little legs kicking with anticipation as she looks up at me with those big, baby blue eyes that could melt the coldest of hearts. I run my fingers over the soft fabric of the pre-party dress we picked out for her first birthday – it's a pale yellow, adorned with tiny, embroidered daisies, delicate and perfect just like her. The party dress is blue, like her eyes and the colour of the summer sky.

As I slip the yellow dress over her head, she babbles in delight, a string of baby sounds that make no sense yet mean everything. She's growing up in a world filled with so much love, and I swear she knows it. She throws her tiny arms around my neck as I lift her up, and for a moment, we're locked in our own little embrace. It's these little moments that I live for.

I press a kiss to her forehead, breathing in her sweet, innocent scent. "Happy birthday, baby girl," I whisper, and she coos as if she understands every word.

With Mia dressed, I set her down to play with the pile of stuffed animals on her play mat. Her little fingers grab a plush bunny, and she gnaws on its ear, content as can be. It gives me a moment to reflect on the whirlwind of these past few months - from the unexpected turns our relationship has taken to the excitement of growing our family.

There's a quick tap on the nursery door, and Henry's head pops in, his face alight with mischief. "I forgot my keys," he says, but I can tell he just wanted another peek at Mia before he left for work.

I roll my eyes playfully. "Sure you did," I tease him.

He winks at me and scoops Mia up for one last cuddle, peppering her face with gentle kisses that make her giggle like it's the best thing that's ever happened to her. "Dada loves you so much," he tells her earnestly, his tone full of promise and love.

Henry finally puts Mia back down and gives me a soft kiss on the lips. "Take care of yourself today," he says seriously.

I nod and shoo him out of the room with a smile. "Go on, you're going to be late."

He leaves with a farewell wave, and I'm left alone with my little girl again. It's quiet now, the house suddenly large and empty without the presence of my alphas. But it's a good kind of quiet, the peaceful lull before the storm of birthday festivities begins later on.

I sit on the floor beside Mia, watching her explore her tiny kingdom of toys with wide-eyed wonder. Each time she discovers a new texture or a new sound, her face lights up with the simple joy of discovery. It's mesmerising, really, to witness the world through such innocent eyes.

Lost in thought, I marvel at how our lives are about to change again as we add to our family. The unpredictability of it all would have scared me once, but now? There's no fear, only an overwhelming sense of gratitude that I'm on this journey surrounded by love and laughter.

Pre Order my next RH Omegaverse: Forget me Knot

Join my Facebook Reader Group for more info on my latest books and backlist: Eve Newton's Books & Readers

Join my newsletter for exclusive news, giveaways and competitions: Eve Newton's News

Printed in Great Britain
by Amazon